Toxic Octopus

A Spy Shop Mystery

Lisa Haneberg

First Printing, 2017
ISBN 0-9987801-0-3

Written Pursuits Publishing
838 High Street #269
Lexington, KY 40502
www.writtenpursuits.com

Cover design by Stuart Bache, Books Covered, Inc.
Book design by Polgarus Studio
Editing by Alan Rinzler, Jim Spivey and Mark Swift

Chapter 1
Day 1, Tuesday

On a muggy Tuesday morning in Galveston, Texas, a young aquarist working for the Biological and Aquatic Research Labs – or BARL – entered the dimly lit home of an octopus named Fred, who lived in the cephalopod tank area. The aquarist was intending to get high on Gorilla Glue before his boss got to work, but instead he found a dead body.

The body was that of Dr. Jane Moore, a marine biologist whom Fred the Octopus had appeared to have pulled into his tank and drowned.

The young aquarist found Dr. Moore's body tightly wrapped in Fred's pulsating tentacles. Every suction cup on the octopus's multiple arms was gripping her, as if in a passionate embrace.

～◉

"Xena! There's been an incident at BARL." Sparky stormed into the meeting room at my spy shop. Sparky, looking a lot like the Big Lebowski in a long cotton jacket that might've been a pajama robe, is my wunderkind chief technology officer and knows more about spy and surveillance apparatuses than I could imagine learning.

Dora poured a cup of coffee. "What happened?"

Dora's my chief operating officer. A former City of Galveston historian and researcher, she takes obsessive care of every detail in the spy shop as well as my private investigator practice.

"Dead body. Heard it on the police radio." Sparky paused to catch his breath. He put both hands on the table. "Special circumstances."

I knew that *special circumstances* was the code phrase to alert the Galveston PD's Level Three Crime Scene Team that something strange or messy had happened ... separated body parts, bloated decomposing, weird positioning ...

"OK, let's go," I said. "Dora, handle things here and I'll text you with what we find."

"You better! I'll monitor the news stations." Dora clicked on the large TV.

I grabbed my bag and keys and we drove to BARL, a privately funded, non-profit research think tank on the northeast side of the island in an old building where the US Coast Guard used to be. It was a city treasure, along with the University of Texas Medical Branch, anything named after the Moody family, and the dilapidated Mardi Gras arch the city was too lazy to fix or remove.

We are *not* ambulance chasers, by the way, readers. We've worked with BARL on several occasions. Two years ago, they asked us to provide them with tiny cameras they could mount onto dolphins they were training to be government assassins. No, they did not tell us that's what the dolphins were doing, but everyone in town knew and most didn't care. This is Texas. We love arming things.

BARL needed smaller cameras because the dolphins were crushing and knocking off the ones they had been using during their mating rituals, which apparently involve body slamming. Who knew?!

That particular species of dolphin, selected for their ability to be trained for complex tasks, happened to also be one of the horniest, which had presented an unforeseen challenge for researchers. Luckily, the Nano Cam XT worked beautifully, so after the BARL job, we've always kept those cameras in stock for newlyweds who like to film their underwater sex scenes.

We also provided and helped BARL install a network of new security cameras about a year ago, so we were curious to learn what was going on.

When Sparky and I arrived at the compound, we saw a fire truck, several police cars, an ambulance, and a few dozen employees gathered by the back entrance of the main building. The employees were held back about thirty feet from the door by a taped-off area and a police officer standing guard at the door. We parked, got out, and moved into the crowd. Several people were crying. I asked what had happened.

"Dr. Moore is dead," one said.

"Awful way to go," whispered another.

The door opened and the group let out a collective gasp when they saw who was on the other side. A man walked outside, took a few steps to the left, leaned against the wall and slid down on the asphalt. He began weeping.

"Who's that?" I looked for someone willing to talk.

"Dr. Pani," a woman with nametag – Roberta – said. "He's our research manager. Dr. Moore worked for him."

"How'd it happen?"

"Octopus," she whispered, and then turned to hug her coworker.

After talking to several onlookers, Sparky found me and pulled me aside.

"I talked with the security manager. He confirmed that a biologist was found dead in one of the tanks this morning."

"Octopus," I muttered slowly as I stared at Dr. Pani on the ground, holding his head. Rocking.

"What? The manager didn't tell me about an octopus."

I needed to know more about what happened, so I ducked under the tape barrier and walked to the police officer I didn't recognize.

"Is BJ in there?" As the captain of the Criminal Investigations Bureau, if anything major happened on the island, BJ Rawlins was there.

"Yeah," the officer replied.

"Tell him Xena would like to talk to him."

The officer scowled at me but went inside using one foot to hold the door open a crack. I heard him call to BJ and have a brief conversation in a hushed voice. I'd helped BJ nail a violent perp on a nasty case the month before, so I knew he'd pay attention when he heard my name.

Sure enough, a moment later, BJ came through the door.

He was wearing a crumpled gray suit, scuffed brown shoes, and his usual frown.

"I'm kind of busy here."

"I know. BARL is a client of ours. We've sold them security and other cameras. Can I help with anything?"

"Nope. The cameras were off, but I don't need them anyway." BJ walked closer. "It was a tragic accident. Nothing more. Nothing you can do."

"Accident?"

"Octopus drowns woman. Can't prosecute the dumb creature. Case closed."

"Wait a minute … What about—"

"I gotta go," he interrupted and then went back in the building.

I turned around to walk back to where Sparky was standing, but stopped when I heard a soft voice.

"Fred didn't do it."

I looked down and saw that Dr. Pani had lifted his head and was staring up at me. He was still sitting on the ground, his long dark hair falling backward except for a few wet strands that were stuck to his face.

"Fred didn't do it," he repeated. His eyes were dark, reddened, and glassy.

I walked over and sat on the pavement with him. "Who's Fred?"

"An octopus."

"They think Fred did it?"

"Yes, but he didn't. I know Fred and I know Jane."

"Did you tell the police?"

"Many times."

"Why do they think Fred did it?"

He was quiet for a moment, before speaking again. "Why were you talking to the police captain?"

"My company has provided security cameras for BARL and we've worked on cases with Captain Rawlins before. I own a spy shop in town and am a private investigator."

"You're an investigator?"

I nodded.

He took out his phone, found a photo and showed it to me. The picture was dark but I could make out a body in a tank with an octopus wrapped around it.

"Wow," I whispered.

"They said there was no sign of foul play. That it must've been an attack or accident. That's not what happened. I know it." He pulled back his phone and extended his hand. "I'm Ari. I manage the cephalopod lab." He noticed that I was about to say something. "Octopuses, squid, nautilus, and cuttlefish."

We shook hands but stayed seated. "I'm Xena. I'm sorry for your loss."

Ari wiped his face and pushed back his long bangs. Our hair looked to be a similar color – dark brown – but his was longer and more rock star than my straightened pageboy cut.

"Thanks." He dropped his head for a moment before looking at me again. "I need to go back in there. They're wrong about Fred."

"Tell Captain Rawlins again. He may be a bit hardheaded, but he's a good man and trustworthy."

Ari stood up and I followed suit. He extended his arm to shake my hand again and then pulled me into him. He towered above my five-and-a-half-foot frame.

"If the police won't listen," Ari whispered into my ear, "will you help me find out what happened?"

"Absolutely," I said without hesitation while pushing back from him.

"I'd have to get it approved."

"Of course." I grabbed a card from my bag and handed it to Ari. "Call if you need anything."

He stared at my card and rocked back and forth. "How about now?"

"Now?"

"Can you wait here for a while? I'll come back for you."

"Of course."

This was getting interesting.

"Thanks." Ari turned to leave. "Don't tell anyone I showed you the picture, OK?"

"Sure."

He put my card in his pocket and went back inside.

I found Sparky consoling one of the employees. He's a hugger. I, on the other hand, believe in the sanctity of personal space. Twenty-four inches, please. As the most sensitive member of our team, Sparky has a wonderful and effective way of making people comfortable. Within minutes they're sharing life stories in rich, juicy detail.

I gave Sparky a look to join me as I walked back to the car.

"This is some heavy shit." He leaned against the trunk. "Did you find out anything?"

"BJ thinks the octopus named Fred killed the biologist. The lab manager says no way."

"Who do you believe?"

"I've no idea yet, but I'm pretty sure we have a new case." I flashed him a smile.

Sparky checked the video camera he'd set up and then talked with a few more employees while I sat in the car and took notes about my conversation with Ari. The Level Three Team arrived and were rushed inside to, I assumed, get Dr. Moore's body out of the tank. I called Dora with an update and asked her to start researching a few things in case BARL hired us to investigate.

"Boo!" investigative reporter Steve Heart proclaimed loud enough to make me drop my phone.

"What the hell?!" I picked up my phone and opened the car door.

"I just got here. Sparky mentioned you talked to the victim's manager."

I got out of the car. "Nice to see you, too."

Steve and I had partnered on several cases, going all the way back to the glorious incident that changed everything. Maybe I'll tell you more about that investigation later, readers, suffice it to say that his reporting of this unusual case and others had earned him several awards and industry accolades. He could've picked any crime beat job in the country but he chose to get off the bureaucratic hamster wheel and take the top reporter job at the smaller but well-respected *Galveston Post Intelligencer*, or GPI, a year after I moved to the island and opened my spy shop. Get your minds out of the gutter, readers, Steve and I were never lovers. I know you were wondering. Steve is an awesome guy but not my type, and likewise I'm not his. He likes big boobs and smaller brains. I'm proudly the opposite.

"Catch me up?" Steve implored while flashing his bright boyish smile. Standing about five-ten, his tanned body, blond hair, mustache, and soul patch could turn some heads.

"All I know is that BJ thinks it's an accident and Dr. Pani doesn't believe it."

"That the octopus killed her?"

"Yes. The octopus is named Fred."

"No way!"

"I kid you not."

"What else did Dr. Pani tell you?"

"That's it. Our conversation was two to three minutes, tops. He seemed nice. Kinda cute, too. Long brown hair. More Yanni than Fabio."

My phone buzzed with an incoming text. *It's Ari. You still here? Can we talk right now?*

Yes, I typed, and hit SEND.

"You mean like that?" Steve pointed toward the door. Ari and another man walked away from the taped-off area. They passed the crowd and headed in our direction. Sparky saw them and followed.

"Can we talk in private?" Ari motioned us to move away from Steve and Sparky. "This is Dr. Mark Larson. He's the lab director here at BARL."

Dr. Larson glanced up and down at me. He looked like a *GQ* model who had aged well with some professional help.

His clean-shaven skin glowed and his eyebrows looked manicured. I felt underdressed in my khakis and *Life is Good* T-shirt.

"I'm sorry for your loss," I said.

"Thanks. This is a tragedy for our labs and for the entire community." Dr. Larson crossed his arms.

Ari cut in. "The police are convinced Fred caused Jane's death. They're closing the case and won't be assigning a detective, but they've agreed to have the coroner do an autopsy. I've asked for and received Dr. Larson's approval to have your firm investigate the case."

"To be clear," Dr. Larson advised, "I've agreed to a limited scope and timeframe of two weeks. The police are probably right about this being a tragic accident, but Dr. Pani disagrees and I respect his expertise."

I watched and listened, calm on the outside, but buzzing with excitement on the inside.

Dr. Larson was taller than Ari but he bent forward and looked down at me over his glasses. "Dr. Pani tells me your firm has done business with us before and that you're a vetted vendor. Is that right?"

"Yes. We supplied various cameras to BARL for security and other purposes."

"What're your rates for this type of work?"

"My rate is $350 per hour and $200 per hour for my team members."

Ari's eyes got wide but he didn't say anything.

Dr. Larson was unfazed. "Two weeks. That's all I'm authorizing. Dr. Pani is your primary contact, but I expect to be briefed on any findings before they're made public or shared with others."

He shook my hand again, turned, and walked back through the crowd and into the building.

I looked at Ari and exhaled. "You don't mess around, do you?"

"Jane was my friend and colleague and she loved Fred. I want to know what happened." Ari's eyes welled up a bit as he talked.

"I understand. My team and I look forward to helping you."

"How does this work?"

"I'd like to schedule time with you tomorrow or the day after to learn more about Dr. Moore, Fred, the tank area, and octopus behavior in general. I need to understand why you think Fred wouldn't have killed Dr. Moore. In the meantime, my team and I will review the police report and collect some initial information."

"I know where Jane kept journals in her office. She wrote everything in those books. Should I get them for you?"

"Yes, that'd be helpful."

Ari sprinted to the front of the building and through the main entrance. He was attractive, although soft and underdeveloped. His olive skin made me guess his family roots included the Middle East or India. His thin, six-foot frame and long hair bounced when he walked.

A couple of moments later, Ari came back out the front door with a bag filled with bound journals. He handed the bag to me and then went back inside through the side door.

Slower this time, hugging several people as he worked his way past the guard and into the building.

Sparky and I looked at each other with knowing eyes. We lived for opportunities like this.

I held up the bag of journals. "I've never interrogated an octopus before!"

"No doubt," Sparky said, "I think animals know more than we give them credit for."

We walked back to the car, locked the journals in the trunk, and talked to a few more BARL employees. Steve and his photographer interviewed several people while a competitor reporter from a Houston TV channel filmed a live shot for the evening news. BJ came out and made a quick statement, telling everyone it was a tragic accident and encouraging people to go home.

Sparky and I watched the police, fire and rescue personnel, and most of the BARL employees leave. We packed up our video equipment and were about to leave when Ari came back out from the front entrance and walked up to us.

"Follow me." Ari glanced around to see if we were being watched. He walked up to Sparky. "I don't think we've met."

"Sparky's on my team, but he's just leaving."

"I am?" Sparky sulked, looking kind of hurt.

"Go back to the shop and start going over the case with Dora," I said. "Take my car, I'll taxi back."

"Uh ..." Sparky held out his hand for my keys. "Call me if you need me to pick you up. There aren't many taxis out this way. Might be faster."

Ari then led me on a circuitous route around the big, old

building to an unmarked door, which he unlocked. He brought me into the tank area and we stood in front of Fred.

Wow!

I was starstruck.

Fred's body was a lovely mottled sable color with a pinkish underside and light purple markings on his grapefruit-sized head.

Ari pointed at Fred. "Fred's siphon, gills, heart, digestive system, and reproductive glands are all crammed into his mantle – what non-scientists would think was his head."

It was cool the way this mantle expanded and contracted with each watery breath. Meanwhile, Fred's tentacles moved in separate directions. Two stuck to the tank's glass and several others explored above, below, and around his head.

"So many tentacles." I traced his shape on the glass with my finger. "It's hard to count."

"Six arms and two legs."

The suckers on each arm were about an inch wide close to the center and thinned out to the width of a pencil's eraser at the tips. I stood close to the tank and watched how each sucker probed the glass independently and flexibly. He was in a constant state of movement and flow.

Fred was strange and magnificent.

"He's a large *Octopus vulgaris*, or common octopus, about nine months old."

"What's their average life span?"

"Around twelve to eighteen months. Not long."

"Oh no." I held my hand over my mouth and mumbled. "Why so short?"

"Fred has a special arm, a kind of cephalopod penis that

he uses to transfer spermatophores, these little packets of sperm, into the female's mantle. Once he's done that, he'll die within a few months."

"That's awful." I felt like crying, but of course would never do that in public, because it would spoil my tough lady image. "What does the female do without him?"

"He'll serve no further purpose for her." Ari was nonchalant. "She can keep his sperm alive inside her for weeks until her eggs are mature, then she lays about two hundred thousand eggs that fasten themselves to rocks and coral. She tries to cover them up and defend them from any predator that wants to eat them, never leaving, never eating, and by the time the eggs hatch, she's starved to death."

I was speechless.

Fred looked around four feet long, including his tentacles, and his head and mantle were about the same size as a frozen chicken from the grocery.

Fred's tank, which he shared with several anemones and starfish, appeared to be ten feet square. A rocky outcrop covered the back wall and left side of the tank, and there was a fake piece of ship wreckage in the center.

"The design helps ensure that Fred feels both comfortable and stimulated," Ari said.

There were three similar tanks in this section of the lab connected by a walkway of metal grating, presumably for feeding and maintenance.

"Those are cuttlefish being studied to learn more about their ability to camouflage even though they're colorblind like octopuses."

And *YES*, that's the correct plural for octopus, readers, I know you were questioning this. *Octopus* has been an English word for centuries and comes from ancient Greek, not Latin. But there's a connection to scientific Latin, so that's OK, too. Two octopuses were chatting about their three friends, also octopodes. That's five octopi all day! All correct!

The third tank looked empty, aside from a few starfish.

"Interesting." I scanned the area.

"And there's another octopus in that last tank. Ethel. She's not as social as Fred."

"Fred and Ethel. Cute."

"We try to have fun with names."

I pointed to chairs and tables set out like in a classroom across from the four tanks. "Do you allow the public in here?"

"No. We occasionally conduct academic symposia and we've hosted the media when our research piques their attention. As a privately funded non-profit organization, we're always seeking grants and donations. On occasion, we host birthday parties for rich donors' kids in the more popular areas of the lab, like the stingray and river otter tanks. Not as much here."

"Otters are cute."

We walked around Fred's tank. I looked up and down the tank surface and remembered the picture Ari showed me and imagined Jane's body inside.

"Yes, but their tank is open, they smell like rotting shellfish, and they often splash and snivel at people, and this presents a challenge to the staff who have to run the parties. Their parents are willing to shell out millions to support conservation but expect us to tame and sanitize the same wild animals they help us save. I hate pandering to rich people, but it comes with the territory."

I walked back up to where Fred clung onto his tank and stared in amazement. Fred's arms twisted continuously, and the tips curled and unfurled like an ancient exotic dancer.

"Did you do this, Fred?" I whispered.

Ari walked over to the staircase next to the tank. "This is the first I've seen him out since we had to use the fresh water to get him off Jane. Looks like he's calm. How about we open the tank so I can introduce you to Fred, up close?"

"Really?" I was excited and scared. "Let's do it."

Ari made a call to his assistant and escorted me up the set of stairs that had a grating platform large enough for three or four people. The top of the tank came to my hip level.

"Xena, this is Roberta." Ari pointed to his research assistant, who now stood at the bottom of the stairs. "Xena is a private investigator. She's helping us figure out what happened."

I waved, recognizing her from the initial scene.

"Roberta is here as my backup. We never open the octopus tanks without one."

"Why?"

"You'll see. Octopuses are escape artists and surprisingly strong."

Ari opened a portion of the heavy lid covering the tank and plunged his forearms in the water with his hands open and faced up. Like a bullet, Fred rushed to the top of the tank, then, as he clung to the side of the tank, three of his tentacles rose out of the water and wrapped around Ari's arms.

"We're good buddies, Fred and me. Not as close as he was with Jane, but we have a good bromance going." Ari stood a little straighter to bring Fred's head and mantle close to the top of the water.

I shuffled a few steps toward Ari, unsure of how close I should get. "It's like he's saying hello or welcoming you."

"That's exactly what he's doing. Touch is an important sense for an octopus and ours is a real relationship. It feels caring, while at the same time alien."

"He's not still angry about all the commotion or Jane's death?"

Ari pulled off one of the tentacles.

"I'm sure he's missing Jane. That's why connecting here today is so important to him. He's lonely. It took him a good hour to get over being blasted with fresh water – he hates that – but we had to do that to get him to move away from Jane's body. After the police left, I fed him a couple of blue crabs. They're his favorite."

Ari paused and used his head to encourage me to move closer. "Let's see if Fred would like to meet you." He then motioned for me to stick my arms in the water.

"He won't bite me? What if he doesn't like me?"

Ari wriggled his arms and moved them deeper into the tank to coax Fred off him. It took some work. "You're not his favorite food." He smiled at me. "If you offer yourself to him, he knows you're not attacking. His parrot-like beak could do a lot of damage if he chose to attack, but he won't. Jane didn't have any bites on her body, by the way."

I slowly placed my arms in the cold water and held them there for a minute. Fred unfurled his tentacles from Ari and moved in my direction. He turned red.

I stepped back but kept my arms in the water. "What does that mean? Is he angry?"

"He's excited or interested. He also turns red when he's angry, but that'd be a much deeper red color, accompanied by flashing and making himself thorny."

"Horny?"

I heard Roberta giggle.

"No, thorny. He'd transform his skin and it would look bumpy and prickly."

Ari stood watching Fred, ready to assist if needed. Fred explored my arms with his soft, gelatinous suckers. He intertwined his arms and mine starting from the thin tip of his tentacle inward toward thicker and stronger suction cups. It was like he was walking up my arm. The suction cups really sucked!

Ari came closer and watched Fred's movements carefully.

"He likes you. What do you feel?"

I bent a bit more and let my arms go deeper in the water.

"I feel weird, but held by … by a warm – warm isn't the right word because it's cold, but warm or maybe loving embrace. Strong. Gentle. His suckers are pulling me a bit, but not too much. It's like he's exploring me, trying to understand me. Is this normal?"

"It depends on the person. I can see that he's taken to

you, which is special because he's usually shy with people he doesn't know. He likely can sense your genuine interest in and curiosity about him. He's both touching and tasting you. Octopuses taste with their entire bodies." Ari carefully pointed to Fred's head. "Do you see how he's looking at you with his eye? Octopuses have a dominant eye but they don't see color."

Fred moved his head close to the surface and looked right through me. I looked at him, too, and we held our position for a few minutes. The thin end of one of his arms moved toward my face and Ari grabbed it and pushed it away.

"Never let an octopus touch your face. He could easily pull your eye out of its socket."

I stood straighter, pulling away. "He'd do that?"

"Maybe. Even a relatively small octopus like Fred could easily pop an eye out. It wouldn't happen out of anger or aggression, but if one of his suckers got ahold of your eye, it'd be gone in a second if he pulled or if we tried to lift his arm off. The Giant Pacific Octopus is much stronger and that struggle would be a whole other ball of wax."

My arms were going numb because the water in Fred's tank was kept at forty-two degrees. The eyeball comment had unnerved me a bit, and Ari kept redirecting the squirmy tentacles away from parts of my body where they didn't belong.

I didn't know how to detach Fred from me. "Let's stop here for today."

Ari pulled each tentacle, some more than once, and several suckers made a popping sound as they released.

He pointed to the round red marks all over my arms. "We call those octopus hickeys. Some may leave a bruise, especially those bigger ones."

Ari reached into the bucket next to him and held out a fish so Fred could see it. Fred immediately turned upside down and showed us where his eight tentacles came together and the soft area covering his mouth. Seeing all those suckers was cool, but I could imagine how hard it would be to break free if I were caught in Fred's grip. Fred grabbed the fish with the slender end of a tentacle and walked it down, sucker by sucker, toward his mouth.

"He's savoring it," Ari said. "Tasting the fish all the way down his arm."

Ari closed and latched the lid, and Fred took his fish into his dark lair in the corner of the tank.

I walked closer to Fred's tank and took another look. He had charmed me with his direct stare and generous touch. The tank looked empty except for a few light pink anemones, two orange sea stars, and a single tentacle that was dancing, twirling, and swaying to a secret waltz.

"That was remarkable. Thank you."

Ari smiled. "He's pretty amazing. All octopuses are, though not all are as social as is Fred. He'll remember you the next time you visit, especially because he has tasted you."

Ari moved toward the stairs to leave, but I stopped him. "Tell me about the safety feature that you said Jane would've used if Fred tried to pull her under. I can tell he's certainly strong enough to do it."

"Yes, he is. To break the hold of an octopus Fred's size

would require about a quarter ton of force. Although octopuses are usually gentle, they've drowned a few people because their hold overpowered the diver's ability to escape. But being physically strong enough to drown a human doesn't mean that he would or did." Ari moved back toward the tank lid. "I had a hard time conveying this to Captain Rawlins. Accidents have happened in the wild. Here in the lab environment we take precautions."

"Can you show me?" I moved next to the tank and bent to look for Fred, who was still in his lair and out of sight.

Ari squatted and pointed. "See that black hose on the side of the tank near where we were interacting with Fred? If I grab that hose, fresh water will flow and drive Fred away. It works every time and pisses him off for a while, too, so we don't use it unless necessary."

"What do octopuses do when they get angry?"

"Suck in a lot of water and shoot it at you. Or if he's pissed, he might squirt a cloud of ink at you." Ari used his hands to mimic the octopus's movements. "If we continued to annoy him, an octopus would attack, bite, and might kill. But that would be rare and entirely our fault."

"Was there any evidence of ink or splashed water, or that Jane pulled the hose?"

"No, but she might've been in the tank for hours when we found her. I'm hoping the autopsy will help narrow her time of death."

Ari stood still for a few moments, pressing his hands on the top of the tank lid and putting down his head on the glass. He looked like he might break down. He had held it together until he uttered the words *time of death*.

"Are you OK? We're done for today. I know this is difficult to rehash." I went down the stairs and Ari followed.

"I know your interaction with Fred doesn't prove that he didn't drown Jane," Ari said. "In fact, it might make the police's theory more plausible. But I wanted you to get to know Fred, so when I tell you I'm certain that he wouldn't have done this to Jane, you'll have a better context for believing it."

I turned and locked onto his dark and glassy eyes. "Ari … I'm on it. My team is already gathering information, we have an initial case review scheduled for tomorrow morning, and we should get the autopsy report soon."

Ari gently clutched my arm. "I'm so glad we found you. This whole thing seems inconceivable, and yet it's real and Jane's gone. I don't want to lose Fred, too."

"I understand and am sorry you have to go through this. It's getting late and there are several things I want to look into before we talk again. Let's meet Thursday morning if I don't call you sooner."

～◎

In September, the evening breeze coming off the Gulf of Mexico was neither hot nor cool – just a courier of sounds and smells from a beach town crawling with people who don't want to let summer go. Given it was a Tuesday, the sounds were more grackle and less Pleasure Pier.

Fine by me. I loved the crackly, piercing songs that a plague of grackles cycled though as they jockeyed for bedtime positions. Many locals and visitors hated grackles because of their creepy and confident en masse movements. I appreciated their opportunistic and resourceful way of thriving in urban settings, like the Randall's parking lot and the trees and power lines along the alley next to my house.

I bought my home on Twenty-Ninth Street two years ago in a moment of emotionally driven insanity that I've never regretted. Built in 1950 by an engineer who wanted to create a concrete-and-steel, hurricane-proof modern home, my house was the most practical and impractical home on the island – think steel and humidity equals RUST equals money pit.

I sat on my second-floor screened porch, sipped tea, and punched in BJ's cell number on my phone. "It's Xena. BARL hired me to look into Dr. Moore's death. You got a minute?"

"They told me. I'm surprised."

"Why?"

"There's no real case here. But hey, if you want to earn a few bucks making the researcher feel better, more power to you. But do me a favor and don't do anything that requires my team's time, because we're already over budget for the month. The case is closed and we have a lot of work to do to get ready for the Shrimp Festival."

I sat forward and looked at my notes. "Tell me why you're convinced there was no foul play. The security cameras were off."

BJ sighed. "Yes, that's unfortunate. Trust me, if you had been inside, you would've come to the same conclusion. The octopus was wrapped around Dr. Moore and it wasn't until Dr. Pani repelled him …"

"Repelled?" Did I tell BJ that I'd already met Fred and knew all about the water hose safety feature? No, I did not.

"It took some creative efforts to pry him off her." BJ paused. "It was one of the strangest things I'd ever seen. Other than the octopus and dead woman intertwined in a tank, nothing was out of place or unusual. No unauthorized entry. No signs of struggle outside the tank. None of the doors were messed with. It's a secure area."

I was quiet for a moment, slumped back, and took a drink. BJ was breathing heavier now, like he was walking up stairs.

"Ari – Dr. Pani – seems pretty sure that Fred wouldn't have hurt Jane," I continued.

"Yes, he told me that, too, but that's not the story the scene is telling. We may never know why or how it happened."

"I promised him I'd investigate. I hope that if we find something, you will work with us to reopen the case."

"I'm always willing to hear what you find, but please be sure about what you have before you bring anything to us, OK? That Peeping Tom case you got us involved with is still causing me all kinds of grief."

BJ's comment caught me by surprise. I hesitated before calmly asserting myself. "But he was guilty, and you caught him, and he was convicted of felony voyeurism."

"And he was the head of Internal Affairs, and he was peeping outside his ex-boyfriend's house, and his wife had no idea he was gay."

The line was silent. I stalled while I decided how far to go with BJ regarding the peeper case. We didn't agree on how it went down but I empathized that it was awkward for BJ and others at the station. Like catching your dad masturbating.

"The bad guy lost," I finally offered. "That's what's supposed to happen."

"Let's use common sense and focus on the *very* bad guys. That's all I'm asking."

With a year to go until he retired, BJ wasn't hungry to investigate new cases. Even so, I knew he'd be there if we needed him. He was right. The most concerning aspect of this case was no signs of forced entry. If Fred hadn't done this, someone else had to have been there. An intruder or someone from BARL.

"OK, Detective Rawlins. I'll play by your rules and won't mess up your budget unless I have a sure thing with real bad guys."

"I appreciate that," BJ replied.

I hung up the phone and headed inside to make another cup of oolong tea. It was time to dig into Jane's journals. I settled into my reading chair in my first-floor office, stacked the eleven journals on my desk in reverse date order, and started reading from the end of the newest journal backward in time to see what I could learn about Jane's final days.

Jane wrote three journal entries during her final week. One shared her excitement for seeing an old friend from college who was in town briefly to attend a meeting at the University of Texas Medical Branch. Another entry touted her frustration with politics and administration. It was the third entry that gave me pause:

Am I doing the right things by Fred? Will I ever know? We have a purpose – a set of instincts … fortified with drive … that shape who we should be and how our lives will unfold. Fred is a deeply feeling creature. Octos think and anticipate and are more adventurous than I'll ever have the courage to be. Are my decisions satisfying my needs or his? It would be hubris at play if I assumed they were the same. I'd like to know how much he yearns to fulfill his destiny as a wild male octopus. Unfortunately, I may never know.

I didn't know what Jane's post meant but it gave me chills. It was clear that she was tormented about Fred's life at BARL and that she was an intelligent, thoughtful professional. I made a note to ask Ari if she had mentioned being conflicted about Fred's treatment.

Next, I read journal entries from the two weeks prior to Jane's death. No big revelations, but they painted an overall picture showing that Jane was troubled and dissatisfied with aspects of her work – mostly politics. Every few days she wrote about what Fred was doing and how he was getting along. She seemed taken with Fred's animated and friendly behavior toward her and proud that she was able to help him get stronger.

Going back three weeks, two of the three entries focused on a project – "Project 67" – she was working on with a colleague named Ansel Homer. Jane was frustrated by his lack of follow-through and she believed he was driven by the trappings of success more than the quality of his work:

> *Frustrated. Ansel is dense, lazy, or manipulating me to further his career. Why must he take so long to analyze the source of the pollution? Has he already completed his report but kept it from me? Is he worried that I'll take over the project and therefore any glory that might come his way at its end? Men can be so competitive!* <u>*Call Ansel.*</u> *Time for wine.*

I agree, Jane. Men can be turds.

I spent the rest of the evening reading all the journals and marked entries that mentioned names of people or projects. No smoking guns, but it was too early in the investigation to know which pieces of information might become important.

I love that I'm paid to be a professional voyeur, readers. Please don't judge me; we all like to look through the hole in the fence. Or maybe you're jealous?

I walked upstairs, poured a Scotch, and sat in my rocking chair on the porch. It was my favorite place to reflect; still is. Surrounded by lush plants that soak in the island humidity and almost never need to be watered. No lights on, which makes it easy to eavesdrop on those walking by below on their way to or from the seawall. I looked down at the octopus hickies on my arm and searched for the meaning trapped underneath the day's events. I liked Ari and admired his courage. I hoped he wasn't the bad guy!

I topped off my Scotch, returned to the porch, and called Gregory, a friend and mentor from my corporate days in Houston. It might surprise you, readers, that human resources and compliance projects require some of the same techniques and approaches as police and private investigation work. In fact, we often contract with outside resources to assist with larger or complex cases. That's how I met Gregory. He owned a successful spy shop and private investigation practice in Houston. He was my best outside practitioner and became a trusted ally and sounding board when I was trying to reduce corruption at my company, Granny's Home.

A few of my business habits rubbed off on him, too. Gregory and I talked nightly, without fail, as part of a coaching process created by UCLA professor and author of management books Marshall Goldsmith. It went something like this: each person selected three questions that'd be the litmus test for whether they acted true to their goals and intentions. Gregory and I asked each other those questions each night or the following morning. It was a simple but effective process that we had been doing for the last three years.

The questions Gregory asked for me were: 1) Did you keep things in perspective? 2) Did you share something about yourself? 3) Did you show someone that you care? And Gregory's from me were: 1) Did you live like a healthy person? 2) Did you get a bit more organized? 3) Did you spend quality time with your wife?

Although different, our questions shared an interest in creating great personal lives on par with our work. We believed it was possible but struggled in our own ways. Our nightly call lasted about ten minutes unless we talked about others things.

"You never answered number two," Gregory persisted, after I assumed we had finished for tonight.

"I thought I did. I'd say that I shared something about myself with Ari today at BARL. I told him about my work and experience."

"You don't struggle to share your work-related skills with prospective clients. This is meant to be a personal question. Unless you've some personal interest in the biologist?"

"I'm a bit intrigued, but that's all. You're right, though, I didn't meet my intention with number two. Can we talk about how you totally avoided your number three?"

"I got in a fight with Lynn today. She wants me to work less."

"She's right."

"I know. The work we do is much more interesting than real life."

"Yeah, I'm stoked about my current case. Maybe the octopus is innocent and Jane was murdered."

"I saw the story online. Be careful, sometimes things *are* as they seem. Don't go creating a case where there isn't one because the client is a cute scientist."

"I'm not overreacting, if that's what you're suggesting. A few things don't seem right." I stood by the porch screen and looked down. Two cats were lying in the middle of the sidewalk. Claiming their territory for the night. "If I'm smitten with anyone, it's the octopus."

"Fred?"

"Yes, I met him up close and personal, and I've been reading about him in Jane's journals. He gave me hickies."

"Don't get too close. He might be a killer."

"Maybe, but … I doubt it," I said. "Jane seemed happiest when thinking about Fred. She was perturbed about a lot of other things."

"Aren't all women bothered about something?"

"Yes, of course! And my gut is telling me something is wrong here."

"Well, your gut is about as well-tuned as any I've seen."

"Thanks."

"You've a special gift, so go forth and figure it out. Don't be too disappointed if it turns out to be nothing. You can date your new client after he stops paying you."

"It's not about Ari!"

"I have a gut, too, Xena."

Chapter 2
Day 2, Wednesday

I named my business the Paradise Lost Spy Shop because we're all one home invasion or one mugging away from feeling forever violated.

Galveston Island is a real place, not an invented theme park like Disney or Singapore. There's crime, poverty, and tanned con artists in wrinkled linen slacks ready to sell you a piece of marshland where swarms of mosquitoes hide in wait for you on the backs of alligators. It's also a lovely place with warm locals, cool art galleries, talented chefs, and natural beauty in every direction.

My team and I are proud that we can help customers protect themselves and also catch bad people in the act. I know that a few criminally inclined dipshits have used our products to victimize others, but the majority of our sales offer peace of mind to honest islanders and visitors.

Each month we sell over a hundred security money belts and at least seventy-five personal stun guns. Our bestselling stun gun is the Vipertek VTS-880, in pink, which delivers fifteen-million volts of power. One zap and attackers fall to their knees, become disoriented, and temporarily lose balance and muscle control. Stunned attackers get caught but don't die and nobody loses their vacation money.

A win-win!

As you walk into the shop, there are shelves on the left and right walls and two aisles with shelves in the middle. Our cash register and a long display case filled with high-end items runs across the store two-thirds of the way back. Our office area and a combo meeting and stock room occupies the rear portion.

That morning, Dora and I shuffled things around to make room for our latest shipment of personal protection devices. We moved the lock picks, lock pick training kits, walkie-talkies and umbrella dart guns from the left wall to a smaller space toward the back of the store. In their places, we displayed our new sexual-assault prevention product line that included fake HIV, herpes, and chlamydia test kits. They were cheap, effective, and – since they were empty printed boxes – returned a seventy-five percent profit margin. Brilliant, yes?

I stacked each type six high. "Do you think they'll be big sellers for the holidays?"

"What mother wouldn't buy them for their daughters and themselves? And the price point makes them a great stocking stuffer. I plan on giving an assortment to everyone in my bridge club, even the guys."

"It's a perfect first line of defense against the average island pervert." I picked up a herpes test kit and held it straight in front of me with my arm stretched. "Step one, show him the box to let him know you're damaged goods. If that doesn't work, step two, pepper spray him in the face, and step three, zap him on the neck with a stun gun."

"That's what I'd do, and videotape it all with my pendant camera!" Dora lifted her necklace to demonstrate. She was wearing our hottest seller from that category, a large heart with an eye in the center. Oh, the irony!

"Maybe we should leave the umbrella dart guns here." I contemplated a real attack. "That could be a nice way to finish things off, with a dart or two to the groin area."

"Excellent idea!" Dora got the umbrellas and brought them back to the display. "I wish they came in prettier colors, though."

We finished the display before preparing for our team meeting in the back room. I put two fresh sheets of flipchart paper on the wall and cleared off the table while Dora made coffee and set out the almond cookies I'd bought at ShyKatZ Bakery on Fifteenth Street. I sat and went over my notes while Dora moved boxes to clear more space by the table. Sparky arrived, poured a cup of coffee, and sat.

"OK, let's get down to business." I drummed a few times on the table. "But first, I need to tell you both about meeting Fred. He's amazing! He looked at me with a steely stare and he's surprisingly strong. Ari had to hold his tentacles back from touching my face. He said that if Fred got ahold of my eye, he could easily pop it out. It scared me because his arms moved so fast!" I covered my eyes.

"Do octopuses like eating eyeballs?" Sparky asked.

"I don't know, but Ari confirmed that if he pulled one out, it would likely be unintentional."

Dora put up her hand. "Eyeballs are eaten in many food cultures."

We could count on Dora knowing and remembering vast amounts of detail about strange and obscure topics and historical incidents. She wasn't just a historian; no, she was much more than that. Dora curated oddball knowledge with the excitement befitting an Italian politician judging cheerleader tryouts.

"Asian dishes often highlight head-on fish with eyes. Some Icelanders eat sheep's eyeballs, and a few paleo-crazed Americans have taken to caribou eyeballs. Apparently, the trick is to hold the eyeball in your mouth for as long as possible to enjoy the fishy flavor followed by the eye's spongy texture. It's a nuanced and acquired delicacy. I wouldn't be surprised if octopuses love them as well."

"Thanks for freaking me out even more!" I shook my shoulders and clenched my hands. "How do you know all this?"

"NPR did a podcast on eyeball cuisine a few years ago. I saved it in my favorites if you'd like to listen sometime." Dora gave me a sly smile.

"I can imagine watching Fred walking my eye down his tentacle – what Ari called savoring his food – with my remaining eye." I covered one eye. "Enough about eyeballs!"

"OK. How about this? I watched several videos of octopus attacks on YouTube this morning. Mostly involving the Giant Pacific Octopus, but one showed a diver being held under by something about Fred's size." Dora powered on her iPad and turned it so that Sparky and I could see it.

"Most of the deaths were accidents, where the octopus held the person underwater until they drowned. One guy got his finger too close to an octopus's mouth and it bit off the finger. He survived."

"It's their grip strength that amazes me," I said. "Each sucker can pull more than you'd guess looking at their size. My experience with Fred made it clear that he could've drowned Jane. Even so, Ari told me the same thing you did, that it would be unusual for an octopus to attack."

Dora showed us a video of a huge octopus grabbing a diver. The octopus squirmed and explored just as Fred had. It grabbed at the diver's mask and nearly ripped it off. The diver held on with both hands and broke free from its tentacles. As octopuses are curious and often steal items from divers, pulling on this guy's mask seemed more like an effort to get a toy than an attack.

"So do you think it could've been an accident?" Dora asked.

"It's possible, but the tank environment makes it less likely because there're more surfaces Jane could've held on to and they've got the freshwater hose that she could've used to deter him. The police report didn't mention any physical signs that she grabbed at the rocks or tried to free herself, but we'll know that for sure once the autopsy is complete. The police and the media have been too eager to brand Fred a killer because they don't understand typical octopus behavior."

Dora put her iPad on the table and started talking with her hands like a teacher. "The mythology and lore surrounding octopus attacks goes way back to the thirteenth century with the Norwegian story of the Kraken beast that attacked ships. French and Japanese artists depicted giant octopuses attacking people and vessels. Sea monsters, in general, have captured the imagination of storytellers for centuries and make for great drama since the oceans are largely unexplored." She then paused to take a sip of coffee.

"Yeah, man, we fear the unknown." Sparky leaned on the table, engrossed in Dora's story.

"Exactly. In more recent times, reports of killer giant Humboldt Squid, who *are* notoriously aggressive, have perpetuated concerns about eight-legged sea monsters. The story is somewhat true in the case of the squid. Attacks on fishermen in the Sea of Cortez and other waterways around Mexico have been recorded. Even these attacks, however, are believed to occur because of human actions that provoked the squid."

I cut in. "I worry that what people know about octopuses comes more from Hollywood's portrayal in *20,000 Leagues Under the Sea* and *Clash of the Titans* than what they could learn if they got off their asses and went to their local aquarium or library. Ignorance could doom Fred."

"Well, that's why Ari has us on the case," Dora said. "We can help ensure Fred isn't vilified because he possesses the strength to kill. If we applied the same rule to people, every horny man would be charged with cheating."

Sparky snorted. "That might be closer to the truth, based on our sales of video cameras and tracking devices."

I motioned to him, "Let's get back on track with the case review."

"We know that police believe the octopus, whose name is Fred, killed Dr. Jane Moore, either by accident or as an act of aggression."

Dora put away her iPad and opened her folder. "Right. Bizarre."

"Is it like those elephants that live in captivity for years, get pissed off, and sit on their handlers' heads, crushing them like raw eggs smashed by a fist?" I was guilty of getting us immediately off track again. "Or maybe this is a survival story. Like when sharks attack and eat surfers, even though people taste foul, because their usual diet of clownfish has been depleted due to every flipping kid in America wanting one in their bedroom aquarium after seeing *Finding Nemo*."

Dora and Sparky laughed.

Is it irony or paradox that the movie, which is about freeing the captured fish, resulted in more being caught? I get those two mixed up. We should think these things through before we release movies featuring cute wild animals. Cycle of life! Every action leads to a reaction!

Dora held up a newspaper clipping. "Steve's story about Jane's death made the front page this morning. And it was the talk of the town last night at my book club. This is big time."

"What's the chatter?" I said.

"Several said they thought it sounded fishy. No pun intended."

"Octopus are not fish," Sparky came back.

"I know!" Dora hissed and air-swiped Sparky across the face. "One lady mentioned that she saw Jane at city council meetings and there were lots of glares and stares between Jane and the council members. She heard Jane was having an affair with one of them."

"Really?" I asked.

"A few of them had heard this. Me, too. Not sure if it's true," Dora said.

Sparky chimed in. "I heard the bit about her sleeping with a councilman, too. I heard it was Block."

I rocked back in my chair. "Interesting."

"Jane's death was the topic at the Poop Deck last night, too," Sparky said.

The Poop Deck is a favorite for locals and visitors and has been on the island for decades. It's three blocks from my house on the seawall, but it's Sparky's hangout, not mine.

"My friend Gail told me Jane was a lesbian, so she couldn't have slept with a city council member – they're all men," Dora said. "She said that lesbians are known to be violent and strong, so maybe one of her lady friends threw her into the tank."

"Dora!" I gave her a disappointed look.

"I don't believe that. The part about lesbians being violent. That's what Gail said."

"Let's make note of these rumors but remember that people are full of shit most of the time."

"I saw a guy get pulled off his kayak by a gator on the Discovery Channel." Sparky leaned into the table and spoke with a creepy whisper. "Maybe the octopus dragged her into the tank, like the gator did to that man. Animals attack people every day."

I glared at Sparky and stood in front of the flipchart paper sheets with a marker.

"Before we move on, I heard one more thing." Dora looked at her notes. "Jenny, who's a server at the Mosquito Café, said Jane was in there last week with a good-looking fellow. They seemed chummy."

"Did she say if the guy had long hair?" I wondered if it might've been Ari.

"Short hair, looked athletic."

"OK, it wasn't our client. Must've been someone else."

I wrote PS, for potential suspects, on the top of one flipchart sheet and PM, for potential motives, on the other and added SHORT-HAIRED LUNCH DATE to the PS list.

"Ari's concern about the cause of death seems genuine but we should keep him on the list of potential suspects." I added Ari's name to the PS list.

It might surprise you to hear this, readers, but those who report crimes, or make the biggest fuss, are statistically more likely to have committed them than those who remain silent. It's true! We always put our clients on the potential suspects list, but please don't tell them this, as it might affect their willingness to pay us on time.

"What do we know for sure right now?" I asked.

"The cameras were turned off in the area, so there's no footage," Sparky confirmed. "Apparently, this is a common practice. Maybe there are cameras farther from the crime scene that recorded something."

"Will you explore that?"

"Sure." Sparky pulled out a stapled report from a folder.

"I got a copy of the police report. They interviewed Dr. Larson, the lab director, who confirmed they black out sections for classified projects. It also says that Larson agrees with the police that this was a tragic accident or animal attack. Did you talk to BJ?"

"Yes, last night," I replied. "He told me the same thing. He said I should go away and leave him alone because there isn't a case here."

"No indication of forced entry. Nothing was disturbed or taken. The police might be right." Sparky shrugged his shoulders, pushed the police report across the table to me, stood, and added FRED to the PS list, and NATURE to the PM list.

I sat and scanned the police report. Sparky and Dora waited for my response.

"Something's off about this case. It might not be obvious, but that's why they need us, right?" I looked at them both. "Dora, what were the actual *facts* about the victim that you found out?"

"Still researching, but here's what I know. Dr. Jane Moore, born January 12, 1970, in Crescent City, Oregon, got her PhD in Biology at UC Davis and has been at the BARL for fifteen years. Extremely successful career. She brought in a lot of research grants and privately funded project money for BARL."

"They're going to miss the money she generated," Sparky said.

I stood and added GRANTS AND PROJECT MONEY to the PM chart.

"She testified against several developers and politicians over the years, mostly related to pollution in the bay and local inlets." Dora grabbed a cookie and continued speaking with her mouth full. "I've requested lists of the cases on which she served as an expert witness or complainant from the courthouse and city council's office. I should have that in a few days."

I add EXPERT TESTIMONY to the PM sheet. "What about family?"

"She didn't have a lot of family and her closest relative is her brother, Bernie, who lives in California. He's a carpenter and has a wife and seven-year-old daughter."

"The police indicated in their report that they contacted the brother as next of kin and he'll be flying into town later this week," Sparky said.

"Maybe I can arrange to speak with him." I added the brother's name to the PS page.

"Anything else we know?"

Dora and Sparky shook their heads.

"OK, this is a good start. I'll meet with Ari to learn more about why he thinks Fred didn't do it. The autopsy report should be available in a day or two. Let's divide and conquer and meet back."

Dora and Sparky got ready to take notes, accustomed to my practical business orientation and clear instructions. You can take the girl out of the corporation but can't take the corporation out of the girl!

I breathed deep, assembled my ideas, and smiled.

"Dora, continue your research on octopus attacks. Are

they common? How many are fatal? Ari will give me another lesson on octopus behavior tomorrow, but I'd like second source of information. Also, dig further into the brother's background. And Ari's. I'd like to know more about our new client."

"You got it."

"Sparky, I'd like you to explore security cameras beyond the immediate area where Jane's body was found and also around her home. I'll ask Ari for a contact in their IT department. Tap into your usual sources to see if Jane left a digital footprint from the last two weeks."

"Should be fun. Traffic cams, too?"

"Let's hold off on that until we can narrow the time of death."

"Sure. I don't think the police checked out the area around her house, so I'll do that."

"Good, thank you. This is an amazing opportunity to highlight our unique expertise. The case has been closed. No one's looking at it, and yet a popular researcher has died in a most peculiar manner. I'm intrigued and have a feeling there's something hinky about this case. When I looked into Ari's eyes yesterday, I saw pain and resolve."

Sparky stared at a stain on his shirt. Dora pressed forward, put her elbows on the table, and held her face in her hands. She looked both curious and sleepy. I sometimes wonder if my team thinks I'm full of shit!

"If Fred didn't do this, it means we may have a murderer loose on our streets. Watch your backs, keep digging, and let's connect regularly to keep each other in the loop. Fred may be an innocent and grieving creature and we only have thirteen days to clear his name."

I caught Sparky rolling his eyes. Dora sighed and smiled at me in a motherly way. Such insubordination!

~⊙

Before the glorious incident that changed everything, I was a human resources executive specializing in internal investigations for fifteen years.

It's a common misconception that human resources professionals are, at their core, people-people who enjoy handing out cupcakes and soothing hurt feelings. Early careerists often start off this way but are quickly disabused of these Pollyanna fantasies or transfer to the marketing department. Those who remain are drawn to the salacious, fascinated with mysteries, and immensely satisfied with poetic justice.

In any case, I advanced up the corporate ladder at several large organizations, including a holding company for a chain of nursing and assisted care homes for seniors called Granny's Home. Gradually, however, I realized that Granny's Home was a gigantic fraud and that my fellow executives were deliberately and steadily siphoning off the immense profits into personal luxuries and flagrantly over-sized homes, as well as depositing the ill-gotten gains into their private bank accounts.

I'd been feeling increasingly uncomfortable and ultimately horrified about what I was seeing around me, but also frustrated about how to stop it.

What finally put me over the edge was when the chief financial officer, one of my several bosses, asked the company to pay for the twins he'd fathered with his executive assistant so his wife wouldn't discover he was in breach of their ironclad prenup. His crony, the chief executive officer, approved the arrangement against my recommendation, saying it was a legitimate business activity because the CFO worked long hours and had unmet carnal needs.

That was it for me. The End. I was mad as hell and not willing to let it continue under my watch at the HR helm. Stimulated by the god-awful happenings around me, I was inspired to devise a secret plan to destroy my bosses and bring down their whole house of cards.

Chapter 3
Three Years Prior

"It's time to sanitize some corporate scum!" I announced as I marched into Gregory's spy shop wearing a rainbow-striped Grateful Dead bear suit. I needed a costume that'd look natural next to the transvestite dance troupe but didn't require me to walk in platform shoes. Lord knows that would've ended badly. I had looked through the inventory at Arnie's Party Supplies and decided the bear suit seemed safe and would offer Gregory options for embedding mini-mics and cameras.

Gregory recognized my voice and quickly waved me back to his office, leaving his assistant to take care the customers. I followed him into his office, took off the bear head, plunked into the chair across from his desk, and grinned.

"I'm bringing down the worst of the worst, Gregory. I'm all in. Carpe diem. Seize the day. He who hesitates is lost. All things are ready if our minds be so. Two roads diverged in a—"

Gregory held up his hand. "Whoa there, Robert Frost. Calm down and tell me what happened. Who's the target of all this hyperbolic zeal?"

"Remember the exec who convinced the CEO to pay his child support?"

"Someone else pregnant?

"That'd be tiny compared to this. His birthday is in a few days."

"So?"

"A reliable source told me the chief operating officer and other executives are throwing him a huge party."

"So …"

"At the 2121 Kirby Penthouse."

"Ken Lay's former Enron palace?"

"Yes, no other. Before Lay was arrested and died."

"That sounds interesting, but I'm still not following you."

"There's a big bash on Thursday night for the cheating bastard's sixtieth birthday. I'm told there will be hookers, drugs, booze, and entertainment."

"Sounds like a fun party."

I gave Gregory a cross look. "Sounds to me like an opportunity to bust several of Granny's crooked executives."

"Going from a rich boy's birthday party to getting several big shots arrested seems like a leap."

"You sound like Oliver."

Oliver, my fiancé at the time, told me to leave it alone. He categorized leaders' actions and decisions into a work bucket and a personal bucket. I saw behavior as a continuum. Situations like these had made me wonder if we were a match.

"These execs have ethics clauses in their contracts," I

continued. "It's one of the first things I changed. They'll have to forfeit their jobs and their seven-figure golden handcuffs if they're arrested and convicted of anything."

"I hope your informant has given you good intel. You'd hate to rush in there and find a string quartet playing Vivaldi for a civilized crowd."

"I confirmed the details through a second source. It's going down. Will you be my wingman?"

"Any day, any place." Gregory grabbed his chin. "It'll be a peculiar surveillance installation."

I placed both of my paws on his desk. "Breakthroughs occur on the fringes, my friend."

"True." He shrugged and then threw his hands high in surrender. "What's the plan?"

I sighed in relief because I knew my idea would work with Gregory at my side. He had helped my human resources team investigate some tricky cases at Granny's, like a third-shift pharmacy crew who was running a meth lab out of the blood bank. He also worked with us to catch an executive assistant who had used her boss's login to hire Max, her cocker spaniel. Max's midlevel management job paid $195,000 a year, plus a twenty-five percent bonus based on performance metrics he always exceeded. And we had partnered with Gregory and the Houston PD to bring to justice a nurse who was turning tricks bedside. Her lawyers argued she was providing important sex therapy and collected cash payments because Medicare didn't have reimbursement codes for the procedures she performed.

"I'm going to attend the party and alert the media and

police if I observe any illegal activities."

Gregory raised an eyebrow. "That's your plan?"

"Pretty much. I know there are details to work out, but I'm using our whistle-blower policy – which I also changed last year – to hold them accountable."

"How'll you ensure you're on the invite list? They don't usually request the presence of the top HR lady at such parties. And these guys don't like you the least bit on a personal level, as I recall."

"I'm shocked." I smiled, scooted forward and whispered for no reason. "I won't have an invite. I'm going in this costume. Incognito. I'd like you to install mics and cameras."

"Undercover? Cool. Who's your media contact."

"Dunno yet. Whom should we use?"

"Steve Heart. He's the best investigative reporter in town and owns the healthcare beat. He's open to nontraditional assignments, too."

"Good, that's important."

"You want me to call him for you?"

"Yes, pplleeaassee," I gave my best femme fatale pose, which I'm sure looked weird coming from a bear.

"I'll ask him to come by the shop tomorrow before we open. Bring your costume back so I can get it ready for the party."

I stood, raised both arms and twirled around, nearly falling when my stubby bear tail got caught in the chair arm. "It's going to be epic!" I exclaimed while righting myself. "I gotta go. I need a Fire-Breathing Dragon."

"A dragon suit, too? Because you know that tail would be even more dangerous to navigate."

"No. Green juice with jalapeño from the Fresh Squeeze. It's called *nutrition*. Gonna need my energy and focus."

~⊚

The next morning, I brought my costume back to the spy shop and handed it to Gregory. He held it high next to me.

"It's a bit baggy, but will work fine." Gregory inspected the suit from front to back. "You're going to need more cushioning around the belly, too."

I flexed my arm muscles and struck a bodybuilding pose. "It's the freerunning."

"Mine is body by meat supreme pizza. I'm rather dedicated." Gregory patted his rounded belly.

"Commit or go home."

"Yep."

Gregory handed me the bear. "Put on the suit. I'll take the extra fabric into account and mark where we want the mics and cameras."

I climbed into the body of the bear and put on the green furry feet. "I'll need to wear cowboy boots or something under these to get them to stay on." I then pulled my hair back into a short ponytail, pinned my bangs out of the way, and slipped on the head carefully. "This part smells."

"The lengths we go for our craft, eh?" Gregory marked several places on the suit with slips of paper and pins and I took the suit off.

A man walked into the shop and looked at the suit. "Should I ask?"

"Hey, Steve!" Gregory greeted him with a smile and motioned to me. "Meet Xena Cali. She's the Senior Vice President of HR over at Granny's Home."

We shook hands, but I could tell Steve was a bit wary about why we were all here. "Great to meet you, Steve," I said. "Gregory tells me you're one of Houston's top investigative reporters."

"Yep. Wait … *one* of?" He smiled at Gregory and relaxed a bit.

"Xena would like to offer you an exclusive on a big story," Gregory said.

"Great," Steve said slowly. "What's the catch? There's always a catch."

"How familiar are you with Granny's Home?" I asked.

"Very. And I must admit that my impression isn't too favorable."

"We're on the same page there." I tried to reassure Steve. "Relax, I'm not going to ask you to do a puff piece. In fact, I need you to follow your nose and write about what you find. Warts and all." Steve looked perplexed, so I cut to the chase. "Granny's hired me to reduce corruption."

"I remember. I wrote about the fraud case and settlement and their announcement that they'd hired you away from Amazon. How's that been going?"

"We've made some progress; mostly midlevel stuff. And that's the problem. Several execs have gotten away with bad behavior for years." Steve put his hand on his chin, nodded, and moved closer. I continued, "I've credible information from an executive secretary that there's going to be a big party. She helped plan it and is pissed at her greedy boss who's paying thousands for the lavish arrangements but refused to buy twenty-five-dollars-worth of Girl Scout cookies from her daughter."

"Seriously?"

Gregory broke in. "You know what they say about scorned women …"

I held up my hand to Gregory so we didn't get off track. "Steve, I'm offering you the exclusive, but you must agree to play by my timing and rules," I said.

Steve took out his notebook and pen. "I'm listening."

"I need you to be on call Thursday evening. We'll send you a live video and audio feed and ask that you write a story about what you see."

"I'll send it from my van," Gregory said.

"I'm wearing this bear suit to the event," I said.

"Sounds like an unusual party." Steve looked at the costume again and raised his bushy eyebrows. "What did your informant tell you?"

"Can't share that now. Once we send the feed, respond to what you see and hear. We'll give you the address at the same time in case you want to go to the scene. You can call the police, too, if you feel it's warranted." I counted on him doing both as part of my plan.

"Call the police, huh?" Steve asked. "This is twisted stuff. I hope you're right about this."

"I am."

Steve looked at Gregory and then back to me, and straightened his stance. "I'm in."

～◎

I arrived early at the underground meeting point for the entertainers and watched each act park and gather as three shuttle buses pulled into the lot. I put on my costume and joined them. As I expected, no one asked who I was or why I was there. The transvestite dance troupe wore elaborate gowns and some towered over seven feet tall in their matching gold lamé boots. One of them cornered a man with six macaws in two large cages.

"Are these giant birds going to crap on my sequin gown?" the dancer asked.

"Certainly not," the handler said. "They never come out of their cages, but to be safe I haven't fed them for three days."

A group of major-league hookers eyed the transvestites as if they might be competition for tips. Three bagpipe players kept to themselves near the front of the third shuttle and seemed uncomfortable with the whole scene. A scrawny guy with tattoos covering every visible patch of skin hopped onto the shuttle at the last minute. He looked like a drug dealer. According to my source, several helicopters would deliver the pharmaceuticals and the guests.

The ride to the penthouse took under five minutes. I could hear Gregory, who was in the control van, laughing in my earpiece. "This is going to be interesting," he chirped between giggles.

He narrated his observations from the cameras and invented stories about the people on the bus because he knew I was a captive audience and couldn't talk back to him without blowing my cover. The bear head contained and amplified the sound like a high-end headset. I concentrated and stared forward, trying to keep it together.

~⊙

The late Ken Lay, may he rest in uncomfortable distress, had a thirteen-thousand-square-foot Enron reward system penthouse condo with its own helipad and ten dedicated parking spots. It was now being rented out by Enron creditors to help recoup their losses, and had become *the* place for ritzy events.

The shuttle buses pulled into the building's garage and we took three private elevators up to the top floor. When we got to the main reception area, which was flanked by staffed pouring stations, we were greeted by a guy who looked a lot like Kenny G playing a saxophone.

"Hey, is that Kenny G?" Gregory asked. "Please don't tell me we're going to get Kenny G busted. My wife loves his music."

"Wife, my ass. I bet you're the fan boy," I said softly. I walked to the liquor stations and whispered to Gregory. "Let's do a soundcheck. Here we have Cristal champagne. Nice."

"I can hear you fine. What's that on the next table?"

I walked over and said, "1800 Colección tequila. Let's test this." I moved to the next table and turned my back to it. "Try to read the label with my butt cam."

"Dalmore Scotch that's ... sixty-two years old! They spared no expense. You're paying your execs too much."

A server walked in front of me and I started to bob my big round head to the beat of the music.

"Ingredients for an amazing party," Gregory said. "Except for the hookers and drugs. Goes without saying."

The event team helped everyone find their places. The outside stage was next to the pool area where the macaw cages added a tropical flair. The transvestites practiced for their live dance production, which was set to popular rap songs. I hung close to them, hoping the staff might assume I was part of their performance. The bagpipe players warmed up at the other end of the condo but were heard and felt everywhere. The guy who looked like Kenny G enjoyed serenading the hookers, who had made a beeline for the bar.

Within the next half hour, five or six loaded helicopters arrived filled with Granny's business partners and has-been socialites needing benefactors for their next plastic surgery procedure.

The final helicopter delivered the chief operating officer, chief financial officer, and chief medical officer, and several other Granny's executives. I tensed as they brushed past me and into semi-private lounge pits in the center of the condo, but not one of them recognized or even glanced at me.

"*Wow*," I whispered, as I was enjoying this interesting turn of events. Just the previous week I had presented the company's slipping employee engagement scores in my best navy suit to these same leaders.

The transvestite troupe rocked their first set while the

booze and hookers were served to the guests.

It was a surreal mix of people in a place designed with Liberace's sensibilities. I was a big hit in my costume, which enabled me to move around without causing suspicion. I posed with guests for pictures as I made my way to where the execs were partying. The drug dealer turned out to be a guy named Waldo – just Waldo – the washed-up former lead singer from the Flaming Monkeys. He passed out pills, powder, and packets as if it was trick-or-treat candy.

I walked inside to see what the executives were doing and assumed the initial rounds of drinks and drugs would be impacting their brain cells by now. The CFO and COO were lounging in a sunken pit upholstered in purple velvet. Opaque silk runners coming down from the ceiling had created a private canopy area that I could film by positioning my furry, camera-injected butt between the breaks in the silk strips.

"Are you getting this?" I asked Gregory.

"Yep. Unbelievable," he replied as the COO, CFO, and CMO enjoyed a pack of attentive naked girls. "Your execs are doing lines and the drug dealer—"

"Waldo," I whispered.

"Waldo … is going on about some revival tour."

"Start streaming to Steve."

"Once I send the video, Steve will be able to hear everything we say, FYI." I formed my fuzzy hands into a thumbs-up, placing it where I knew Gregory could see them from the cameras.

"OK, streaming … now …" Gregory confirmed.

The bagpipes had ended up being a bad idea. They started playing after the transvestites finished their first set, squawking out Beatles songs at decibels that'd make a deaf Scottish virgin cringe. Two fucked-up hookers, including one who was in the middle of giving the CFO a blowjob, started screaming and holding their hands over their ears. The CFO roared and launched after the hooker, but tripped over his pants and face-planted into thousands of dollars of now bloodied coke. Was it a nosebleed or was it really broken?

"Holy shit!" Gregory yelled.

Macaws screeched and banged around in their cages trying to escape the offensive noises. The handler opened their doors to let them out so they didn't hurt themselves.

"Birds in flight!" Gregory screamed even louder. I grabbed my bear ears in anguish. "Sorry!" he then hissed.

The event manager convinced the bagpipers to stop. They stomped off stage, stole the bottle of Dalmore, and demanded a helicopter lift back to their cars.

"What moron would book hookers *and* bagpipes?" Gregory asked.

I didn't answer. I was focusing to ensure my cameras caught what was happening in the purple pit. Waldo told everyone to chill out and enjoy the party. He escorted the distressed hookers into another pit where he had set out opium pipes, tequila, and vodka Jell-O shooters. He introduced the embattled CFO to a woman with tits the size of beach balls and everything seemed OK again.

"Freak. Of. Nature," I muttered and started grooving to the beat of the DJ's music.

"That's not Mother Nature's work. She's Candy, from *Candy Is Dandy*. It was a best-selling porn film about ten years ago … I'm told … and stop that dancing, you're messing with my video feed. Wait … heads-up. Three o'clock!"

The starving macaws had escaped from the handler and were jumping from guest to guest, pecking at anything that resembled food, including jewelry, Quaaludes, Chex Mix, and Jell-O shots. Two landed on me and it was difficult to control my every urge to scream so I didn't reveal my identity. The handler and a few waiters lured the macaws away from guests using baskets of hot sopapillas.

"Turn around. Check out the pool area," Gregory said.

I did so and saw the CFO, COO, and the CMO dancing half naked in a Rockettes-style kick line with several transvestites. They urged the ex-porn star to pull off her halter top and join the line while Waldo danced in the opposite direction to pass out bong hits. Some guests cheered while others joined in.

"She should have left that on," I concluded after Candy went topless. "I had no idea implants could fall so far."

"Listen, Xena," Gregory interrupted. "Steve just told me that he and the HPD drug enforcement and vice teams are heading up to the condo."

"Nice timing!" My plan was coming together.

"Better warn Kenny G," Gregory pleaded. "I don't want the police to arrest him or I'll be in trouble at home again."

I bounced over to whisper a warning to the sax player. He grabbed a bottle of Cristal and jumped into a down elevator.

Steve and the police's narc and vice squads arrived a couple of minutes later. At first, the execs thought the break-in was part of the entertainment. The naked CFO asked the police to handcuff him, which they did. He laughed as they threw him on the ground, sure this was part of his birthday present. The CMO realized something was wrong after the vice squad evacuated several elevators filled with screaming guests. Steve and his photographer were busy capturing the scene as best as they could without getting in the police's way. I kept off to the side with Steve, who told the police I was his informant.

They let the transvestites and the event staff go and arrested the execs from Granny's Home, their guests, the hookers, and Waldo. The police cited the macaw handler for endangering a threatened species. The SPCA later rushed the birds to the Gulf Coast Emergency Clinic; Steve told me they tested positive for cocaine, alcohol, barbiturates, and marijuana.

I overheard the executives tell the cops they believed it was going to be a classy charity event and the hosts must've drugged them to coerce them to make large donations. But even in spite of the CFO peeing in the bucket of high-end tequila bottles and the COO teetering, grabbing a silk runner for balance, and spinning down to the ground like a top, the police captain sounded open to their version of the facts.

"No, this can't happen," I protested to Steve. "They can't talk their way out of this. Get ready."

I took off my bear head and walked over to the CFO and police.

I can still remember the confused, pissed, and fearful looks on the faces of the Granny's execs when they saw me. It. Was. Awesome.

"Hello, Harold," I announced to the CFO.

"What the hell?" He then mumbled something unintelligible about this being a bad birthday gift.

"You're right, Harold, this is a most unwelcome surprise. Imagine when the board finds out their highest-paid executives snorted away their careers and risked the company's future for a few jollies."

The CMO and COO started screaming at me about loyalty and how dare I deceive them and that my career was over.

"Have a nice time sobering up in your cell!" I snapped with a smile as the police took the execs downstairs in the elevators.

I told the police who I was, that I had tipped off Steve there was something illegal going on, and that's when he had called them.

"Why didn't you call 911?" the sergeant in charge asked me.

I danced around the question, knowing they didn't care. Juicy busts like this were gifts however they came wrapped. "I contacted Steve when it looked like a story and before things got ugly. Had I known everything that was going down …"

They let me go after I had provided a full statement. I put my bear head back on and took the elevator to the first floor. Once in Gregory's van, I took off my costume, and we both busted out laughing. We then sighed and got serious for a moment because we knew this was a moment of truth. A bell we could never unring, not that I'd want to.

~⊙

Steve's feature story got national attention. Several in-depth pieces about corporate greed and corruption at Granny's Home came out in the coming weeks. The board suspended the entire executive team pending the outcome of both the criminal and internal investigations. The executives who had attended the party were fired and the company sold their nursing homes to their largest competitor.

I "resigned" from Granny's with a three-year severance intended to keep me quiet about anything else I might be aware of. And I know plenty, dear readers, and have a box of investigation reports and notes stashed in a safety deposit box at an undisclosed location in Houston. Just in case.

~⊙

The Granny's Home sting operation was indeed a glorious incident that changed everything. Everything!

First, I spent a month hiking from distillery to distillery in the Scottish Highlands and another two back in Houston thinking about my career alternatives and life choices. I loved the quaint, awkward, imperfect, and personal feeling of small towns like the ones I had hiked through. I also needed the complexity, intrigue, and action that bigger cities offered.

I know only one place like that in the world.

I asked Gregory to meet me for lunch to share my decision.

"I'm thinking about moving to Galveston," I announced.

"Why Galveston?"

"I like its contradictions and quirks …"

"Sure, but—"

I swayed back and forth in the chair. "Mansions, cottages, and roach motels that rent by the hour …"

"Roaches? Yes, it's—"

I cut Gregory off again while conducting each word with my hands. "Haunted shacks, pirate myths, and technology breakthroughs …"

Gregory laughed, gave in, and relaxed backward.

"RICH med school students, beach-loving CON artists, and cruise ship tourists from Bread. Basket. Towns … ALLIGATORS on one side, SHARKS on the other and DRUNKS WITH GUNS in the middle …"

He held up his hands. "I get it! I get it! Sounds like a perfect setting for an interesting life."

I beamed and perked up straight.

"You should definitely go there," he said.

"And …" I hesitated and looked at Gregory like someone who was about to ask her dad for a $500 prom dress. "And I'm thinking about opening a spy shop and PI practice."

I paused again, not sure how Gregory would feel about the idea.

Gregory was quiet, too, and took what seemed like a thousand sips of his iced tea.

"I LOVE that idea!" he said, putting me out of my misery.

"I don't want to compete with you …"

"I don't work that far south," he assured. "I'll help you get the store ready. We can collaborate on bigger cases."

"Really?"

He nodded his head.

"I'm so relieved you like the idea." I took a folder out of my bag. "I found a shop on Twenty-Fifth," I said. "Between the Antiques Warehouse and Urban Resort. It's two blocks off the Strand."

"That's a cool part of town." Gregory looked at the real estate listing I'd handed him. "What'll you call it?"

"I'm thinking … Paradise Lost Spy Shop."

"It's perfect. How does Oliver feel about this change?"

"I called it off with Oliver. I don't know how to say this without sounding full of myself, but he didn't challenge me. He thwarted me and acted as though my interests were pedestrian compared to his beloved art scene."

"People don't understand what we do. That it's science and art combined."

"That's true!" I agreed.

"Sorry. I know it must've been tough to break things off, even if the choice was clear."

"Yes. I'm also relieved. It'll be a fresh start all around."

"Paradise Lost Spy Shop on Galveston Island … I can't wait to see it come together."

Chapter 4
Three Years Prior

The transition from corporate executive to small business owner and private investigator has been natural and easy for me, but my mom and dad still have had a hard time understanding it all. They had hoped I'd use my law degree to go into private practice. From my perspective, that's exactly what I've done! But they don't see it the same way.

My role in the glorious incident that changed everything at Granny's Home hit cable news stations and was seen by Mom and Dad in my hometown of Cincinnati, Ohio. They each struggled differently with how to talk with me about what happened. My dad had grown up in Greece, so he was accustomed to believing that corruption in government and business was a normal part of progress and economic growth.

"How is that relevant to how well they do their jobs?" he asked me. "What they do in their personal time is personal. They'll have to pay for it when they get home to their wives."

My mother vehemently disagreed with Dad and was proud that I took a stance, but she worried about how the media attention would affect how others treated me.

"What if your friends think you're in a dark and dangerous line of work?" she warned. "Or customers are afraid you'll find out something bad or shameful about them and call the police?"

She had been raised in a small Scottish highland town called Killiecrankie, where neighbors knew everything about everyone but being a discreet community member was expected.

My parents were wonderfully right for each other even though they sometimes held opposite views on things. They had met and fallen in love at college in London. Dad was studying engineering, Mom education and gymnastics. Her specialty was the uneven bars and she almost made the UK Olympics team.

They had moved to Cincinnati before I was born, after my dad got a great job offer to work for Procter & Gamble designing packaging for Pampers, Ivory Soap, Crisco, and Crest toothpaste. Mom taught English and was the gymnastics coach at our high school. Because I shared her strong, compact physique, Mom started me in gymnastics early and had hoped I might someday make the US Olympics team. That never happened because I fell in love with martial arts, especially aikido, and had used what I knew about both disciplines to excel at parkour, also called freerunning – the art of efficient movement.

After earning a degree in employment law from Georgetown University, I then passed the bar, but my internships with law offices were disastrous and I got into major disputes with the partners when I'd find complex and fascinating cases that didn't have paying clients attached to them. I wanted to be where the action happened – inside the belly of the corporate beast – so I worked inside corporations instead of as an attorney in practice.

Like my dad, I love solving tough puzzles, and my career took off. By the time I landed the top HR investigations job at Granny's, I had earned a reputation for getting results, albeit sometimes using unconventional, though always legal, approaches.

Before the glorious incident that changed everything, my commute to work had taken one hour each way through Houston's clogged highways. In Galveston, the trip from home to work takes between three to fifteen minutes, depending on whether I drive, bike, or walk. The east end of Galveston Island is only four miles long and a mile and a half wide, so everything's close.

The Paradise Lost Spy Shop is located on the west side of downtown, at 419 Twenty-Fifth Street. It's close to both the Strand and the seawall, in an edgy neighborhood with lots of entrepreneurs and artists.

There's a mural on the alley-facing wall of our building of a woman in a bikini videotaping mating pelicans. Tourists like to take photos in front of the mural, and many wander into the shop. This is one reason I get more foot traffic than you might guess, given the nature of my business. I'd hired a local artist to paint the mural according to my specifications and it was the best $1,500 I've ever spent for advertising!

Another reason tourists come into the shop is that Dora helps attract cruise ship passengers and local retirees to the store. She got Paradise Lost added to the shopping route for cruise ship shuttles, and identifies products that'd appeal to those consumers such as pepper spray, antitheft bags, ministun guns, hollowed-out books, pen video cameras, and, everyone's favorite, the seagull-shaped drone. Female passengers who worry their pathetic, sex-starved husbands had tampered with their, or other women's, drinks, purchase our Bill Cosby special drug detection drops.

Dora's bridge club hosts self-defense classes at the shop for single retirees. The first part is taught by a local Muay Thai master who shows them how to use eight points of contact to combat an attacker. Dora also shows her seniors the latest gadgets they can carry when they leave their houses, and security measures they should implement at home. She lives in an old Victorian one block off the Strand with two other widows. All three take their independence and welfare seriously and are walking billboards for our personal safety products.

Dora is old enough to be my mother, but we share common interests and would be girlfriend material if she wasn't my employee. It's a golden rule to never befriend your employees, you know that, right? I've seen leaders get trapped in swirling cesspools of misunderstanding and incorrect assumptions after befriending team members on Facebook or going out for drinks after work. We humans do stupid shit after two drinks or under the cover of what seems like a private online network. Ha! Nothing is private anymore.

My leadership mantra is to cultivate within my team a connection to the business and a passion for the work. I show interest in them, but only so far. We never go out socially, connect online, share videos from our vacations, pitch Girl Scout cookies, or talk about our love lives.

Never.

Well … almost never. It's a small town, after all.

Dora is an avid murder mystery reader who knows everything about Galveston. Her retirement from being the Galveston City Historian lasted about six months before she got bored and went back to work. The Paradise Lost Spy Shop is the perfect gig for her because it taps into what she loves about mysteries and history.

You already know that Sparky is my other full-time employee at the shop. He's in his early thirties and looks like a hippie with long, straggly hair, organic cotton tie-dyed shirts, and drawstring pants. He drives a dilapidated 1974 VW Thing and lives in a crappy neighborhood just north of Broadway and west of downtown in a seven-hundred-square-foot shotgun cottage. No one messes with him, though, because the place is wired and streams 360-degree video 24/7.

Unlike many hippies, Sparky is brilliant when it comes to new technology. He's my gadget guru and can videotape, bug, surveil, and find electronic footprints better than anyone I know. I hired Sparky because he was buying more stuff from the shop than he could afford and knew more about what we sold than I did. I was looking for an assistant who could help our more sophisticated clients select and buy the right products.

Sparky was reluctant to come on board because he feared that a regular job would get in the way of his community activism. We worked it out so Dora or I cover for him when he attends demonstrations or other events. It's worth accommodating Sparky's outside commitments because he's *that* good with spy technology.

Sparky's family has lived in Galveston since the *Open Era* of the 1920s and '30s, when the island nurtured its dark side. In those days, it was a major tourist destination for those interested in illegal gambling and other endeavors that'd ordinarily get the vice squad's attention. Celebrities, beatniks, and famous mobsters rushed to Galveston, where repressive beliefs and laws were rejected by many, including local officials, who usually looked the other way.

There's a noticeable difference between true locals like Sparky and more recent transplants, like me and thousands of others. For Sparky, community progress and setbacks are deeply personal. He believes the city council ought to ban Target stores, Chick-fil-A fast food emporiums, and cookie-cutter apartment complexes. He favors fueling the economy by providing low-cost housing for craftspeople, tax breaks for small, locally owned businesses, and collecting tax revenue from recreational drug sales (after making them legal). He's led or been active with several grassroots organizations that aim to keep Galveston small, special, and livable for locals.

~⊙

Have you been to Galveston? It's like a do-it-yourself version of Las Vegas with the grittiness of New Orleans thrown in for good flavor. Naughty and uninhibited are on the to-do list for most visitors.

Within two years of opening my spy shop, every upscale hotel concierge had us on speed dial. We sell two popular packages to this clientele. The first, called the Viral Adventure Tracker, includes a nearly invisible video cam and portable light source that can easily be attached to ceiling fixtures or doorknobs. Hotels buy and resell VAT Pacs to wandering husbands who enjoy making high-definition recordings of their Viagra-enabled screw-fests to show their buddies back home. We also have a multi-hooker upgrade that we routinely sell out of during the high season, from Mardi Gras through the end of summer. The VAT Plus Pac offers two camera angles and Google Glass for a 360-degree production.

Our second most popular package is purchased primarily by those suspicious of their piece-of-shit spouses. It includes audio recording devices, GPS tracking, and a tiny, snake-necked video camera that's able to go under doors or up three stories.

It has been an awesome business, readers. I don't make the cheaters cheat; I help them fully cultivate their potential before they get caught. It's an important and valuable community service!

My first big case on the island – shutting down a brothel doing business under the name Mancation Adventures – earned us some thanks from Detective Rawlins of the Criminal Investigations Bureau. Here's how it happened …

A pediatrician from Seattle hired me to find out what her

husband was doing in Galveston. The pictures he was sending her showed him participating in various sport-related activities, but the GPS app she used to keep track of him showed he had remained in one position. She looked it up on Google Maps and discovered he was in an old hotel on the west end of the island. She then googled *Galveston private investigators* and found me.

Our landside stakeout couldn't tell us much because the entrance to the property was gated and locked. So I kayaked by one evening wearing night-vision goggles and found an entry point onto the hotel grounds. I tied my kayak to a docked boat, jumped on the dock, and got close enough to the building to hear and videotape what was happening on in the patio. Several men were bragging about hour-long erections while gorging on pulled pork sliders and beers.

Topless girls were waiting on the men while others escorted the men back and forth from the inside of the house. The windows, unfortunately, were blacked out.

Back at the spy shop, Sparky found and followed the business' electronic trail including several password-protected chat rooms and online sales videos. Dora researched the property-related permits and real estate transactions. We soon discovered that Mancation Adventures had moved their base of operations from Bangkok to Galveston, presumably because the poor dollar-to-baht conversion rate was killing their business. MA marketed all-expenses paid trips to middle-aged men who could talk their wives into letting them take a vacation with their buddies.

They were called bro-packs.

A fake website and brochures gave Mancation Adventures a look of legitimacy. They even had a studio where they mocked up photos of the bro-packs fishing, kayaking, or touring NASA that the men could email to their wives.

This, of course, was a well-orchestrated sham. While the wives thought their husbands were participating in sports, Mancation Adventures provided high-priced escorts who gave customers the time of their lives, all fueled by readily available Viagra, uppers, downers, booze, and bottomless vats of BBQ.

Once we figured out what was really going on, I told my client in Seattle so she could get her husband out before it all went down. She chose not to contact him. I also called Steve Heart and told him the story was about to break. Even though it was outside his regular healthcare beat, he drove from Houston that night.

My third call was to BJ Rawlins at the Galveston Island Police Department. After he heard my synopsis of the case, he asked me to come to the GIPD headquarters on Fifty-Fourth Street. We spent the better part of the morning with him going over all the meticulous evidence Sparky and Dora had prepared.

"This is well done, Miss Cali," BJ offered.

"Please call me Xena."

"Seena?"

"No, like a *Z*. 'Zeena'," I explained. "And is it OK for a reporter named Steve Heart to come along if he stays out of the way?"

"Well, ordinarily I don't like to publicize a bust, but these sleazy folks deserve it."

That very evening, BJ led a team of detectives and patrol officers on a midnight raid at Mancation Adventures, arresting twelve women in various stages of nudity and twenty pissed-off customers. It was our first time working with the GIPD and we earned a good deal of credibility because it was a major bust that made them look good.

A year later, Steve moved to Galveston to work for the *Galveston Post Intelligencer*. The official press release said that he was taking his career in a new direction, but he told me he was fired after he had discovered and exposed that a former mayor of Houston was growing and selling hallucinogenic drugs. John Reiner was found running naked, except for his custom-made cowboy boots, in the Discovery Green Park downtown with a pygmy goat named Sue he had liberated from the children's petting zoo.

Reiner's publicist was spinning the event as an acute medical incident, but Steve had retraced the ex-mayor's steps to a head shop called Smoke Signals in Midtown that had a large grow room and lab on the second floor. Records had showed the shop was owned by Southern Botanicals, which was owned by a shell company of which Reiner was the majority owner. His cockatoo, Jasper, was the minority owner. The judge presiding over the case held Jasper in contempt of court after he answered every question with songs from the musical *Tommy*.

Steve's story had exposed that Reiner had been supplying the region with psilocybin mushrooms, peyote dots, and DMT for twenty-five years, including the eight years he was the mayor of Houston – a big embarrassment for the fourth largest city in

America. And while Steve's excellent investigative reporting had earned him well-deserved recognition, it was a problem for his paper's president, who happened to be Reiner's cousin.

I've already told you that Steve could've moved anywhere but chose the Galveston Island for many of the same reasons I did: easy access to recreational drugs ... Kidding!

Chapter 5
Day 2, Wednesday (Continued)

Dora and I shared a delicious muffaletta for lunch from the Maceo Spice Company, which was one block from the shop. I turned on the large TV in the meeting room and used it to open the Galveston Municipal television channel website, where the city council meeting was being streamed live. We'd promised Sparky we'd watch because he and a group called Keep the Island Small and Successful, or *KISS*, were going to picket outside the City Hall building and address council members during the meeting.

"It looks like the meeting is about to begin," I said, looking at the TV screen.

"Yep. Here comes Sparky and several protestors. They've filled the last four rows. Standing room only," Dora observed.

"Do you know why it was so important to Sparky that we watch? I'd like to prep for my meeting with Ari."

"Not sure," Dora smiled. I could tell she knew more than she let on.

Dora tidied the store shelves and I made notes about the

case as we half listened to the city council meeting. Each councilman reported on the Neighbors Night Out block parties and thanked local police and fire houses for participating. They approved a new parking lot permit for the Jack in a Box being built on Broadway and three houses were granted Galveston City landmark status.

The meeting secretary then introduced a signage variance request for a new development, and he invited the property owner to the podium to submit her testimony. A woman came forward and said her name was Vicki Moon, owner of Cerulean Sky.

"Here we go," Dora announced. "This is Sparky's cause."

The video camera showed the backside of Vicki Moon and I could see that she had a dark pageboy cut like mine. When she started to talk, the video feed switched cameras to a tight shot from the front.

"Holy shit," I exclaimed.

"She looks exactly like you! But older, of course," Dora patted me on the arm.

"Who *is* this person?"

"Sparky called her the devil incarnate. But you know how he is. She's building the big mall and hotel development three blocks west of us and south of the cruise terminal. On the old brewery site."

"I've seen the construction site but I've never seen *her*. She even has tattoos."

I have a large Chinese dragon tattoo on one arm (because I was born in the Year of the Dragon) and a Celtic spiral on the opposite forearm. And a few others on my back and legs.

Vicki raised her heavily inked arms as she explained pictures of her proposed signage. She looked fit and toned.

"Is that a koi fish on Vicki's arm?" Dora asked.

"Looks like it. Nice work, and very realistic. I wonder where she goes."

"Wow," Dora said. "She even talks like you! So professional and smooth. Were you adopted? Maybe you and Vicki are twins separated at birth."

"Stop it, no!" I objected and Dora laughed. But she was right; Vicki seemed intelligent and charming.

Sparky and two other protestors stepped up to the podium after Vicki was done and stated why they believed her signage permit should be denied. They argued the large neon lettering would detract from the Victorian charm of the Strand. Vicki then came back for final testimony and showed pictures of how the signs would look at night. The lights from the ship channel industrial operations and two parked cruise ships dominated the sky and overshadowed the street lighting from the Strand. The neon sign on top of the Cerulean Sky building seemed tame in comparison.

"That's pretty cool, actually. I like the pink and blue," Dora admitted.

"I won't tell Sparky you said that."

The city council granted Vicki Moon her sign permits. No surprise there; the council supports business owners most of the time.

"He'll be in a crappy mood later," Dora said.

"No kidding." I moved closer to the TV screen and watched as Vicki left the meeting room. She put on large, round sunglasses that accentuated her thick, dark bangs.

Dora stared, too. "She may've had some work done on those lips. Otherwise, she's a dead ringer for you!"

"I'd never wear my nails that long."

~◎

Early that evening, I changed out of my work clothes and into a pair of yoga pants – not that I ever dressed up or practiced yoga – poured a glass of wine, and nuked leftovers from the Mosquito Café. I heard voices and went out to the porch to investigate. It was my friend Sally and her Segway tour group stopping in front of my house. This is a common occurrence because my house is a landmark, but more important, it's a convenient midway point between the Pleasure Pier and Broadway. Newer Segway Personal Transporter riders need frequent breaks.

I went downstairs. "Hello, Sally."

"Meet the Robinson family. They're here from Buffalo, NY, and just got off the *Carnival Magic*."

"Hello!" I said to the Robinsons. "Thanks for checking out my house."

"This is Xena, the owner of what locals call the Stanley House. It was built in 1950 by a well-known engineer out of concrete and steel. It's unusual to see a house like this in Galveston."

The Robinsons didn't seem very interested. The mother hadn't gotten the hang of the Segway, so was unsteady and jerked back and forth. She looked as though she was about to throw up. The three kids were spinning in place as the husband took frequent swigs from a chrome flask. Sally, bless her heart, was either oblivious or honestly thought the family were enjoying themselves.

She continued, "The Stanley House is an example of the International Modern Style. Notice the corner windows and lack of adornment."

The father turned to face the opposite direction while the kids took selfies.

"I've been told that engineer Paul Stanley built an airplane in the garage," I said.

That's true.

Still nothing from the Robinsons. The mother was looking down, likely for an exit strategy.

I tried again. "And that his plane was shot down by Snoopy the Red Baron and crashed into the Ferris wheel on the Pleasure Pier. The explosion set off a chain reaction, and that's why they had to rebuild everything on the pier."

Not true. Hurricane Ike demolished the pier, but I wanted to see if I could get a response. Sally darted her eyes at me, not happy that I'd degraded her carefully narrated historical tour with my ridiculousness. I smiled and winked, but Sally turned and signaled that it was time to move on. The Robinsons politely bobbed their heads, which bobbed their Segways.

After I went back inside, I ate dinner and finished a second glass of wine while listening to my favorite jazz playlist. OK, it was Yanni, but remember I'm half Greek. It's like New Yorkers and Sinatra, Canadians and beer, or Seattle and coffee: expected. Does it help that I also like The Fray,

Arctic Monkeys, Glass Animals, and My Chemical Romance? We are all complex beings, readers, with banal pleasures that nonetheless ring our chimes. How else can we explain the continued success of Spam, Busch Light, cheap rubber flip-flops, official Rachel Ray Cookware, and Honda Accords?

I thumbed through Jane's journals again to review the entries I marked last night. She wrote as if she was talking to a friend and it made me wonder who her friends were. I added a question about Jane's friends to the list I was drafting for my meeting with Ari the next day. She mentioned Ansel in a few posts, including this one:

> I went to see the crew of the Elissa because they asked me to stop by to check out something new in the water. It's not organic, that's for sure. It's some sort of pollution that looks lighter than the usual oil-and-gas slick you might expect in a busy ship channel. The source can't be far away. Ask Ansel to check it out.

That post, dated six weeks prior to Jane's death, marked the beginning of the situation involving Ansel. I made a note to visit the *Elissa* crew. I chuckled at a post about Fred, where he rejected a fish because it was still frozen. Picky octopus! In the dozen or more posts about Fred, Jane never mentioned any kind of aggression or aberrant behavior. If he was getting angry, wouldn't she have noticed and written about the signs?

I reread a long post about Judge Buddy Sassoon, who

apparently had crossed paths with Jane during legal cases where she was an expert witness. It was clear that she hadn't thought highly of the judge:

> *Judge Buddy is a misogynist, sexist scumbag. The laughing stock of Galveston. He can't uphold and represent the law while simultaneously breaking it. How does one get caught with a fifteen-year-old, have the story plastered all over the paper, and get reelected with seventy-five percent of the votes? What are people thinking? He gets reelected because locals like the entertainment value he brings to the community. Today he disregarded testimony and advice to rule in favor of greedy oyster farmers who are surely padding his bank account. Oyster populations will suffer! I won't let you win the next one, Buddy. The flounder case is too important to the ecosystem. I don't care about your cronies; I won't let you ruin the bay. Need to bring everything I've got. Call the media?*

I know Judge Buddy Sassoon, by the way, because he's a regular customer at the spy shop. Jane was right that he is a decrepit human being. The case with the fifteen-year-old hooker had, in fact, been all over the papers, and it was inexcusable the way Buddy's lawyers had discredited the girl to make sure no one would believe her story. I looked forward to learning more about the flounder case and made a note to add Buddy's name to the potential suspects list.

After taking a few more notes for my meeting with Ari, I

called Gregory. We went through our daily questions and then sat in silence for a moment.

"We both failed today," Gregory argued. "Why are we even bothering with these questions?"

"Our problem is that we're like pyromaniac firefighters," I said.

"What? We're not setting fires."

"In a way we are. Hear me out. There's a disproportionate number of firefighters who become pyromaniacs. It's documented. Firefighters love fighting fires, but what do they spend most of their time doing?"

"Cleaning fire trucks."

"Exactly. The part of their job they love the most accounts for about five percent of their time. Some set fires so they've more to put out."

"What?" Gregory seemed unconvinced.

"Again, documented. Look it up," I said.

"How are we like that?"

"We love the thrill of solving crimes but spend a small fraction of our time doing that. Maybe we're creating mystery where there's none so we have more to solve. As a result, we fail to take care of other aspects of our businesses and lives."

"We're making new work because it's the work that fulfills us?"

"It's always been my challenge and perhaps it's been yours. We'll never run out of rocks to look under because we'll keep asking questions even if no one else is, or cares."

"Like your octopus case?"

"No, not like that! There's something off about Jane's death. I feel it, and I need to prove it."

"You do that. I gotta go and put out the fire in my wife's eyes," Gregory said. "She's ticked that I forgot to pick her up for lunch today."

"Make her a fancy cocktail. Double strength."

"Great idea. Lynn loves my banana margaritas."

Chapter 6
Day 3, Thursday

The BARL was an ugly, three-story brick building that housed some of the most advanced marine research facilities in the world. Not that I noticed any of this on the way to meet Ari. I was deep in thought about how I might handle this case.

The bright and open lobby had enormous photos of turtles, dolphins, and scuba divers lining two walls. I followed Ari to his office, where we sat at a small table overlooking the Galveston Ship Channel. Ari looked cool in a pair of skinny black jeans and a lime green polo shirt that made his dark features pop. Even so, I could see that he was still in a lot of pain.

"The last few days have been excruciating." Ari slumped into his chair. "Jane was a highly respected researcher … she was a friend, and … she was my mentor."

I thought about how to ease into the topic of the day without putting off my new client. "I can't imagine how you're feeling and I'm sure that it's worse since you don't believe her death is being given the attention it deserves."

Ari nodded.

"From what BJ told me, the scene and circumstances point to Fred. But you think they missed something. Is that right?" I asked.

"I don't know what the full story is, but I know Fred and Jane, and I know they wouldn't have generated the Detective Rawlins version of the narrative. I'm sure of it, but I don't know how to prove it. I tried telling him about octopuses and why it makes no sense that Fred did this, but I'm sure I sounded like an idiot." Ari's passion was palpable in the way his shoulders moved with his words.

"I doubt that you sounded like a fool, you're a respected expert in the field. It's just a strange situation, all of this is. What reasons did you give BJ for Fred's innocence?"

"I had two counter-arguments," he declared. Ari spoke the language of business; right up my alley. He leaned in, sat tall, and showed conviction with his hand gestures and solid eyes. "First, octopuses are intelligent and complex beings. Fred and Jane had a strong relationship, and Fred wouldn't have acted in aggression toward her."

"What about the pissed off elephants that crush their handlers' heads?"

Ari cocked his head sideways and squinted. "Where'd you hear that? I think you saw that in a movie. That ancient practice is something humans train elephants to do as a cruel form of death penalty. Elephants don't choose to crush people's heads in aggression or anger."

I suddenly remembered that I did see it in a movie and felt dumb. I looked down at my pad of paper to avoid eye contact.

"Captive animals sometimes attack their handlers, and octopuses have hurt and even killed humans," he continued. "But octopuses are different because their love or fear or hatred is specific to situations and individuals. They feel emotions and form attachments."

"You're anthropomorphizing and so will I. Based on what I've learned working with law enforcement over the years, most killings are emotional and the deeper the love, the farther the killer cuts."

"Fred didn't feel scorned or jealous, and I'm not talking about romantic love. Fred was found near death by a group of nature-loving baby boomers on a yoga retreat. They called animal control who suggested the group bring him to BARL. He had been slowly poisoned by toxic runoff from a plastics plant on the Mexico side of the Texas border. He's much better now because Jane nursed him back to health." Ari cupped his hands as if Fred were sitting in them. "He knew she saved him and he loved her. In fact, I believe Fred was embracing Jane and mourning her death when they found her."

Ari sat back in his chair and looked out the window as a big tanker ship sailed by on its way out to the Gulf. This was tough for him to talk about.

I moved forward to connect to his gaze. "If that's true, it's quite tragic. Could it have been an accident? Maybe something that started out as play or affection?"

"The police asked this as well and that leads to my second argument. Even if I'm totally wrong about Fred – which I'm not – Fred couldn't have killed Jane because of the safety measures we've in place in the octo tanks."

"Like what you showed me when I met Fred?"

"Yes. Fred, like all octopuses, hates fresh water. The hose may not look like a sophisticated safety device, but we've one installed in each tank and it never fails to get the octopus to move away if it gets too clingy or when a part of the tank needs maintenance. If Fred were pulling Jane under, she would've been able to use the hose to get him to release her. We practice drills every month. We know these are wild animals."

"Let's say that I buy your arguments. If Fred didn't do it, what happened?"

Ari grabbed his hair and reclined back. "I don't know, nothing makes sense. At first I wondered if she had a heart attack or suddenly died and fell into the tank. But she seemed healthy, and it's not common that Jane, or anyone, would open the tank while alone. We generally work in teams when handling larger or dangerous animals."

"Do you think someone might've killed her?"

"I doubt it. Jane was beloved. She never mentioned any threats or conflicts. She had to testify against politicians on occasion, but we all do this."

"So let me get this straight. Fred didn't do it, you don't believe Jane had a medical condition, and you doubt someone killed her. Something bad happened yesterday. Are you and your team willing to share everything you know to figure this out? I'm not saying that you did it, but you likely have information I'll need to solve this mystery."

Ari paused, took a deep breath in, straightened tall and met my eyes. "Yes. I don't know what might've happened, but I'm confident Fred didn't kill her. I want you to explore all possibilities so I know that I've done everything I can to get to the truth. I worry that I'm too close to the situation to see what's out of line and the police are too busy to explore the case further. I need your help."

"OK. The investigation will be intrusive and you might not like what we conclude. I know the police have already interviewed your team, and we've reviewed their report, but we might want to talk with them again."

Ari nodded and then added, "One more thing. I know the director authorized two weeks, but there's an even tighter deadline. I found out this morning the lab's board has called a special session next week to discuss Fred's fate and may vote to euthanize him."

"Next week!" I tried not to sound alarmed but my voice sounded like a total screech.

"That's right. Thursday. And I don't think Director Larson is on Team Fred. He's into sharks, not cephalopods. I doubt he'll advocate for more time."

~⊙

When I got back to the shop, my phone beeped. It was a text from my friend, Melissa Romero, the Galveston County Medical Examiner.

"Sweet," I said to Dora. "Jane's autopsy report is ready."

I started texting her back. *Can you meet me in twenty minutes at the Mod? I'll bring the twenty-five bucks as usual.*

That's not a bribe, readers, it's the cost any citizen pays to get an autopsy report. Most people, however, don't get theirs hand-delivered by the Medical Examiner herself.

I grabbed my bag and hustled three blocks east to the Mod at Twenty-Second and Post Office Street, my favorite place to go for coffee in Galveston. I love the bohemian, industrial, scrappy vibe of the place. Wood floors, walls, and ceilings cause sounds to bounce, and make the place seem busier than it is. Local artists of widely varying talent hang paintings for sale under lumpy couches and chairs that look as though they had been picked up at the curb on free recycle day.

The air inside the Mod smelled incredible, like warm butter and Grandma's biscuits, especially right after the baker pulled misshapen cookies and puffed-out muffins from the shop's oven.

I got comfortable at a small wooden table by the window and sipped my usual double cortado. Melissa walked in and ordered a cappuccino before joining me.

"It's been forever."

Melissa nearly spilled her coffee. "Too long. We've been short-handed and up to our eyeballs in dead bellybuttons."

"The motorcycle rally?"

"No. Boating accidents. We allow anyone with a pulse and a credit card to operate jet skis and speedboats. When things go wrong it's worse than an auto wreck. Body parts everywhere. Blunt-force trauma. Propellers always win. Most of the bodies I've worked on have died high or drunk. Sad and totally preventable." She sighed and sipped her coffee, but rebounded with a perky smile.

It's amazing, readers, how we become so numb to the grisly bits of our work, don't you think?

Melissa was the lead Medical Examiner and well-respected by Galveston law enforcement. We met two years ago during a zero-to-hero training program for the Bike Around the Bay charity bicycle ride, which was two days and 190 miles long. We both rode at a seventeen-miles-per-hour pace and finished the ride vowing we'd never do it again because the winds coming off the Gulf kicked our asses.

"But not so with your Jane Moore," Melissa confirmed, interrupting my thoughts.

"Great transition. You must be in a hurry."

"Yeah, sorry, I got a text after I parked. Rush job coming."

I sat forward and opened my notebook. "No problem, I appreciate you bringing the report to me. Jane wasn't drunk or on drugs?"

"No. Nor did I find anything else in her system that wasn't supposed to be there. The final tox results will take a couple of weeks but our quick test, which is ninety percent accurate, showed nothing unusual or suspicious. Jane Moore's cause of death was a straightforward strangulation and drowning, likely at the same time, judging by the volume of water in her lungs."

"How'd you determine strangulation?" I asked.

"Two signs. She had bruising around her neck and the trachea was partially crushed. Whoever or whatever did this was strong."

"What do you mean, whatever?"

"I read the papers and know BJ likes the octopus for this. Was it strong enough to strangle a woman?" Melissa downed half her cappuccino in one gulp.

"Likely yes," I admitted.

My mind reeled because we could now eliminate accidental death from the list of possible explanations. Jane didn't die of an acute medical incident, and it seemed less likely that Fred killed her by accident. Either Fred attacked Jane or someone else did.

"There were a few smaller bruises on her arms, but only the ones on her neck contributed to her death. I can't tell you who did this, I only know how she died," Melissa said. "Nothing else was out of order."

"Was she pregnant?"

"No. Nor did I see evidence of recent sexual activity."

"Any signs of a struggle or defensive wounds?"

"No, in fact her nails seemed too clean for the end of a working day." She held out her nails in example, turned her hand palm up, and finished her coffee. "Maybe she washed her hands a lot. It's all in the report."

"Time of death?" I asked, not sure how much information she'd be willing to discuss here.

"About 10 p.m., give or take an hour. It's hard to pinpoint due to the water temperature in the tank. I sent an electronic copy of the autopsy report to the police last night and it has been filed and finalized. It's good to go." Melissa noticed that I looked puzzled and bobbed her head in reassurance. She handed me the report, and I gave her a check made out to the Galveston County Medical Examiner for $25. She finished her drink, stood and grabbed her purse.

"Gotta run. Let's go out for a ride soon."

"Yes, we have to do that. See you later."

I knew it was unlikely that we'd ever follow up on our

intention to ride. There's entirely too much gear involved in biking. And the clothes are so unflattering!

I ordered a second cortado and read through the autopsy report. I stared for a long time at a drawing of the marks found on Jane's neck, several inches long and about an inch wide. Fingers might've made marks like this, but Fred's tentacles were about an inch wide, too.

My heart sunk. Was Jane's trust in Fred misguided?

I called Ari and asked if I could come back to his office right away.

Ari looked tired and his office was more cluttered than it had been just this morning. Stacks of paper spilled over the trays on his desk. His eyes were red, like he'd been crying.

I sat at his round table overlooking the ship channel and considered about how to begin. I cut to the chase. "I have the autopsy report and the ME has concluded that Jane drowned and was strangled. Nothing else seemed out of whack. She didn't suffer a heart attack or die of natural causes before falling into the tank."

I stopped to let the first fact sink in.

Ari sat silent and still for a moment before speaking. "What do you mean strangulation? Around the neck?" He held his hands to his neck.

"Yes. The medical examiner's report determined this was the cause of death, along with drowning, because of bruising on her neck and her trachea was crushed. There's a diagram, but it's pretty disturbing."

"I want to see it," he insisted.

I pulled out the autopsy report and thumbed through the pages to locate the drawing of Jane's neck area and handed it to Ari, who looked at it for a long time.

"I knew it," he whispered. "Any pictures?"

"No, pictures are rarely available without a subpoena. Knew what?"

"Fred couldn't have done this."

"How do you know? Those bruises are about the width of his tentacles, right?" I pointed to the marks drawn on Jane's neck.

Ari bounced over to his computer and started typing. "Octopuses don't make marks like that. Their suckers make distinct and individual bruises; they don't run together like this." Ari typed fast, stopped, and typed again. "I'm looking for a report Jane did a few years ago that has a picture of bruising from an octopus attack."

He paused, typed more, and straightened. "What the hell?" he shrieked. Ari typed harder and cursed under his breath. "*Shit! Shit! Shit!*"

"What's happened?" I asked.

He spun around and looked at me. "All of Jane's reports have vanished. They're gone. This is impossible. Her backup folder is gone, too." Ari turned back around and tried again with the same result. "I can't believe it. Her work is missing. I looked at it yesterday. It was here."

"Could it be a glitch?" I asked.

"Maybe, but I doubt it."

"Could it be that her files were moved into a safe place

by someone else? Maybe security or legal? In the corporate world, we'd put a litigation hold on files that might be needed for legal cases."

I stood behind him and watched as he looked again for the files.

"It's possible but unlikely. I'd be the person to do that." Ari stopped and rested his hands lightly on his keyboard. "And besides, I'm the only one who thinks there might be a case. I'll look into it further after you leave." Ari moved back to the table and I followed. He looked at the autopsy drawing again. "Trust me when I tell you that Fred didn't make those bruises."

He leaned back in his chair, grabbed his hair and head, and covered his eyes with both hands. He suddenly jerked forward and looked at me. "Wait, do you have any hickies left from your visit Tuesday with Fred? Look at your arm."

I pulled up the sleeve of my turtleneck and looked at my arm where Fred had grabbed me the hardest. There were still several pinkish-red marks from where Fred had tasted me. They looked like stepping stones that showed the path of his hold on me and looked nothing like the bruising pattern on Jane's neck. Ari touched the red marks to emphasize the number and size of each one.

"What if he squeezed hard, would the suckers slide and make longer bruises?" I asked.

"That wouldn't happen. The suckers are the source of the hold, not the squeeze. He's not like a boa constrictor." Ari plucked at my hickies and squeezed my arm to demonstrate. "Octopuses don't squeeze prey to death. They grab it with their suckers, bring it to their mouths, bite, and kill it."

"What if Fred held on to Jane's neck in an embrace with no ill intent?"

"Same thing. We would've found the hickies, not this," he said, pointing to the diagram of Jane. "The autopsy results prove that Fred was innocent."

"If Fred didn't do it, then it means that—"

"Jane was murdered," Ari answered.

Each neighborhood in Galveston offers its own picture of urban renewal, decay, and transition. The closer to the water, the more extreme these differences are because wealthy owners pour big money into transforming storm-ravaged wrecks into over-the-top dream beach houses. On the east end of the island, you can drive along nearly any street and see million-dollar homes flanking on both sides right next to bird-and-bum infested shacks. Jane's house was something in between. Lovely, up-to-date, and in a great location, one block off the seawall near Porretto Beach.

Ari agreed to take me to Jane's home so I could see if there was anything there that'd shed some light on who might've wanted her dead. He knew where Jane's hide-a-key was because he watered her plants when she'd go out of town to do field work or attend conferences. He quietly opened the door and we went inside. It seemed undisturbed and was tidy both inside and out.

Ari plunked on Jane's couch and I sat next to him. His eyes welled up again.

"I'm sorry," I offered. "Maybe we shouldn't have come here tonight. I know this is hard to take. I wanted to see it before we meet with BJ tomorrow, in case he opens the case and tries to restrict access."

"It's OK." He looked around and sighed. "The last time I was here, Jane was heading out on a dive to explore manmade reefs she had created in the bay. She was happy and excited to see how they were doing."

Although Ari believed in Fred's innocence from the beginning, he hadn't seriously contemplated what that meant. Murder is a heavy concept and was no doubt beginning to fill his mind with new questions. Did someone associated with one of her projects kill her? Why was she targeted? Who'd want to do this? Was anyone else in danger?

I had to consider whether Ari played a part in this. I didn't believe so because he could've let Fred take the fall. And he convinced BARL to hire me to find the truth. Even so, it was something I needed to evaluate. Psychopaths, in particular, like to insert themselves into investigations. Both my head and my heart hoped he wasn't involved in Jane's death.

As we looked around her living room, I noticed that I wasn't being as nosy or intrusive as usual because Ari was there. But I took lots of pictures with my cell phone, and hoped I didn't miss any important clues.

I sat behind Jane's office desk and called out to Ari. "Was Jane always this neat?"

He joined me in the office. "Yes, even her BARL office is tidy. Other than her journals, Jane kept few paper copies because she was a big environmentalist. Makes the disappearance of her computer files even more disturbing. I hope we can find backup copies somewhere."

"I can ask Sparky to work with your IT people. He's got a few tools he uses to restore deleted files."

"That'd be great."

"Absolutely."

I rummaged through her top-right desk drawer and found a ticket to the Galveston Bay Foundation's gala at the convention center for the coming Saturday.

I handed the ticket to Ari. "Did you know that she was attending the gala? Would she be going as part of work?"

"I didn't know she was attending, but we hadn't talked recently."

"Why?"

"We were both busy on projects. Seems silly now."

"Are you attending the gala?"

"Not this year. BARL always has a table, and several of us go each year because we partner with the Foundation a lot and like to show our support. It's also a good event to schmooze with past and potential donors. I avoid big events if possible. I bought a ticket and gave it to Roberta."

Ari handed the ticket back to me.

I smiled inside. "I know what you mean about big parties. I can handle a get-together of three or four people, but parties are a colossal waste of precious time. I devise my exit strategy the minute I arrive if not before."

"Exactly," Ari agreed.

I considered the ticket. "Are you OK if I hang on to this?"

"Sure."

"Do you know if she was seeing anyone? Perhaps she was going to the gala with him or her?" I treaded lightly with this question because I wasn't sure how close Jane and Ari were.

"No." Ari paused. I waited for him to say more. "I heard rumors now and then."

"Rumors? A friend of Dora's told her Jane was having an affair with a city council member. Do you think that might've been true?"

"People have mentioned this, but I've a hard time believing she'd be with a married man."

I sensed that Ari hoped the affair wasn't real. Was he a friend talking or an ex-lover? And why didn't she mention her lovers in her journals? Maybe, as the autopsy suggested, she wasn't involved with anyone.

I sat and twirled around in Jane's chair. The two bookshelf cases behind the desk were filled with marine biology and environment-oriented books.

"No desktop computer?" I asked.

"She used her work laptop for everything," he explained. Large framed photos of coral reefs, shipwrecks, and fish were on the opposite wall. "She has similar photos in her office that she took herself. Jane was an avid diver."

"All the more reason that it doesn't make sense that she accidentally drowned in an eight-foot-high tank."

"Yep. She knew how to manage breathing and herself underwater," Ari confirmed.

I found a mostly empty notebook under a stack of professional journals. In it was a printed agenda for the following week's city council meeting.

"Did she attend a lot of council meetings?" I took a picture of the agenda.

Ari sat on the corner of her desk and scanned the agenda. "We all do when the council is voting on topics we care about or are working on. It's amazing how quickly politicians forget about their responsibilities to preserve the ecosystem when they're charmed in a different direction by rich businesspeople waving potential new tax revenues in front of their faces. We testify when they need to be reminded of the long-term issues or downsides of these short-sighted development projects."

Ari watered the plants while I looked around some more. There wasn't a lot to see, but I took pictures of each room, including her bedroom. Jane's closets contained a limited and mostly casual wardrobe except for a formal gown that still had tags; she must've bought it to wear at the gala.

"I'm surprised she doesn't have fish tanks," I mused.

"Most of us don't. Our field work takes us offshore, sometimes for weeks. Fish tanks require a lot of work and nearly daily maintenance. At the BARL, there's a team of twenty people who do that full time."

"Well, that explains a lot."

"What do you mean?" he asked.

"I've tried to keep fish tanks several times but have each time ended up feeling a tsunami of depressive guilt after every living thing inside the tank died. I was under the impression, obviously wrong, that they were low maintenance!"

Ari laughed and smiled for the first time since we arrived

at Jane's house. "Thanks, I needed that mental diversion."

I walked to Ari and placed both my hands on his shoulders. "You've been through a lot. I know this is a tough process." I looked into his eyes and softened. "And the investigation is just getting started."

Ari held my gaze.

"I'm here for you," I assured. I caught myself being drawn to him. Every bone in my body wanted to embrace Ari. But luckily, I was able to take a deep breath, pull myself away and back into the investigation. "This is what I do."

I knew I'd need to come back to Jane's house. Alone. There was far too much raw emotion in this room right now to hear or see what the scene might be trying to share about Jane's life and death.

Chapter 7
Day 4, Friday

It was a typical Friday morning on Broadway Avenue as people flooded onto and off the island like ants traversing through a chewed-up cocktail straw. Buses, vans, and rental cars loaded with hopeful vacationers clogged entry points for the beaches and cruise ship terminals, while locals needing to get to work off the island tried in vain to avoid them.

Ari and I were among the crowd, snaking through side streets to the Galveston Island Police Department, next to the courthouse and county jail. I had no idea how BJ would respond, but needed Ari there because our argument to reopen the case relied on his expert analysis of the bruising pattern on Jane's neck.

The front desk receptionist confirmed our appointment. After several minutes past our appointment time, she took us down a long, beige hall to BJ's office. He was behind his desk and stood up as we came in.

"Sorry for being a bit late. Thanks for coming." Then, before we could say a word, he jumped right in. "I read the autopsy report, and have seen the medical examiner's diagrams and photos, and it seems that both support our theory the octopus caused her death. My understanding is that these animals are strong and could easily have strangled Dr. Moore." He paused and cocked his head. "Given that, what can I do for you?"

So this was how it will begin, I thought.

"Thanks for agreeing to meet with us," I said. "We'd like to share information that we believe will make you feel otherwise about the manner of death. While we didn't see the medical examiner's photos, when we reviewed the diagram and description of the bruising patterns on Jane's neck, Dr. Pani confirmed that Fred couldn't have made these marks. We believe someone murdered Jane."

BJ looked at something on his computer screen as we were talking. He shook his head. "Murdered? That's a big leap, Xena. What's so obvious about the bruise pattern that you could know for sure the octopus didn't do it? As I remember it, the animal's tentacles are about the width of these marks."

Ari straightened forward as he was eager to talk. "May I?" He handed BJ a folder of photos of octopus hicky marks. "The octopus's holding strength is found primarily in his suction cups, of which he has over a thousand. If Fred grabbed onto my neck and held tight, the marks that'd be left behind would look like round track marks, not long solid marks. These pictures show bruises made by octopuses." He gave BJ a minute to look at the photos. "Do these look like the pictures or diagram in the autopsy report?"

BJ looked at the pictures with some interest. "No. The

picture of Dr. Moore's neck shows long streaks of bruising. But what if the struggle included several instances of the octopus grabbing her neck, wouldn't the bruising pattern overlap? We've one octopus and one dead body in a confined space, and no indicators that anyone broke into the building. Are you ready to say that you or one of your colleagues killed this lady and framed the animal?"

I broke in. "BJ, don't you also think that if Fred were grabbing and releasing Jane's neck that we would've seen signs of a struggle somewhere at the crime scene or within the autopsy report?"

BJ handed the photos back to Ari, sat down, turned in his chair, and reclined back. "You and I both know the scene was never perfect and lots of evidence was gone by the time the body was found." He paused. "You and your team have been asking lots of questions, right?"

"Yes."

"Tell me one possible motive you've uncovered."

Ari fidgeted and sat back.

That's the one question I hoped he wouldn't ask because we don't know this yet. Crap!

"It's too early in the investigation, BJ. We don't know what the motive was, we only know that Fred didn't cause Jane's death," I said.

"Give me something. Anything else you've learned," BJ pleaded.

Shit. Crap. Shit. Crap.

I told BJ about the people named in Jane's journals, even those who I knew weren't potential suspects. I recounted the gossip I heard from my team and shared the information Dora had uncovered about Jane's brother. My shotgun data dump was complete after I shared what we knew about Jane's work, her missing files, and that she routinely testified against developers and company executives. I watched Ari closely because I hadn't shared most of this with him yet.

BJ leaned back farther, planted his elbows in his chair arms, and talked with his hands outstretched. "Most of what you've shared is a stretch or gossip, but let's go through some of it. Everyone knows about the affair with Sam Block. He and his wife, Laura, have what they call an 'open marriage.' Laura romps around, too, and neither cares much about the other. Unless Jane was pregnant, which we know she wasn't, there isn't a motive associated with the affair."

I tried to get a word in but BJ raised a finger and asked me to wait.

"Judge Buddy's a harmless twit who doesn't have the balls to get involved with murder. Racketeering, prostitution, and corruption? Sure. Anything involving sexual depravity? You bet. Did you uncover anything pointing to a relationship between the victim and Buddy?"

"Not yet," I admitted.

"She's not his type. Too normal. But you go right ahead and talk to him all you want. Dr. Moore's brother was in California when we called to notify him as next of kin. So he couldn't have killed his sister himself, and he didn't strike me as someone with the resources or connections to hire an assassin. Furthermore, if a hitman were employed, he sure as hell wouldn't have concocted this bizarre manner of death."

He was right about that. Assassins were simple, clinical death machines and wouldn't have had the imagination needed to frame Fred.

I felt embarrassed that Ari was witnessing my verbal lashing and tried to think of a comeback that'd convince BJ that a crime had occurred. But BJ continued before I could get a word in.

"Additionally, my understanding is that Dr. Moore brought in a lot of money for the labs and was worth much more to this community alive than dead. I don't give a shit if she was a lesbian or bisexual or whatever. The autopsy report, the missing files, and Dr. Pani's expert opinion make this case less tidy. But who wanted her dead? I've yet to hear one possible motive that'd convince me to reopen the case and spend department resources to investigate it."

I was about to respond when Ari touched me on the arm and motioned for me to hold on. He stood and readied himself. "Captain Rawlins, octopuses are powerful and sometimes lethal creatures, but let me explain how octopuses kill. Unlike the boa constrictor snake, octopuses don't have the ability to squeeze their prey to death. They hold on with their suckers, subdue with their ink, and bring the prey to their beak-like mouth sucker by sucker where they bite, kill, and eat it. The ink doesn't sedate humans, by the way."

Ari lifted my arm and used it to demonstrate, using his arms as the tentacles, winding them around mine and squeezing. He went on, "I can see no scenario where Fred could've caused either the bruising found on Jane's neck, or the crushed trachea the medical examiner indicated in her report. Even if he grabbed her multiple times."

Ari sat and I smiled at him.

BJ moved forward and rested his forearms on the desk. "I appreciate your explanation. It's fascinating, and certainly raises questions. But I lead a cash-strapped organization that's already working overtime to prepare for the Shrimp Festival. I must consider how I spend the people's money. Don't take my previous criticisms the wrong way. You have a good little investigator working for you."

Good little investigator? What a patronizing dinosaur!

"If Xena and her team can vet and narrow their leads to one or two persons of interest who might've had a motive to kill Dr. Moore, I'll consider reopening the case. I've no reason to believe that others are in danger." BJ then looked directly at me. "If you uncover something or someone of concern, if any of these or other leads pan out, I expect you to contact me *before* going too far, getting hurt, or into trouble."

"Of course," I said.

"If anyone can figure it out, you can." He chuckled. "Seems like you get all the strange cases." He glanced at Ari. "No offense."

"None taken," Ari said unconvincingly.

BJ stood and moved toward the door. "Now if you will excuse me, we have to rehearse our plan for evacuating the Strand in the event of an active shooter during the chowder-tasting competition. Last year two roux masters nearly killed each other and several bystanders. They all carry and many take our little charity competition way too seriously."

He then imitated a crying child – "Waaa, you stole my recipe, so I'm going to kill you. Waaa" – and laughed. "Shit, it's just god-damned fish soup."

~⊙

I sat on my porch with a tall glass of Edradour Scotch and reflected on the day's highlights and lowlights before giving Gregory a call. Overall, it ended in an OK place because we got BJ's attention and could proceed with the investigation. It would've been better if he had reopened the case, but it was a partial win in that he'd left the door cracked open for us in doing so. And what about Ari? He was smart, assertive, and articulate. His dark, bushy eyebrows looked beautifully intense. What did I do? Nothing but make a fool of myself!

Gregory picked up on the first ring.

"I totally blew it today and Ari witnessed it," I complained to Gregory. "I got frustrated that BJ wasn't listening and I overreacted."

Gregory sighed. "I bet it wasn't as bad as you think."

"Yeah, well, I had to do something. There's a killer walking around Galveston right now. This is a big effing deal. He's more worried about the Shrimp Festival than catching a murderer!" I paced back and forth. "Some emotion was warranted."

Gregory didn't respond. I hated it when he let me stew and simmer in my own words. After a couple of minutes, I sat and exhaled loudly. "I could've been more focused. I wish I had been better prepared. We believed the diagram was enough, and it wasn't."

"Ari didn't fire you, right?" he asked.

"No. He said that BJ was being unreasonable."

"It's going to be fine. Maybe you shouldn't have shared the half-baked tips and leads, but I know of no one except my younger self who's better at this kind of work than you are. Ari's lucky he found you."

"You always know what to say. You're awesome."

"I know, but would you please tell my wife? She doesn't believe me when I tell her." We both laughed. "Now that you're sure there *was* a real crime, can I help?"

"Yes." I thought for a moment. "The motive was likely love, money, or fame."

"Always is."

"I need to know who might've had a financial incentive for killing Jane. Her will isn't public and her lawyer is in Houston. Can you track that down for me?"

"You got it. I'll also do a search for life insurance and beneficiaries."

Love, money, or fame, dear readers. We all want these outcomes, but some covet one or more to a degree that warps reality, bloats courage, and splinters judgment. Turns smart people into raging morons. Job security!

Chapter 8
Day 5, Saturday

Parkour, also called freerunning, is a lifestyle that's rooted in the belief that we should know our limits and transcend them. It cultivates total kinesthetic awareness and confidence and enables us to recognize all possibilities and power forward.

Sounds cool, right?

Parkour originated in France in the early 1900s as a method to build fitness and strength in the natural world. I first fell in love with it when I was nineteen years old, after watching two guys practicing along the river in Cincinnati. They were fast, elegant, and almost ballet-like. Not soft and refined ballet-like, but fluid with full body extension like ballet. I was transfixed by how they vaulted, tumbled, and jungle-gymed forward through the park. It was like a raw urban ballet meets a big-budget 007 Bond movie chase scene kind of thing.

I fell for the art and the guy who taught me freerunning, which disappointed my mother because it made her beloved gymnastics seem tame and boring to me. I quit gymnastics and my relationship with the guy didn't last, but I've been practicing parkour ever since. I freerun on Saturday mornings before the beach umbrella rental guys stake their claim on the shoreline.

I was more distracted on this particular Saturday than most for many reasons, including that the BARL board's vote whether to euthanize Fred was just days away. I walked, skipped, and jogged the three blocks from my house to the seawall and down to the beach to stretch. The tide was low and the surf quietly lapped in and out. I took my time doing several seated stretches and warm-up exercises. I looked up, with my back to the water, and noticed for the first time octopuses painted on the seawall mural where it intersected with my street. Was this a sign? Each segment of the 2.4-mile-long mural – the world's largest and longest – featured different sea creatures and beach scenes, and the octopuses had been looking at me all along.

Amazing!

I took a deep breath in and nearly gagged.

Have you noticed how cities that were luminous and lively at night seem dank and grimy in the morning? Gulf Coast towns often smell sour, mildewy, sweet, or a combination. We call the more humid months on the island, which are all of them except January, the season of rot and mold. No, not everything rotted or got moldy, but things are saturated, like your whole house covered in morning dew, to a point that you imagine rot and mold. Even so, it is enchanting. We all have a little rot and mold going on inside.

Done with my stretches, I vaulted over benches, held handstand balances on a few railings, and double-jumped sets of stairs going up and down to each segment of the beach along my freerun. I was going through the motions but was struggling to remain present and focused on perfecting my movements.

I needed a dress for the gala that night but hadn't found one yet. Even though I hated parties, I thought it would be helpful to see who might've been expecting Jane and what people from the environmental movement were saying about her death.

I searched for a dress after Ari and I met with BJ with no luck. Who knew that Walmart didn't carry formal gowns! I shopped about as often as Paula Dean cooked low-fat. And getting the dress was just the first step. I'd then need to get it to Sparky so he could implant surveillance devices.

I faced a third distraction about halfway into my freerun: a guy sitting in his car in the Ben & Jerry's parking lot, engine running. He was wearing a gray sweatshirt, hood up, and this struck me as odd since he was inside a presumably climate-controlled car. This same guy, or someone who looked a lot like him, had been parked two blocks from my house earlier this morning. And Ben & Jerry's wasn't open for breakfast.

Maybe it's not the same guy, I whispered to myself. *Maybe he thinks you're hot. Maybe he's a fan of parkour and admires your form* (don't laugh, readers, I often draw attention when I freerun, because it's cool-as-shit-urban-raw-ballet-like stuff).

Don't overreact, Xena.

Crap, who am I kidding?

The ten-mile-long seawall is lined with hotels, restaurants, and souvenir shops, and there are many places from which someone can hide and watch. I usually turn around at Ben & Jerry's because it's about a mile from my start, making for a nice two-mile freerun. It seemed too obvious to turn around right by the guy, so I kept going past the San Luis to the convention center at Fifty-Seventh Street and crossed over to the north side of the street and headed back. My plan to get a closer look at the guy was foiled because he wasn't there as I passed the ice-cream store, and I didn't see him anywhere on the way home.

It was likely nothing... I thought to myself.

No, it was definitely something, my instincts answered back.

There was nothing I could do about the guy at that moment, so I returned to obsessing about what I'd wear to the gala. I had the brilliant idea to delegate the shopping to Dora. That was a notion I later regretted.

I called Dora and gave her my size, budget, and offered to cover the spy shop while she found my dress. The caveat was that I needed it later this morning.

~⊙

I couldn't be too hard on Dora because I'd assigned her the nearly impossible task. And to be fair, I'd told her I didn't care what the gown looked like as long as it would fit and accommodate the devices Sparky needed to embed in the dress. I should've known better. Note to self!

What she found nearly left me speechless. Have you heard of a *quinceañera*, readers? It's a coming-of-age event for fifteen-year-old girls in many Latin cultures similar to the debutante balls found in Europe, but with more flair. The flair was most evident in the "slightly used" *quinceañera* dress Dora had found for me to wear to the gala. My dress might've qualified as an exemplar.

The bottom layer of the skirt was made of black satin with large green, orange, and blue flowers embroidered on the bottom twelve inches or so. The next several layers were made of sky-blue taffeta gathered to create a thick, puffed-out body. On top of the taffeta was a silk skirt with a hand-painted desert scene of agave and yucca cacti, butterflies, and blooming prickly pear. The top, sleeveless part of the dress was black satin with bright embroidered flowers to match the bottom layer of the skirt. Sewn on each layer of the dress were dozens of colorful plastic gemstones in yellow, clear, red, and blue.

Dora told me this was a special dress made by the renowned designer Roberto Salazar and was expensive when it was new.

Dora had found my dress on Craigslist.

"You're one lucky lady that you've such a trim body and can fit into teen sizes."

Sparky laughed so hard he snorted coffee.

I put on the dress while Dora and Sparky used binder clips to mark where Sparky would place the video cameras, mics, and communication devices. Dora helped him sew everything securely. I jumped up and down and waved my arms to test whether the dress was going to slide off me – my parts slipping out – because its former teen owner was more voluptuous than I.

"I'm not sure I want to stand out this much," I replied, stating the blindingly obvious.

My plan had been to blend in, move around the room like a ninja at night. In. Out. Slicing through the crowd like vapor. No chance of that now! I started thinking about how I could use the dress to my advantage.

"The plant theme fits right in with the Galveston Bay Foundation's mission," Dora argued.

"It's an awesome dress! I can put a lot of surveillance devices in this dress and they'll look like more decoration," Sparky said. He looked like a kid in a candy store. But my dress already looked like the whole candy store – and I reminded him that we'd have to undo everything before I could give away or sell the dress.

"You're going to be the belle of the ball!" Dora said, trying to make me feel better.

"I hate parties," I whined. "Now help me find something to fill out the top of this dress!"

"How 'bout a couple of MoonPies?" Sparky suggested. "I know how much you like MoonPies, and they always run out of food at these events."

"Yeah, that'd work," I muttered, only half kidding.

～◎

Sparky set up the van in the Kroger parking lot next door to the convention center. As I walked into the main reception area, a gala attendant took my ticket, swiped my credit card for the auction, and put on me an armband printed with my table assignment and a barcode for purchases. He told me, while trying to keep a straight face, the first hour would include a cocktail reception and silent auction in the grand foyer. At 7:30 p.m., the ballroom would open for the dinner seating, and there'd be a live auction of higher-priced items during the dessert course.

I ordered a Scotch and found a relatively quiet corner to do a mic check with Sparky. Things were working OK except that my dress made a loud swishing noise when I walked. It was drowning out the audio and Sparky told me to walk more quietly.

"That's not going to be easy unless I walk like I'm a sloth or on Quaaludes."

"Could you?" Sparky snarked. "Thanks. Heads up, you've a visitor coming up behind you."

I turned in time to see my ex-fiancé and Houston-based artist, Oliver Jenson, and his new wife. Both were dressed in head-to-toe classic black and looked gorgeous.

"Well, look who it is!" Oliver's face communicated, *What the hell?* "Xena, you remember my wife, Tiffany?"

"Yes, nice to see you both." I air hugged them by bending at my waist and sticking out my ass to reduce the space the skirt took up in front of my body.

"That's a unique dress. Are you part of the entertainment?" Tiffany asked.

My mind flashed to the scene in *Pretty Woman* where the clothing shop owner basically tells Julia Roberts's character

— a hooker — that they don't sell clothes to her kind. Entertainment? Having cacti on my skirt at a gala honoring the environment doesn't make me part of the act.

They smiled like they were holding in a cackle.

Bitch.

"No, I lost a bet with a friend," I replied. "Had I won, he'd be here in a pink tutu and tiara. That's the last time I count on the Texans for a win."

They laughed with me. Or at me.

"You're a good sport," Oliver said.

"I see that several of your pieces are featured in the auction," I said.

"Yes, I donated five. I love what the organization is doing for the bay."

We stood silent for a few awkward minutes. I noticed how attractive Oliver was and how uninterested I was in him nonetheless. No feelings. No regrets. I smiled wide but didn't break the quiet.

"It was lovely to see you, Xena. I hope you win the next bet." Oliver coaxed Tiffany away.

"Nice," Sparky offered into my earpiece, which was hidden by the silver dollar-sized plastic pineapple earrings I was wearing. They came with the dress, in case you were wondering.

The Galveston Bay Foundation was a local non-profit organization with the mission to preserve, protect, and enhance the waterways and their associated ecosystems. They funded and hosted local conservation projects, education, and research. The scientists at BARL did most of their research related to marine life, so the two organizations had a strong partnership.

The silent auction area was huge, with six rows of donated items on both sides to bid on. As I sashayed slowly down the first row, people coming in the opposite direction squeezed to the side to make way for my dress. A few offered comments like, "Wild dress," or "Interesting dress," but most people smiled and pointed. I was officially a spectacle while undercover. Ha!

"Judge Buddy and the mayor, ten o'clock," Sparky announced.

I whispered to myself, *You can do this. I'm doing this for the case*, and headed toward them.

"Judge Sassoon, good to see you here." I then turned to the mayor. "I'm Xena Cali, a local business owner."

Buddy whispered to the mayor, "Spy shop on Twenty-Fifth."

The mayor smiled broadly. "I love meeting our small business owners."

"That's QUITE the OUTfit." Buddy seemed delighted. "It gives you a SPIrited youthful look. I ... had ... NO idea you were so much FUN!"

"I'm not, actually," I confirmed. "I'm wearing this dress in honor of micro-lending programs that help women in poor countries start their own businesses to support their families and villages. This was sewn by four women whose dressmaking business has been so successful they built the first-ever water well in their community."

Buddy was staring at my chest ... MoonPies ... oblivious

to what I'd said and the mayor was looking from side to side for a way out of our conversation.

"Now everyone has access to fresh and healthy water." I stepped closer to the mayor. "I'd love to see the City of Galveston support programs like this." The mayor nodded politely. Time to change the subject. "I'm sure you both heard about the untimely death of Dr. Jane Moore. She gave testimony in your court and at city council meetings. Did either of you know her?"

"Yes, Jane came before the council many times," the mayor said. "Such a tragic loss and a reminder that wild animals are sometimes unpredictable." He looked over at Buddy.

"Wild people, too," I said.

"I knew Jane. Not REAL well, but our paths crossed a few times. Smart lady, always seemed a bit PISSed off about something. But she certainly didn't deserve to be eaten by that fish," Buddy proclaimed.

I looked at Buddy's eyes because his voice went high when he talked, and he'd sway back and forth on his cowboy boot heels. BJ was right, he's too stupid to orchestrate a murder. The mayor continued to look around and pulled at Buddy to move on.

"Excuse us, there's someone I needed to catch up with," the mayor said.

"She wasn't eaten and the octopus isn't a fish," I corrected as they were leaving.

"'Micro-lending'?" Sparky asked. "You might be enjoying this too much."

As the cocktail reception continued, they played video

vignettes on large screens next to each bar station highlighting the work the foundation had done for the community. It was getting crowded and my dress was causing traffic jams in the silent auction area. I placed a bid on a painting by local artist Ray Heard of an octopus that looked a lot like Fred, and moved into a clearing near one of the bars. Three people walked to me asking where the restrooms were.

I'm not part of the event staff, I whispered.

Sparky laughed and ordered a pizza into my earpiece.

The doors to the grand ballroom opened and so I sashayed slowly to table sixty-seven, which BARL had reserved for their attendees. I got some funny looks as I walked to the table, but Amy, one of Ari's researchers, recognized me from earlier in the week and welcomed me.

"Xena is here using Jane's ticket," she explained.

Several bobbed their heads in acknowledgement.

"Ari invited her to join our table," Amy continued. "This is Peter, he specializes in seaweed research, and you've met Bob. He's our small mammal expert."

We all shook hands.

"I don't think you know Dr. Mark Larson. He's the executive director for BARL, and he's also well known for his research of shark predation patterns."

"That was so long ago, Amy, but thank you," Mark said. "Ms. Cali and I met the day Jane died."

It took me two tries to sit. Amy helped fold my skirt to reduce its height. The director looked refined and polished while the others were like fish out of water at the gala. No pun intended! Larson's tailored suit and skintight turtleneck emphasized his developed pecs – which ironically resembled MoonPies, too – and he looked very New York, except the sleeves were too long. His gelled-back hair and manicured hands completed his style. It was all part of becoming a figurehead.

Amy broke the ice. "That's a distinctive and colorful dress."

"Yes!" I said. "I'm wearing it in honor of the cacti replanting project the Galveston Bay Foundation is doing to rehabilitate old EPA Superfund sites. I understand that a portion of this evening's proceeds will be earmarked for this work."

"That's cool," Peter replied, as the others nodded in appreciation.

"You're *too* good at this," Sparky quipped inside my ear.

The dinner tasted delicious. The head chef at Blvd Seafood, one of my favorite restaurants and only two blocks from my house, had created the menu. He paired the seared scallop appetizer with a white wine that had strong herbal notes. The blackberry pork chops main course harmonized well with the bold Zinfandel they served. As we ate, the table conversation stayed light with the occasional discussion of BARL projects. They mentioned Jane several times, and it was clear that she was well-respected, even beloved, by her colleagues. Most found the idea that Fred killed her surprising, yet possible. But they didn't know what the autopsy report had revealed.

I got up to go to the restroom before the dessert course.

The director stood and walked over to me. He smoothed his suit jacket, pulled his sleeves down straight, and pushed his glasses to the top of his nose bridge.

"I want to confirm a few things about your investigation into Jane's death," he said.

Seemed like an odd time for this discussion.

"Sure, what's on your mind?"

"I'm supportive of your work, but I think Ari might be the outlier regarding what happened in that tank. I hope that you don't drudge up things that'll affect Jane's reputation. Or BARL's, which are both deservedly stellar."

"I can appreciate what you're saying, Dr. Larson. Investigations uncover all kinds of things. We've no desire to share irrelevant, but embarrassing information that could mar Jane's reputation. She was the victim."

"Thank you."

"But we also want to make sure that we find the truth, especially if Ari's correct about Fred's innocence."

"Of course. I'm glad we are on the same page," he advised softly while staring into my eyes. He excused himself and went across the room to talk to people at another table.

"Do you want to meet Sam Block?" Sparky asked into my earpiece. "You know, the guy who was supposedly having an affair with Jane?"

"Yes!" I whispered. "Where is he?"

"Three o'clock. Tall guy standing with the woman in the cream-colored gown. That's his wife, Laura."

I spun around, found the couple Sparky was describing, and slinked over to them.

"Excuse me, Councilman Block?"

He nodded and looked up and down at me. Same as I'd gotten all night. I called it the *Oh shit, what am I going to say about that dress?* look.

"I'm Xena, a small business owner downtown. I wanted to say hello and thank you for your support of new businesses."

"Well, thank you, Seena. This is my wife, Laura. I've always believed small businesses would rule the world!"

"I own the Paradise Lost Spy Shop, and I'm also a private investigator." He nodded blankly like he'd never heard of it. "I'll be investigating the death of Dr. Jane Moore, who was a biologist at BARL."

Laura's glass slipped out of her hands and onto the floor. She apologized and tried to clean it up.

"That's OK, honey. The help will take care of that," Sam said. "What were you saying?"

"Dr. Moore's death."

"Oh, yes, I read about that in the paper. So sad."

"Did you know her?"

He looked at Laura who was standing again with a new drink.

"We've met her at a few gatherings like this," Laura said. "She testified at several council meetings. Right, Sam?"

"Could be, I don't have much of a memory for everyone who comes and goes at city council. But I do remember talking to her a few times. Smart lady."

I focused on Laura, who seemed a bit looped. "You're right, Laura. Jane has testified at city council a few times," I clarified, and watched her reaction carefully.

"Unbelievable, really, and I—"

"It was nice meeting you, Seena," Sam interrupted. "We're going to check on our silent auction items. Laura has her heart set on the deep-sea fishing trip."

"That's you, Sam. You're the only one who wants it, and the only one who'll go if you win," Laura corrected.

On the way to the restrooms, I whispered to Sparky, "I don't think Jane would've been attracted to Sam Block. Lights on, no one is home. He's not her type."

If you ever need to go undercover at a formal gala, please take my advice and make sure that you install a kill switch on your dress to mute the audio and pause the video while in the restroom. Did I learn this lesson the hard way? Yes, I did. But that was years before this case, and so I engaged the kill switch and confidently entered the ladies room.

The convention center's restrooms were huge with twenty or more stalls in each section of the building. I took forever to straighten all the layers of my dress and make sure no padding was sticking out. The chimes sounded, signaling it was time to take our seats. I turned around after washing my hands and nearly knocked over a petite woman in a beautiful black gown. I apologized and realized I was standing face-to-face with Vicki Moon.

"Well, hello. Aren't you decked out!" she exclaimed.

We eyed each other, noticing our similar features.

"Yes, I'm …" I trailed off because I was startled and at a loss for words.

"You're the most interesting person I've seen tonight, that's for sure. I love people who make a statement!" She straightened. "I'm Vicki Moon." She smiled and extended her hand to me. We shook, and she held my hand in hers for a moment.

"I'm Xena Cali. I own a spy shop in town." I thought about how to explain the dress. "This dress was a gift from a family I sponsor in Guatemala. I promised them I'd wear it proudly the first opportunity I had."

Vicki touched and examined the top layer of my skirt. She walked around me and returned and stopped when we were again eye-to-eye.

"And that you have," she declared as her smile broadened. "A spy shop? How fascinating! I bet you live an entertaining life, Ms. Cali." Vicki continued to look directly at me as we both walked out of the restroom.

I disengaged the kill switch to turn the audio and video back on.

"Holy shit!" Sparky blasted as he saw Vicki. "What've I missed? How'd this happen?"

I tried to keep my cool, even though I couldn't escape hearing Sparky having a fit. Vicki and I paused before the now-closed doors into the grand ballroom.

"This is such a lovely event, don't you think?" I asked.

"Yes, it is," Vicki said. "You know, I might one day need something from your spy shop. Could you tell me its name?"

"That witch. Don't you dare encourage her to come to the shop," I heard Sparky say in my earpiece.

"Paradise Lost. It's on Twenty-Fifth, near Market. Please come by anytime. We'd love to help you." I beamed, accepting Sparky's challenge.

"That's close to my new development, Cerulean Sky. Have you heard of it?"

"No," I lied. I was curious how she'd describe it.

"It'll be the best shopping destination in Galveston. Hell, in Texas! I'd love to show you around some day." Vicki handed me her card, sky-blue with a phone number and no name. She ran her hand down my arm, smiled, and went through the doors to take her seat across the room.

"What're the odds of you running into that witch at this event?" Sparky asked.

"Weird night, that's for sure," I replied. "I can't create one more story about this dress."

I left the gala with my octopus painting, which I won after rebidding three times and paying $1,650. It was for charity! I got inside the back of Sparky's van, and he stepped out while I changed back into my street clothes. I gave him the all-clear sign and we sat next to each other in front of the monitors. "Did you get anything good?" I asked.

"Not sure. Lots of interesting clips, but who knows if any of it relates to the case," he said. "I loved your dress stories, by the way. Inspired stuff."

"What was I supposed to do? I stuck out like a sore thumb." I pointed to the dress, now hanging at the front of the van.

"True, but you still managed to talk to a lot of the people on your list."

"And then some."

Sparky was playing clips from the various conversations. I asked him to hit the PAUSE button when he got to Oliver and Tiffany. "Oliver looked good, as usual. I should've known he'd be here. He loves the attention."

"You guys were going to get married, right?"

"Maybe. Sort of. I suppose technically we were engaged. Then disengaged after I decided I didn't want to move into his house." I hit the PLAY button and then fast-forwarded to the next clip.

Sparky let it drop, which I appreciated. I don't need to tell him about why it didn't work out with Oliver, but I'll tell you, dear readers. I didn't want to commit. I didn't want to slow down or become dependent on Oliver for my happiness. I loved Oliver's passion for life, and I missed that. He wanted more from me than I could offer him, or anyone, at the time.

"I'm not finished scrubbing the footage from the cameras in the back of the dress, but I'll work on that tomorrow after the demonstration." We both stared at the raw footage on the screen.

"OK. Maybe I'll stop by and see you at the demonstration before heading to the Shrimp Festival."

"Cool. Do you want me to drive you home now?" Sparky asked as I got up to leave.

"No, but hang on to the dress and bring it to the shop on Monday so we can remove our gadgets. I'm going to make Dora sell it again."

"Sure. Nice painting, by the way," he said.

"Thanks. It looks a little like Fred." I left with my

painting and walked home on the business side of the seawall road. I scanned left, right, front, and back all the way home but saw no one suspicious.

Chapter 9
Day 6, Sunday

Timing is everything in politics, activism, and sales. Planned well, a tiny story about killing an endangered species in a paid hunt can reverberate, go viral, and topple a political candidate who had a comfortable twenty-point lead over his opponents. And bad timing renders brilliant plans inert. Imagine a famous, big-time author with a new book set to launch on the same day that the Kardashians announce a new line of nipple jewelry ideal for wearing under see-through suit blouses. All the rage on Wall Street! Millions of dollars of media spent and publicity arrangements go down the drain!

I knew that Sparky made sure I saw Vicki on the video feed from the city council meeting because he wanted to pique my interest in this cause. The encounter at the gala was luck and icing on the cake for him. Great timing. I guessed Sparky would be spending a lot of time on this movement and wanted me in his corner when he asked for time off from the spy shop. It was funny, and totally unnecessary, because Sparky could take whatever time off he needed! Did I share my unwavering support with him at any point during this build-up? No, I did not. I found his efforts entertaining.

Sparky picked a perfect morning for a demonstration. It was the second day of the Shrimp Festival and locals, visitors, and the media were packed into the streets and businesses. I sat with him in his van as he tested camera feeds and mics. Several dozen demonstrators assembled near the main entrance of the Cerulean Sky compound. The Mod served coffee from a van near the south border of the demonstration site. People carried signs with phrases like: KEEP GALVESTON SMALL, DON'T RUIN THE ISLAND LIFE, and CERULEAN SKY = DARK SKIES FOR THE STRAND. I remarked to Sparky about several signs that said: KEEP IT REAL, KEEP IT SMALL, WE DON'T NEED YOUR STINKING MALL.

"That's the official chant for the demonstration," Sparky said. "The KISS Board came up with it at our last meeting."

He zoomed his cameras in and out to ensure everything was working. I looked at the center screen – a wide shot of the main building. "What're you hoping for?" I asked. "What impact do you want this demonstration to have? It seems like the place is nearly complete."

Sparky fidgeted with several of the controls for the third time; I could tell my comment displeased him. I should've kept my mouth shut.

"We want the community to reject Cerulean Sky so it never opens or is a commercial failure." Sparky checked the batteries in his mics. "We can do this. Several building permit issues still need to come before the city council. We want to influence the outcomes of these decisions by showing council members that, if they let Cerulean Sky break or bend the rules, we'll hold them accountable. We've been a presence at city council meetings for the last year and have affected several important changes."

I reminded myself I was here to support Sparky. This wasn't the time to challenge him, even if I didn't understand how bringing more business and tourism dollars into a struggling community could be a bad thing. It had been an ugly, dilapidated site before Cerulean Sky built here.

"That makes sense. What's the plan for this morning?"

Sparky relaxed. "We'll begin the march around the complex in about ten minutes. Our group leaders will address questions from the media. We're hoping that Vicki Moon might speak to the group as well. It's not likely. We've been told she's pissed that we're here today." He smiled and stood. "She had to reschedule an event with several potential investors today. Ha! We'd love to come back and disrupt her dog and pony show when she reschedules."

"It's about the money," I argued.

"Always."

Sparky and I left his van to get coffee. About 150 people stood at the intersection of Church and Thirty-Third streets. It would be a good-sized group anywhere, but especially here on the island where community support can be spotty. Two group leaders provided direction about how the march would work and how to hold signs to ensure the greatest visibility for the media.

Two Houston media outlets, each with a reporter and videographer, set up about a half a block up Church Street. Steve Heart was covering the event, too, and walked over to us by the Mod's coffee van.

"Thanks for coming." Sparky extended his hand to Steve.

"Hey, man, I wouldn't miss it, but I do have to shift over to the Strand by 11 a.m. Our entertainment reporter is on sick leave, so I need to cover the crowning of Miss Shrimp Festival." Steve shrugged his shoulders. "Xena, how have you been?"

"Things are interesting, as always," I said. "In fact, I've been meaning to call you about our a new case and would like to pick your brain. Can I take you to lunch tomorrow?"

"If you're buying, the answer is always yes."

"Olympia Grill on Pier 21. Eleven thirty?"

"It's a date." Steve pulled a notebook out of his pocket and turned to a fresh page. "Sparky, will you introduce me to the demonstration leaders? I'd like to get their statements before these knuckleheads from Houston try to take over."

The march began. I watched for a while, fascinated by the energy of the protestors. This big development had gotten under their skin. Galveston was a funny place in this way. Scrappy and backward in some respects but always rooted in community connection.

I liked the smallness of Galveston but knew the city needed money. For example, we had to rebuild the beach every few years with sand shipped from sources hundreds of miles away to keep the island from eroding into the Gulf. I'm worried, readers, how imported sand will affect our ecosystem because it's not just sand. We also bring in tiny flora and fauna from the source. Seems like we're messing with Mother Nature in ways we don't understand. *The Revenge of the Mississippi Nano Crab.* I made a mental note to ask Ari about this problem.

I stopped to see Sparky back in his van before I left. "Cerulean Sky is a big place. It took fifteen minutes to walk around one time."

"Yep. And when it's topped out it will tower over a hundred feet high. It'll be the island's white whale." He held his arms high and wide.

"It's been a ramshackle site for a long time."

Sparky gave me that look again, like I was pissing him off. He focused back on his main screen and whispered into it. "Come on Ms. Moon, let's see what you have to say."

"I don't mean to seem unsupportive, I'm trying to understand things better."

"I get it. You're always investigating." He gave a slight smile.

"Perhaps."

I stayed with Sparky until the demonstration finished and the media left. There were no Vicki Moon sightings.

"I gotta get some gumbo. I'm starving," I declared.

"I love the food, hate the lines."

"Yeah, tradeoffs for sure."

A fifteen-dollar donation to the Galveston Food Bank entitled me to generous samples from over a hundred gumbo booths competing for the title of Best at the Festival. I left the demonstration determined to try as many gumbos as I could get to before falling over, filling up, or wearing out.

~⊙

I carried the little plastic gumbo cup and spoon they gave me when I registered and headed for the far end of the first line of booths that ran on both sides of the Strand between Twenty-Second and Twenty-Fifth streets. There were more gumbo booths one block north and south of the Strand on Twenty-Fourth and Twenty-Third streets. Car traffic was blocked from the area and there was a thin strip in the middle of the road, lined by the backs of each booth where non-gumbo-eating people could walk. It was packed, so my strategy was to begin on the northwest side because it was the farthest from the registration tent and parking.

Truth be told, half the gumbo tasted like crap, usually because some manic wannabe chef burned the roux or added too much salt. It was also common for cooks to water down gumbos or add more celery than seafood to maximize the number of people who could be served within their budget. All these culinary mishaps were worth wading through, however, for the other half. I loved the velvety concoctions that oozed personality, had a bite, and were filled with big chunks of local seafood. Ruthless in my assessment of gumbo, I had no problem throwing away samples that wasted my taste buds' time.

The Shrimp Festival was particularly crowded because the weather was beautiful. Seventy degrees with a soft breeze coming off the gulf. Two cruise ships docked a couple of blocks from the Strand added ten thousand more potential gumbo eaters.

After an hour of tasting, my favorite was from the team at Shrimp and Stuff – a popular restaurant with locals. Medium spicy, a well-developed sauce, and full of whole shrimp. Bubba Gump's entry tasted great, too, but I hated to admit that because it was a chain restaurant and I favored independents. BG's gumbo had a good balance of everything and the best hot sauce offerings at the festival.

Yes, readers, I recognize the irony of my remarks, given what I said about Sparky's demonstration and the value of new developments! It's a complex and contradictory world, no?

After consuming a gallon of gumbos, I took a break and walked toward Harborside Drive where the Shrimp Festival parade was getting underway. As I walked north, the scene changed from gumbo booths to kiosks with cotton candy, smoothies, and domestic beer. A young guy carrying a green sno-cone nearly crashed into me and my white T-shirt.

At the corner of Harborside and Twenty-Third, I looked left and saw the beginning of the parade coming east, led by a gigantic fiberglass shrimp carrying the newly crowned Miss Shrimp Festival, a title awarded to the local high school senior whose parents sucked up the best to the judging panel with donations and favors. Pageants teach important and marketable skills!

As her float went by I admired the craftsmanship of Miss Shrimp Festival's get-up. The body of her dress was the unforgettable deep orangey-pink color that shrimp turn when scalded in boiling water. Her tummy and breasts were covered in sections of fabric in the same color augmented with two rows of four articulated, furry pink legs that heaved up and down when she waved to the crowd. The Miss's long hair was spiked up and came to a point like a shrimp's head and she wore round black sunglasses to emulate the shrimp's eyes. Curiously, the designers had turned her hands into red claws with flamenco castanets that clanged when she squeezed down on them. Miss Shrimp Festival got into her role with a dance performance that seemed part Charo, part John Travolta. *Pulp Fiction*, not *Grease*. Shrimp do have tiny claws, readers; I know you were wondering.

After Miss Shrimp Festival went by, I checked out a few of the floats. All of them were artistic renditions of large shrimp including one made of crab shells, which seemed odd since crabs prey on shrimp. Perhaps the float creators didn't know this or maybe this float was more intellectual than I gave it credit for, like a John Waters interpretation of the dark side of being a shrimp, representing its nightmares. Perhaps it was a statement on the beauty of revenge since several thousand crabs must've died to make the float. It seemed like bad juju either way.

There were many people on both sides of the street watching the parade, including another guy with a green sno-cone opposite me. Or was it the same guy? There was something about this guy that seemed fishy because he looked as though he wasn't enjoying himself. I went back down Twenty-Third and turned right to cut into Saengerfest Park. After maneuvering through the crowd for about five minutes, I turned to look for the guy.

Waited.

Waited.

He turned the corner, ditched his sno-cone, entered the park, and acted as if he was in line at one of the gumbo booths. But he didn't have a plastic gumbo cup. This was telling because people couldn't *buy* gumbo from individual booths; you had to register and carry the official festival cup. This guy was following me.

I kept going but moved slowly to allow him to catch up to me, which he did. When he was ten feet behind me, I turned and yelled, "WHAT?!" like the Muay Thai master taught us to do in our personal safety class when approached by a stranger. Except that I wasn't fighting off an attacker; I was trying to figure out why this guy was following me, so it might've been the wrong thing to do because I startled him and he ran away.

I ran after him back up Twenty-Third and to the right at Harborside. He was fast, a challenge because the streets were crowded with people. I made up some distance by vaulting over several railings separating the street and sidewalks.

The guy looked back to see if I was close, which I was, but then he wiped out Miss Shrimp Festival, who was taking pictures with fans. She fell toward a passing truck and the crowd gasped in horror. She was OK, but the bottom part of her shrimp-colored Miss Shrimp Festival dress got caught in the truck's tire and ripped off, revealing her silver lamé thong to anyone who cared to see it. Which was everyone. It looked oddly appropriate for the occasion, except there were little kids staring at her bare ass cheeks.

Two of the pissed-off parents chased after my guy.

I needed to get out in front of them and looked around for a shortcut. I saw Sally and her Segway tour group, who had stopped to watch the parade.

"Sally, I need your Segway."

"No!"

"I'll bring it right back."

"No!" she replied, but it was too late. I had hopped on her Segway and was going after the guy, who headed west toward Twenty-Fifth. I took Sally's Segway because I knew the other Segways were in a safety speed limiter – or turtle – mode and would only go about 6 miles per hour. My guy might be running that fast. Sally's could go 12.5 miles per hour for twenty-five miles on a full charge on smooth pavement, which this wasn't; it was broken, rutted, and undulating.

I tilted forward on the Segway to get it to go fast. The guy ran south on Twenty-Fifth Street, toward my spy shop. I waved to Dora as I went by in case she was watching, but I don't think she was. The guy cut into an alley and I turned in pursuit, closing in. I was twenty feet away from him when I rode over a hole with one tire and sailed sideways and forward on the Segway. I rolled onto the rumbly brick alley. It hurt a lot, but nothing was cracked or broken. I thanked God, which was stupid, because I'm an atheist.

The Segway shook and growled because it was doing something that it shouldn't, like crashing, but I got it started again and it stopped growling. You should wear a helmet if you try this at home, readers, but I was OK and I zoomed out of the alley in time to avoid hitting a group of gumbo enthusiasts with matching pink T-shirts that read BAYOU GIRLS ARE HOT AND SPICY. They were all men, but maybe they were hoping to find bayou girls or they lost a drinking bet and their friends were watching and laughing their asses off across the street.

I was going full speed but didn't see the guy and was back in the area with all the gumbo booths. It was packed with people. I drove up the thin strip in the middle, looking both ways to find the guy. I looked for cops, too, because I doubted that Segways were allowed here, since it was for pedestrians. Maybe Segways were a gray area, but I was lucky because the closest cops were busy cuffing a guy wearing a shrimp stocking cap, probably hand-knit in Portland.

I gave up trying to find the guy and brought the Segway back to Sally, who huffed and stared me down as she grabbed her Segway from me.

"Sorry, extenuating circumstances," I shirked.

"I'm not insured for this kind of thing," she scolded in a whisper. Her tour group applauded me and said that this tour was way better than the alternative, which apparently was riding the John Water's-inspired shrimp float in the parade. I hoped they tipped Sally extra for the entertainment value.

I was upset that I'd lost the guy but typed a description of him into the notes app on my phone so I didn't forget. About six foot, skinny, late twenties, short light brown hair, fast runner, tanned to the point his arm hair was bleached. Boney, wide shoulders. I wrote a few questions such as: Why was this guy following me? I was eating gumbo; who cares about that? Have I met or seen him before? He seemed somewhat familiar to me but I wasn't sure why. This happens a lot in small towns and it does not take long to see most of the locals enough that they become known to you.

I was hungry again, but I'd lost my gumbo cup during the chase and was too cheap to buy another one, so I walked back to where I locked my bike and headed home. I didn't go the most direct route and checked several times to see if I was being followed, which I wasn't. When had the guy started watching me? At the demonstration? Or after that? I tried to remember details about the guy from my freerun along the seawall and considered whether it might be the same guy. If it was one man, trying to lose him would be a waste of time because he knew where I lived. I was disappointed it took two hours and his green sno-cone before I noticed him. Bad investigative work. Something was affecting my attention to detail.

Maybe Fred.

Or Ari.

I'd been daydreaming about both all day. For different reasons, of course!

~⊙

I looked out my window for the twentieth time and went downstairs to my office with a bottle of Sauvignon Blanc from the Marlborough Sounds. I grabbed one of Jane's journals from toward the middle of the stack, flipped through, and stopped when I saw Fred's name:

Fred is growing. Larger, stronger, bolder. I opened his tank lid today and he floated to the top immediately to see me. His eyes met mine and the webbing between his arms billowed like sails. I plunged my arms down and he grabbed them. Roberta gave him two capelins and he took them in separate arms, passed them to his mouth, and devoured them. She gave him a third fish, but instead of taking it he sucked in and let loose a water bomb at me. I was soaked! Roberta had to help me get untangled from Fred. He sunk to the bottom and went into his lair. We think he did it because the heads of the capelins had been removed and that was his favorite part. Such spirit! This discrimination and preference is a good sign – he's recovering.

I speculated whether Jane had taken the heads off as a test or if this was a coincidence? And I wondered if Fred missed her? Not her fish or her attention, but *her*. Octopuses are not social beings; they don't live in groups. Maybe the emotion involved in loss is acute for them because they form fewer but deeper connections.

Before I called Gregory, I texted Sparky and Dora and asked them to meet me at the spy shop early the next morning. Someone knew I was working this case and was nervous enough to have me tailed.

Excellent.

Yikes!

Where is he now?

I put on a moody David Sanborn album, poured a second glass of wine, and reclined in my chair, letting the moment get heavy. Aloneness – as distinct from loneliness – can be bewitching, don't you think? I turned off all the lights, opened the blinds and watched nature's shift change occur.

Chapter 10
Day 7, Monday

I got to the spy shop by 6 a.m., groggy from lack of sleep but excited to get into the tricky bits of this case. Before Sparky and Dora arrived, I turned the meeting room into a war room, adding LOOSE ENDS for open items we need to close and KNOWNS for facts we know for sure to the PS (potential suspects) and PM (potential motives) flipchart posters that were already on the walls.

I moved several cases of products out of the way. New stuff for the holiday gift-giving season, like twelve dozen "TV Terminator" remotes that turned off any TV set by sending out the power-off codes for nearly every television set manufactured in the world. It would be a huge hit for people who lived in nursing homes, drank in bars, or had annoying spouses or siblings, which covered most people on the island and all their friends. If you pushed the TV Terminator button twice, the TV was disabled until its reset button was pushed, which few people ever managed to find.

I put on the latest Foals album and transposed from my notes the names of people I had come across in association with this case. They all went on the PS chart for now, joining the names from our previous meeting including Fred, Ari, and Bernie. I crossed off Fred's name and added Ansel, Ralph, Judge Buddy, Sam and/or Laura Block, skinny guy, friend from out of town/lunch, BARL Director Mark Larson, the mayor, and BARL employees Roberta, Amy, Peter, and Bob. Each name was listed on its own sticky note so we could categorize and organize them as highly suspicious, somewhat suspicious, or likely nothing. On the Loose Ends chart I captured all the questions and open items that we each were working on.

On the Knowns chart I wrote: FRED DID NOT KILL JANE, JANE WAS STRANGLED, JANE WAS NOT PREGNANT, NO TOXINS IN BLOOD, TIME OF DEATH ABOUT 10 P.M. MONDAY.

Dora and Sparky arrived with a cortado from the Mod for me; they don't open until 7 a.m. I told them about Sunday's chase.

"Xena, you need to be careful! Why chase the guy?" Dora asked.

"To figure out who he was and why he was following me," I replied.

"I'm going to look at the street cameras and see if I can pick up any of it," Sparky said. "Did you do any of your running mumbo jumbo?"

"A little," I admitted.

"What time was this?"

"About 2 p.m." After he jotted all that down, I then asked for updates on open items.

"The IT guys worked all weekend at BARL and managed to get back most of Jane's files. Everything looked normal, but most of the company names are cloaked." Sparky crossed off the item on the chart and sat.

"We don't know what we're looking at, but I can get Ari to take a closer look and cross-reference the company codes with their records to identify them," I said.

"Ari was there yesterday," Sparky confirmed. "I stopped by after the demonstration wrapped up, and he told me that he didn't see anything out of the ordinary in the files. He's going to take another look at them today. By the way, I see why you're taken by Ari. He's smart and has a great presence. Not too flashy. Seems like a generous soul." Sparky raised his eyebrows up and down and smirked.

Dora laughed.

"Who said I was taken by him? Anyway, he's not at all athletic," I insisted.

"True. You could totally take him in a fight," Sparky mused.

I motioned for us to get back on track by pointing to the charts. "Did he say he could decode the company names?"

"He thinks so. And he needs to get permission to share that with us."

"If nothing was there, why delete the files?" I asked.

"Just in case? Maybe the killer doesn't know," Dora suggested. She stood and crossed off EXPLORE ARI'S BACKGROUND from the open list.

"While we're on the topic of Ari," Dora said, "let me tell you what I've learned about our client. He's forty-one.

Never. Been. Married," she added slowly and looked at me with a grin.

I'm thirty-eight years old, readers, I know you were wondering.

"Ari has been at BARL for four years and came in as the cephalopod team manager. Was at the Seattle Marine Institute before that, where he was considered a rising star. He spent a year researching with Cousteau right after getting his PhD from UC Davis."

"That's the same place Jane got her degree, right?" I asked.

"Yes, but it doesn't appear they knew each other, because Jane was four years ahead of Ari," she said. "Ari's research interests have included the migration of nautilus and the effects of pollution on the giant pacific octopus."

"He *is* an octo-expert," Sparky decided.

"In fact, he authored a well-known study that measured high levels of caffeine in the bloodstreams of Puget Sound sea life, including octopuses. The caffeine came from storm drains and runoff from Seattle. There's a coffee kiosk on virtually every corner there."

"Fascinating!" I quipped.

"Great story for my happy hour crew. I'll want to remember that," Sparky said.

"Ari was trying to determine what, if any, behavioral differences the caffeine might cause and found that local octopuses were more aggressive than those up in British Columbia," Dora added and closed her folder.

"Well, Canadians are more relaxed than Americans.

Everyone knows that," I said. "They soak cheese curds in Crown Royal."

"Really? Cool, man," Sparky said, not realizing I was kidding.

"What else did you find about Ari? Any other connection between Ari and Jane?"

"Not that I could find. Their careers didn't intersect until Ari came to BARL," Dora replied.

"I wonder how she felt about a younger researcher being her boss. If there was any jealousy."

"You should ask him, Xena," Dora suggested. "To finish up about Ari, he has a clean record and has lived a quiet life. His parents are second-generation American, and his grandparents came here as refugees from Pakistan and Iran."

"I see that you added the name Ralph on the list of potential suspects. Who is that?" Sparky asked.

"I'm not sure," I replied. "Jane mentioned that she needed to meet with Ralph about a case because his science was wrong. I got the sense he's an expert witness on the opposing side. I'm going to ask Steve about him at lunch."

"Do you want me to research what he's been working on?" Dora asked.

"Great idea."

I added that to the Loose Ends chart and looked out over all the charts and pictures.

"I'd like the two of you to spend some time looking at everything we have and come up with a list of questions that we should be asking but aren't. We're missing something and we don't have a lot of time to figure it out. I need to spend some time prepping and then I'm meeting Steve for lunch, but text me if you think of anything I should be asking him in particular."

~⊙

The Olympia Grill on Pier 21 – as distinct from the one on the seawall – is my favorite place to sit waterside and enjoy a Greek salad with grilled shrimp. Local shrimp, of course. From an outside table, you can see the cruise ship terminals to the west, the *Elissa* tall ship, and shrimp boats being followed by seagulls and pelicans. To the east, the BARL compound is visible if you knew what you are looking for.

Steve sat and we ordered iced teas.

"Thanks for joining me for lunch," I said.

"I never turn down lunch. And besides, I'm dying to know what you were doing speeding through the Strand on a Segway yesterday!"

"You saw that?"

"Some of it. I was covering the Miss Shrimp Festival crowning, remember?"

"Did you hear what happened to her dress?"

"I heard, but didn't see it, myself, darn it. I included the disrobing of the Miss in my story, but the entertainment editor thought it was too edgy and cut that part." Steve then lowered his voice. "Did you have something to do with her extra exposure?"

I slumped forward against the table. "No, I didn't! But the guy I was chasing caused it."

"So, by association, you did! Something I might want to write about?"

"No. I don't know enough, and I don't want you to scare off my suspect."

"So this was related to the BARL case?"

I nodded.

"How's that going?" he asked just before we paused from our discussion to order lunch and check our phones.

"Can we be off the record if I promise you the exclusive when I'm ready to share?" I replied.

He sulked. "Yes, I suppose." Reporters hate off-the-record conversations.

"Dr. Pani and I believe the autopsy proves that Jane was murdered. I'm investigating."

"And BJ?"

"He's not convinced and won't reopen the case."

"You know I need to go public the moment he does."

"I know."

"And even if he doesn't, if the evidence is convincing."

"Yes."

He took out his notebook. "I'm going to take notes, off the record, for when I need to write something."

"OK. Can you tell me about any open cases that Jane was working on?" I asked. "Perhaps something you heard about at the city council or courts?"

"Not sure I know much," he offered and then leaned back to think for a moment. "I know she was testifying on the permit challenge for the new crab joint on Tiki Island."

"The same case Ralph Miller was working?"

"Yes. You know Ralph?"

"No. Jane mentioned him in her journals."

"He's good people."

"Good to know. Tell me about him."

"Geologist. Math genius. Has been on the island a long time."

"Were he and Jane friends?"

"Maybe, but I doubt it. Ralph is in his sixties and doesn't get out much. I'd guess there would've been mutual respect – both had great reputations."

A soft breeze made the temperature feel perfect. Low 80s. Two feral cats stared at us while we ate. I tossed shrimp tails to them, and Steve offered them pita bread. We tried to be coy so the restaurant staff didn't see us. Two tourists at the next table took pictures of the cats as if they were lions on a safari. Their urban adventure.

"Any other cases you know about involving Jane?" I asked.

"She was scheduled to testify about a big home site expansion on the west side of the island that'll take out some of the marsh," Steve replied. "No big deal there."

"Anything involving pollution?"

"No, not that I know of. I heard one of the other BARL guys was mucking about on Pelican Island, something about water samples. The fishermen out at Seawolf Park like to gossip."

"Do you know who?"

"Can't remember."

"Ansel Homer?" I suggested.

"Sounds familiar. Not sure though." Steve moved closer and lowered his voice again. "Do you think Jane's death was linked to dumping in the bay?"

"Don't know. That's one lead." I sat back and put both my hands up to stretch. "The motive is always love, money, or fame, right?"

"Right. I don't know if she had a love interest," he said. "I heard she was messing with a councilman. But she seemed smarter than that."

"I heard that, too." I finished off my last shrimp, broke the tail into two pieces and tossed one half to each of our newly devoted felines. "Can we switch gears?" I asked.

"Sure."

"BARL has been tight-lipped about revealing company names associated with their projects. Do you know what's behind that?"

"Yes. They were sued for defamation last year because a draft report included derogatory information that damaged the company. The final report cleared up everything and they issued a correction, but the damage was already done in the media and public opinion. The company's stock tanked. BARL paid a judgment in the case. Since that happened, it's been harder to get information from them on any case."

"I knew it had to be something." I paused, took a few deep breaths, and looked at Steve. "Have you seen Jane and Judge Buddy go at it?"

"Once. Some oyster case. She was tough!"

"She lost that one."

"Yes, but she did all she could. Money talks and the company promised the city jobs. We need jobs."

"Do you know anything about a case involving flounder?"

"Some. It's just getting started. Fascinating situation.

There's a company that thinks they've figured out how to create a successful flounder farm in the bay. Many have tried but no one's ever done it. Something to do with the fish returning to the right spawning ground."

"Can you get me a copy of what's been filed so far?" I asked.

"Sure. Is this related to the case?" Steve took some notes and checked his phone.

"Not likely but I want to eliminate it from my list."

"OK." Steve moved forward and whispered, "Buddy's on your suspect list?"

"On the list, but not high."

"I doubt he'd have the imagination or ability to execute."

"That's what everyone thinks!"

He bent forward and grabbed the sides of the table. "Xena, I want in on this case. It's right up my alley."

"I know," I whispered back with a smile.

"And it's wild stuff!"

"I agree!" The waiter took our plates and gave me the check. I put my notebook back in my bag and signed the receipt.

"Before you leave, let's go back to what happened yesterday. How'd you end up on that Segway?"

I told Steve about the guy with the green sno-cone and Sally's tour group and how I crashed and how the guy crashed into Miss Shrimp Festival and how the parents of the defrocked beauty queen joined the chase and how I lost him in the gumbo booths.

"I love gumbo," Steve announced.

"Me, too."

"You didn't hurt yourself?"

"I'm sore and have a big bruise on my leg."

"I had no idea those things could go that fast."

"I'm thinking of getting one for my two-mile commute to the spy shop."

"Cool."

I agreed to keep Steve in the loop and he said he'd look for anything that might be interesting regarding Ansel and Buddy. Steve was itching to write about this now, but he had promised to hold off until we knew something more concrete.

"I never thought I'd say it, but this case might eclipse what happened in Houston with Granny's Home," Steve remarked as we walked off Pier 21.

"You might be right."

Chapter 11
Day 8, Tuesday

As Ari and I walked into the Carnes Brothers Funeral Home, I couldn't help but notice that he looked like an assassin in his black suit, with his hair pulled back in a ponytail and his dark features. Too cool for Galveston.

I, on the other hand, looked like Mother Hubbard. I wore a long black skirt borrowed from Dora with a gray wrap scarf. I wondered the same thing you are, readers; where was *this* skirt the day of the gala? I could've saved myself a lot of humiliation. Dora said she thought it was too casual for the gala and the color explosion that had been my dress was better. Paybacks are hell, I reminded her.

Ari and I entered the already packed hall where Jane's service would be held and stood in an open area toward the back. I recognized several folks from BARL and Ari introduced me to a few I hadn't met. I typed their names into my phone in case I wanted to speak with them later.

"Xena, you remember Roberta," Ari said.

"Yes, nice to see you again. I'm sorry it's under these circumstances."

"Thank you for taking on this case," Roberta said. "I love that eight-legged guy. Jane did, too."

"How'd Fred seem during the days leading up to Jane's death?" I winced inside because it seemed rude to ask these kinds of questions at a funeral. Luckily Roberta was eager to talk about it.

"No different. He was getting fat, growing long, thick tentacles, and showing signs of middle age," she said.

"What signs?"

Ari jumped in. "Thinking about mating, mostly. You can see it in how octopuses explore their environment. Fred is more interested in others. It takes very little to get him to come to the top of the tank and interact. Likely because he's feeling better. When he came to BARL, he was nearly dead from the toxins that were pouring out of the Mexican plant near where he lived."

Mark Larson then arrived. I watched as he stopped to talk to each lab employee and several others whom I didn't know.

"Hello, Dr. Larson." I extended my hand as he walked up to the group. "It's a wonderful showing. It's obvious that Jane was loved by many people and well regarded by the community."

"Yes, she was," he agreed. "Every facet of the environmental movement in Galveston and Houston is represented here." He stepped closer and spoke more softly. "Any new leads in the case? I'm afraid the deadline is approaching."

"We're following up on several pieces of evidence and I'm confident we will get to the bottom of who killed Jane before the two weeks are up," I replied, choosing my words carefully.

"I saw in the paper that you got into a minor scuffle on the Strand. Was that related?"

Ari flashed his eyes at me because I hadn't told him about the Segway chase during the Shrimp Festival.

I know Steve didn't write about it, so how'd the story make the paper? I asked myself.

"Chase, not scuffle," I clarified. "It's hard to tell if it was related, because the person who was following me got away. I didn't realize it had hit the news."

I was disappointed the director mentioned the chase in front of Ari. Now I'd have to tell him about the skinny man, which could open a can of worms. I needed to switch the subject. "It looks like it'll be a lovely service. Is that Jane's brother, Bernie?"

I pointed to the man at the front of the room. I already knew it was Bernie, of course, because Dora showed me his picture.

"Yes, he's here from California," Roberta said.

"He came by BARL yesterday and we took him to meet Fred," Ari added. "Seems like a great guy. Jane was his only sibling."

"He stood in the tank area and stared at Fred for a long time," Roberta said.

"Angry at Fred?" I asked.

"Gosh, no," Ari answered. "He admired Fred and knew Jane had dedicated her life's work to sea life like him. We told Bernie we didn't think Fred killed Jane."

"We don't know what happened. We might never know the whole story," Dr. Larson said.

"We will uncover the truth. I have faith," I declared.

Jane's brother talked to the funeral director and greeted those who stepped up to look at the urn on display that contained her ashes. I took and sent Dora a furtive picture of a woman sitting in the far-right seat in the second row. The woman looked distraught and had separated herself from others.

Dora texted back: *Laura Block. Is Sam there?*

No. Just Laura.

I remembered how she dropped her drink at the gala when I mentioned Jane. Now she's here and he's not. Perhaps the affair, if there was one, was with her, not her husband.

Ari and I sat in the back row because that was the only place with seats left. The funeral director opened the service and handed it over to Bernie. He shared a poignant story about how he and Jane were competitive siblings who fought for the love and attention of their only parent before their mother died when he was ten and she was thirteen. After she passed, Jane assumed the role of parent and they both lived with their grandparents until they started their own lives. The grandparents had both passed away since.

Dr. Larson and several other BARL staff members, including Ari, spoke about Jane. Ari struggled to get through his story and his voice cracked. It was a lovely service that lasted about an hour.

I could see Ari was itching to leave.

"Go ahead," I said, "I'd like to talk with Bernie. Can we meet tomorrow? I've some things to share about the case."

Ari glared at me. "I gather. And I want to hear all about it, but tomorrow doesn't work for me. Come by my house later this evening, I'll make dinner and we can talk." Ari spoke softly so others wouldn't overhear.

He cooks! Add ten more points – maybe twenty – to Ari's already high attractiveness rating.

"Deal," I responded without thinking. I'd need to get my information organized before going over there.

"I'll text you my address. Seven?"

Did I tell Ari that I already knew his address and a lot more about him? No, I did not.

"Sure, see you tonight."

Ari turned to leave and ran into Dr. Larson. They walked out together.

I stood at the end of the line of people paying their respects to Bernie. Laura Block got up from where she was siting and left without acknowledging Bernie or anyone. A few people admired Jane's urn. It was painted a beautiful opalescence blue like the water she loved so much. One man took a selfie with it.

The hall was nearly empty when it was my turn to address Bernie.

"Hello, my name is Xena. I'm sorry for your loss."

"Thank you. How did you know Jane?"

"I never had the pleasure of meeting her, although I'm getting to know her through her journals." Bernie cocked his head with curiosity. "I'm the private investigator Dr. Ari

Pani hired to investigate her death."

Bernie perked up and moved closer. "Ari told me about you. Thank you for what you're doing. I'd love to learn more about your progress on the case."

I spoke softly. "We're following up on initial leads, so I don't yet have anything concrete to share. I understand you went to see Fred yesterday?"

"Yes, it was fascinating and painful."

"Based on what the police and the folks at BARL have shared, and what you know about your sister, do you have a theory about what happened?"

"No." He slumped and sat in a chair in the first row. We were now alone in the room. "I know one thing, my sister wasn't careless in the tank. So if one of your theories is that she didn't pay attention or forgot how to work with an octopus, you can cross that off your list. Her discipline annoyed me when we were kids but it took her far."

I eased into the tough part. "I understand Ari shared that we believe she was murdered. It's fine if you don't want to talk about this right now."

He acknowledged that and motioned with his hands for me to sit next to him and continue.

"The police aren't convinced, but Ari has confirmed that those marks on her neck didn't come from Fred," I confirmed. "Do you know of anyone that might've wanted to hurt your sister?"

Bernie held his face in his hands for a moment, then replied. "No. But to be honest, although we were close, we didn't talk much. I can't imagine anyone wanting to hurt

Jane. Last time we talked, during the holidays, she seemed happy overall, but was clearly perturbed by the politics of business. I'm the same way, and it's why I'm a carpenter."

"Have you found anything unusual in her belongings?"

"I haven't gone to her house yet. I'm arranging to have everything sold and the proceeds donated, per her wishes. I'll go to her home on Wednesday morning before I leave to take a couple of mementos for myself." He stood. "I'm sorry I couldn't be more helpful, but if I give you my number will you keep me up to date on the investigation?" He pulled out his wallet and handed me a simple card with his name and cellphone number. "I'm not much of an email guy. My daughter tells me I'm out of step."

We shook hands and I offered to help him carry things to his rental car. He declined and said he had to settle up with the funeral home. "I'm trying to close out as many things as possible before I leave," he explained.

"One more question. Do you know if Jane had a love interest?"

"No, I don't."

"Would you mind telling me if her lovers tended to be male or female? It could help me make sense of information I uncover."

He sighed and shrugged nonchalantly. "Mostly women. A few guys in high school. She never told our grandparents she was gay and only told me after they both passed. I already knew, of course."

I handed Bernie my card and promised to call him when we got a break in the case. I drove home while reflecting on

Bernie's answers, Laura Block's appearance at the funeral, and my upcoming dinner at Ari's. I needed to decide quickly how much to share with Ari and wondered if he knew or suspected Jane was gay.

~⊙

As I got in my car that evening, I reminded myself this wasn't a date or anything like a date. It was a business meeting that included a home-cooked dinner. Maybe it wouldn't be home-cooked. Maybe Ari ordered fancy takeout. That's what I'd do. I shouldn't have said fancy, readers; it might've implied more meaning to this dinner than a routine business meeting, which is what it was.

I arrived at Ari's house on Barracuda Lane in Fish Village, an area of town that people called a locals' favorite, which was good when used to describe restaurants but not always true when referring to neighborhoods. In this case, Fish Village had an undeserved bad rep that kept housing values lower. The houses were small, close together, and some of the streets seemed a bit dodgy, but it was also a cool part of town. And besides, there were a lot of dodgy streets in Galveston, especially on the east end. My street was no different and we were all one or two blocks – or houses – from being in the wrong part of town.

Fish Village got its name because it was where fishermen lived. I'm not being sexist; this was during a time when all people-who-fish-for-a-living were men, and they lived there because it was close to where their ships docked in the Galveston Ship Channel. Ari likely lived here because it was close to BARL.

He greeted me with a big smile and welcomed me into his house. I noticed he was wearing jogging pants and a moisture-wicking runner's top, although he didn't look like he exercised. It could be like how I wear yoga pants everywhere even though I don't downward dog, or how people buy four-wheel-drive SUVs and never take them off-road.

What I should share, readers, is that he looked hot in his jogging suit, so whether he ran or was a couch potato was irrelevant.

"Would you like a drink?" Ari asked as he motioned me to take a seat in the small but neat living room furnished with a large beige sectional and a matching armchair.

"Sure, anything is fine. A glass of wine?"

I sat in the chair.

"I've a Pinot Gris that'll go nicely with the appetizer." He headed back into his kitchen. I could hear him say that he had looked online for the article the director mentioned but couldn't find it.

I hadn't yet decided how much to tell him about how the case was going. This is normal, and always a balancing act because it makes sense to withhold some things. I wouldn't have mentioned the chase scene through the Strand because it might not be related, although I was sure it was. But the director had blown my cover and so I'd have to tell Ari at least some of what happened. But all the other leads and meetings? The guy on the seawall? I wasn't yet sure.

Ari sat in the sectional next to the chair and set a shrimp cocktail and two glasses of wine on the coffee table.

"This looks delicious," I said. "I wondered if you ate seafood, since you're a marine biologist."

"Farmers eat wheat, right?" He laughed. "I get what you mean. I love fresh, sustainably raised seafood, but don't eat octopus or squid. That's too close to home." Ari dipped a shrimp into the sauce. "The sauce has lots of horseradish in it."

I brightened because I loved the *pow* of horseradish. I grabbed a shrimp, covered it in sauce, and ate it. I tingled from the top of my skull all the way down my back. "That packs a punch!"

"My personal recipe." He smiled and sat back. "So how are things going since I saw you Friday morning with BJ? I heard that you made quite an impression at the gala." He laughed again. "Was that part of your plan? And Mark mentioned the chase."

I thought through the best way to tell Ari, without sounding like a fool, that no, wearing the most garish and over-the-top dress on the island, maybe in the state, wasn't my strategy. How could I tell him about the guy from the seawall and maybe the same guy chasing me through a crowded Shrimp Festival? How could I tell him that despite all these happenings, I knew little more than I did two days ago and time was running out?

So I fibbed a bit.

"The gala was memorable, for sure. The dress wasn't part of the plan, but it ended up a fine conversation starter."

"I saw it in the paper. I had no idea dresses like that existed!"

"Nor did I." I sat forward and changed the topic. "Things

are going well. I've continued to review Jane's journals, I talked with a local investigative reporter and will be meeting with him again later in the week." I grabbed another shrimp and sipped on my wine. Ari listened closely but didn't speak. "How do you feel about all this? I assume this is the first time someone close to you has been murdered? It must be hard."

"Yes, for sure. And I'm involved in the investigation, to boot. This is surreal for me and the team. We live pretty mundane lives as marine biologists."

He shifted to the side and rested his head on one hand. His hair fell forward. Nice.

I decided to test Ari's comfort level and looked straight into his eyes. "I understand that this is a heavy topic, and I don't mean to make light of the situation by rattling off tasks and bits of information. There's a lot going on and this is normal. It's too early to tell which clues are material to the case."

"I want to hear about the chase," he pleaded. "Were you in danger?"

I sighed and let it all out – or nearly all. "I noticed someone following me during the Shrimp Festival, so I tried to confront him to learn his identity. He ran and I chased him." I animated the chase with my hands and Ari's eyes seemed to keep up. "I was never in any danger although I was in hot water with my friend Sally because I borrowed – commandeered – her Segway to try and catch him, but he ran into the gumbo booths and blended in with the crowd. He was young, about six feet tall, and skinny. Sandy brown hair. It means we're getting close to something. It's a good sign."

"That's it?"

"Yep."

"I think there might be more to it," he assessed. "I trust that you'll tell me what I need to know. Be careful, OK?"

"Promise."

We both sat in silence and drank our wine.

"Can I ask you a few questions based on what I've read in Jane's journals?" I then asked.

Ari sat up straight and put his wine on the table. "Of course."

"What can you tell me about Ansel? Jane mentioned him and something called 'Project 67' in her journals a few times. She seemed frustrated with him. Was there tension?"

"Ansel works in another group. I don't recall a Project 67 but I can inquire about it. It isn't unusual for a project to have a number and no names in the early stages."

"Do you know Ansel? Did he and Jane butt heads?"

"Yes, I know him. If anything, Ansel was jealous of Jane's success and standing." Ari paused, as if he was searching for the right words. "He's driven by title and money and isn't well-respected by peers. That said, he doesn't seem like the type to take those feelings and do something extreme like killing someone." He paused again. "Stealing files or cheating …? I could see him doing that."

I took notes before asking the next question. "How'd Jane feel about working for a younger boss?"

This question seemed to surprise Ari, but he answered. "I don't know, but I didn't act like her manager, so I doubt she minded. I looked up to Jane."

"While we're on the topic, what was the nature of your relationship with Jane?"

Air responded quickly. "Colleagues who were also supportive friends. We weren't drinking buddies, not that close, but we cared for each other. We were never romantically involved, if that was what you're asking."

"Yes, thanks. Did you know she was gay?"

"Yes, and she talked to me a few times about how creeped out she was when guys hit on her and wouldn't let it go. I remember her saying a judge tried something."

"Judge Buddy?"

"Perhaps. I don't remember."

"Why didn't you tell me she was gay when we were at her house? We talked about the rumors she was having an affair with a councilman and you didn't mention that a big reason it didn't make sense was that she was gay."

"You have me there. I didn't think it was relevant. I hate to see people's private business dragged through the media."

"This was a murder investigation."

"You're right. I'm sorry. No more holding back."

"Thank you." I gave Ari a slight smile.

I could tell by the way he was hesitating that Ari was ready to say something. "You're a mysterious woman. I'm glad to have you on my team."

Ari put his hand on my shoulder, stood, and went to get the wine bottle to refill our glasses.

"I've a set of questions that I'd like to ask a few more people at BARL. How soon can we do that?"

"I can have Roberta help organize that as early as tomorrow morning.

"Let's do it in the afternoon. I'd like to talk more with

Roberta, the director, and Ansel."

Ari refilled our glasses. "Sure, no problem."

"And I'd like your help thinking through something."

"Of course."

Ari shifted to the edge of the cushion to get closer and face me. His eyes stared softly at me. He extended his hand to encourage me. I grabbed my notebook and moved to sit next to him on the sectional.

"Assuming Jane was murdered," I began, "Fred might've witnessed the crime and might know who the killer is."

"Yes, that's true," Ari agreed.

"I'd like you to think about how we might test this. Is there a way to help him share what he knows with us? You've told me – and I read Jane's journal entries where she wrote – how intelligent octopuses are."

"It's true. But how we communicate with him is another matter. Can I research this and get back with you?"

"Sure," I said.

"And speaking about Fred, I meant to mention the board agreed to a one-week extension to decide Fred's fate. So we have a bit more time."

"That's great news. Now, I've a list of basic questions I haven't yet asked *you*."

"Fire away."

"Where were you last Monday evening between 8 p.m. and midnight?"

"Home, reading, alone."

I paused and sighed, because this means he doesn't have an alibi. I went on, "Did anything unusual or different happen that last Monday or the week before?"

"No."

"Was Jane preparing for any big projects or cases?"

"Fred was a big project, she was the lead on the cuttlefish project, and she had two expert witness cases – a flounder case in the court and a permit hearing against a bar owner."

"Did you know of any conflicts between Jane and others?"

"Nothing beyond the usual style differences."

"Did you turn off the security cameras in this area?"

"No. They had been off for a while and I don't remember who turned them off at that time. It wasn't me. I haven't worked on a classified project in years."

"Thanks. This concludes the interrogation portion of the evening," I announced. I closed my notebook and smiled at Ari. It was a bit of a risk talking to Ari about Fred as a witness, I know. He was still in the PS list and if he had anything to do with the crime, my suggestion could've endangered Fred's life. But I was confident that Ari had nothing to do with Jane's death.

"Let's eat!" he suggested and stood. I followed Ari into the kitchen, which looked much tidier than mine and twice the size. I watched as Ari made spicy grouper sandwiches with homemade coleslaw. From scratch. Using pots and pans.

His dining area was fun, like a sixties diner booth, upholstered in blue sparkle plastic. The fish sandwich was tender, crunchy, and spicy. Everything was delicious. We exchanged stories about the culture shock of moving to Galveston after living in larger cities, our childhoods, and our favorite places on the island.

"Would you like some coffee?" Ari asked after picking up the dinner plates. "I've a terrific decaf."

"I'd love coffee. One cup for me, and then I'll need to leave." I was glad he didn't offer more wine, because we each had consumed three glasses and I was feeling a bit buzzed. "I need to prepare for the interviews at BARL tomorrow."

We returned to the living room with our coffees.

"Why marine biology?" I asked.

"It's a whole different world down there. Like going to another planet and finding no humans." He brightened and sat straight. "I love new adventures."

"I do, too."

"Why investigations?" Ari asked.

"I like to unravel messes and figure things out. And I like to see deserving people get justice."

"I do, too," Ari said.

Neither of us spoke for a moment. It was awkward.

"I should go." I stood up to leave.

Ari walked me to the door, but held onto my elbow. I turned around before opening the door.

"I enjoyed this evening. Even the interrogation." He smiled. "More than I expected."

"Likewise," I confessed softly.

Ari stepped closer, took my face in his hands, and kissed me. Not a long kiss, but tender. "I'm sorry," he said. "I probably shouldn't have done that."

"Done what?" I replied and winked. "Thank you for a lovely dinner and your company."

I walked out and got in my car. Stunned. Buzzing. Happy. Worried.

~⊙

I was on the phone with Gregory ten minutes later, happy because we both did well with our daily questions.

Finally!

Perhaps this was because we were too busy to get in our own way. How existential. It was a quiet night with light winds. I could hear the rides and music coming from the Pleasure Pier. I replayed what happened at Ari's house in my mind.

Did I tell Gregory about the kiss? No, I did not.

I shared what happened at Jane's funeral, including my conversation with Bernie.

We were quiet for a moment until Gregory cut into my daydreaming. "Do you want to hear what I've learned about Jane's finances?"

"Of course!" I said. "Let me guess. The brother gets everything."

"Nope. Jane left everything in her estate to the BARL research foundation, earmarked for studies that promote conservation."

"Wow, I didn't see that coming."

I took notes.

"You were half right, because the brother is her life insurance beneficiary, and his wife, in the event he died before her. It's $250,000, not a huge sum."

"Not enough to kill for that's for sure. I don't see him as the doer anyway."

"Agreed. I did a quick check on the brother's finances. There are no filings for bankruptcy or any lawsuits pending against him, so while he doesn't have a lot of money, he also isn't in dire straits."

"Do BARL and the brother know what they're getting?"

"Yes, Jane's attorney notified both at the time she designated her wishes and again last Friday."

"How much was she worth?"

"Her assets are estimated at around two million. Sizable enough."

"She brought more than that into BARL each year, so the money doesn't seem like a powerful motivation." I doodled with the numbers Gregory was sharing.

"Agreed. Jane's money isn't the motive for her murder."

"Love, money, or fame. The search continues. I've a few people I want to talk to, including Ansel, Buddy, and Laura."

I decided to cross off Bernie from the PS list. Laura, on the other hand, would go higher on the list. I described to Gregory the beautiful aqua urn that held Jane's ashes. It had been luminous, complex, and striking – like I imagined her.

Gregory and I hung up, and I returned to my sensual daydream. My hips hurt like hell from the Segway crash and I was still a little drunk from the wine at Ari's house and the Scotch I'd had at home. All I could think about was the supple strength of his hands cupping my face, the softness of his lips, and the sweet kiss he gave me.

My … oh … my …

There was something undeniably appealing about Ari.

His looks, yes, although I usually went for a sportier type. It was his absence of ego in the presence of his brilliant mind that had me reeling.

Chapter 12
Day 9, Wednesday

Successful human resources leaders know how to compartmentalize things. They can stand up to a slimy executive in one moment and treat him like a respected peer an hour later at the senior staff meeting. They bring down the house with a rousing keynote honoring top performers in the morning and unravel a sticky sexual harassment situation in the afternoon. Imagine knowing something so sad that you want to hide in your office and weep. Instead, you emerge positive and engaged and give something much less important your full attention because that's what you need to do. It's not fake or disingenuous to compartmentalize. Each situation is unique and requires we show up accordingly.

The ability to compartmentalize is a learned skill that has served me well throughout my career. I needed to practice it to focus on the case and leave my warming feelings toward Ari for later. There were several potential suspects who had some connection to Jane, but I had yet to uncover a motive for murder.

I sat in the lobby at BARL and gazed up at the large

photos of marine life, especially the one showing a scuba diver who looked a lot like Jane. On my notepad I wrote LOVE, MONEY, FAME. And GO DEEPER. I stared at the words for a few moments and decided on the fly to switch up my interview questions.

Gregory's research indicated that Jane's money wasn't the motive. I needed to understand the other sources of money she affected. When considering the motive of fame, I considered how others might've felt overshadowed by Jane, her notoriety, or her work. Or perhaps the reverberations of her work. And did the love-related motive come back into play if Jane and Laura Block were in a relationship?

Roberta walked up and jarred me out of my thoughts.

"Hello, Xena!"

"Hi. Thanks for meeting with me." I stood and threw my bag over my shoulder.

Roberta smiled wide and we shook hands. "I'm sorry we couldn't get everyone on your list lined up for today. Ansel and Director Larson are at a client site all day."

"Understandable. Can we get the meetings for them set up for tomorrow?" I asked. We walked down a hall and went into a small meeting room.

"Ansel suggested an early meeting at the Starbucks on Harborside. He has another appointment in the area later in the morning. Does that work?" Roberta motioned for me to sit and closed the door.

"That's perfect." I sat and took out my interview questions.

Roberta sat across from me and folded her hands in front of her on the table. She seemed nervous and kept fidgeting.

"Is there anything you need before we get started?" she asked.

"No, this is fine and it won't take long at all. As you know, I'm looking into Dr. Moore's death. You're not a suspect, but as someone who worked closely with her, you might have information that could be useful."

"Of course. I'm happy to help. I've never had anyone close to me die. Lucky, I guess. I'm not sure how I should feel or act." Roberta held back tears, her voice cracked, but she sat tall and kept it together. "Jane was the best mentor and boss I had ever had."

"Tell me about your relationship and role."

"I assisted Jane with her research for two years. I came to BARL after I got my PhD from Miami." Her speech started to level out as she talked about her work. "I never worked with octopuses before meeting Fred and Ethel. They're fascinating. I'm planning on switching my research interests to octopuses. Maybe follow in Jane's footsteps."

Roberta looked up and smiled.

"I understand your interest. I've been charmed by Fred, too." I paused and slowed my speech. "Did Fred ever scare you or Jane or did she ever mention behavior that seemed concerning?"

"Yes. At first, I was intimidated by Fred. He's so strong." Roberta leaned in. "Jane taught me how to interact with octopuses properly and I became more confident when I was with them. I respect their wildness, though. Always."

"What do you mean?"

"We never forget that our subjects are wild animals and

therefore unpredictable. We always followed handling protocols."

"So there would've been no reason for Dr. Moore to open Fred's tank on her own?"

"None. It didn't happen. Would never happen."

"I read in one of Dr. Moore's journals that she was conflicted about how Fred was being treated. Do you know anything about that?"

"Jane loved to scuba dive because she could see marine life in their natural state. Octopuses are adventurous, smart, and destined by their nature to live short lives."

"Because they die shortly after mating?"

"Yes, for males. Females die after their eggs hatch. And even if they don't mate, they don't live long." Roberta was quiet for a moment. "Fred is in his second or third quarter of life and shows behavioral signs that he wants to mate."

"Like what? I know we talked about this briefly at Jane's funeral."

"He's harder to contain. He tries to escape daily."

"But the tank cover was open the day Dr. Moore's body was discovered. Why did he stay?"

"He loved Jane." Roberta looked down. "He wouldn't have left her alone like that."

"Roberta, this is going to be a tough question," I started and paused. "The three most common motives for crimes are money, fame, and love. Do you know anyone who might've had a reason to hurt Dr. Moore?"

"I've thought about this a lot." Roberta looked out the window. "Jane was a purist in some respects. She ruffled some feathers, especially politicians', and made some people at BARL jealous of her rock star status." She paused again. "But I can't imagine any of this provoking a feeling so strong that it would've led to her murder."

"Was Ansel envious of Jane's notoriety?"

"I'm not sure. Maybe. He seemed like the type but I never saw or heard anything firsthand."

"Just a couple more questions," I said. "Tell me what you remember about the day Dr. Moore died. Did you see her? At what time did you leave work and was she still there?"

"We worked with Ethel, the other octopus, until about three in the afternoon. I wrote up our findings at my desk until I left."

"When did you leave? Was Dr. Moore still there?"

Roberta pulled out her phone and looked at her calendar. "I left at about 5:30 p.m. to meet a few people from BARL at the Spot. They serve half-price burgers on Mondays and a live band. Jane was in her office. I asked her if she wanted to go. She said no, that she was waiting for a call."

"Did she say from whom?"

"No," Roberta sighed. "I didn't ask."

"It's OK."

"I'm of no help and I can't believe she's gone," Roberta lamented and laid her forehead on the table.

I remembered reading that much of the team was at the Spot the night Jane was killed, but asked anyways.

"Who was at the Spot with you and how long were you there?"

"Several of us were there until about eleven. Peter, Bob, Amy, Xavier."

"Was Ari there?"

"No."

"Ansel?"

"No, we don't hang with his team."

"Director Larson?"

"Oh no, he doesn't eat at the Spot!"

Great, none of the people on my PS list were accounted for.

"Roberta, can we visit Fred? I'd like to see how he's doing."

"We won't be able to open the tank because Ari is in meetings, but we can see him and maybe feed him."

~◎

The octopus tank area was dim and peaceful. I stood close to the glass at Fred's tank, wondering if he could see me, and if so, if he'd remember me.

"Hellooo, Fred!" Roberta called while standing next to me.

Roberta danced in front of Fred's tank, waving her arms and legs. She looked like someone who was trying to do jumping jacks after dropping LSD with a tequila shot chaser. She waved and motioned me to join her.

"What're you doing?" I asked with a chuckle.

"Speaking his body language! Come on … have you ever meowed at a cat? Wagged your butt with a dog? Flapped your arms with seagulls? It's the same thing. I'm being an octopus. Join me! Let's show Fred we *get* him." Roberta kept up her spastic rhythm and hummed Fred's name.

I've never wagged my butt at a dog, readers, and was relieved when I saw Fred coil out of his lair and onto the rock outside it.

"It's amazing how each tentacle moves independently," I observed.

"Like my dance," Roberta agreed with a smile. "Fred's movements are actually coordinated. Not exactly independent. But definitely looks that way."

"He sees us?"

"Yes. We've done tests with the octopuses from this view. He's watching us. See his eye there?" Roberta pointed to Fred's right eye. "That's his dominant one. Stay here and keep him company. I'm going to go get a crab for him."

I knelt to get closer to Fred's eye and stared back.

"Hi Fred. You look great. Do you remember me?"

Fred propelled toward the glass and stuck onto it. It startled me and I was worried I'd upset him. I noticed Roberta standing behind me with a crab in her hand.

"I guess he can see through the glass!" I said.

"Oh, yeah. He loves crabs." Roberta walked up the staircase and gave Fred the crab through a special feeding chamber. Fred grabbed the crab and took it into his lair. He was gone.

"Cool. Can we say hello to Ethel, too?" I asked.

"She's shyer than Fred, but we can try."

We walked to the last tank in the room. It looked empty, like the last time I visited.

"Ethel prefers fish."

Roberta walked to the back room. I raised my arms and

did a little octopus dance but stopped when I heard Roberta coming back. She walked up the stairs to the side of Ethel's tank with a fish in her hands. As she opened the feeding chamber, she called to Ethel.

"Ethel! How are you? Would you like a fish?" She placed the fish in the chamber and closed the door. The fish fell into the tank. Roberta could see I was interested in how the chamber worked.

"It was designed by one of Ari's old colleagues in Seattle. It works because everything is sealed one hundred percent. If there were any cracks or openings, the octopus could escape or might die trying. Before we had these newer tanks, we had to have two people on hand to feed them."

"Amazing. So even if Jane were feeding Fred, there would be no chance that she would've opened the tank lid."

"None," Roberta confirmed. "Look," she whispered.

Ethel had emerged and was heading for the fish. She was much smaller than Fred and her tentacles were thinner, more delicate looking.

"Is she the same type as Fred? She's so much smaller."

"Yes – they're both Common Octopuses. Fred's a big boy for a Common. Jane fattened him up because he was so much fun to work with. They had a special bond."

Ethel turned darker pink, close to orange, and took the fish and retreated into her den.

"I'd love to meet Ethel one day, up close and personal," I said.

"Me, too!" Roberta said. "I've yet to get her to visit me. Every octopus has a different personality. Some like the interaction, some have no interest. It's normal. Fred is special. Most are like Ethel."

I walked over, looked at Fred's tank again and stepped back to look at the surrounding area. I tried to imagine how the killer might've done it. What could've happened that resulted in that outcome – Jane dead with Fred's eight arms wrapped around her? How'd she get there? Was she alert? How'd the killer know what to do? As my mind cycled through ideas, I was energized and headed to the spy shop to map out each possibility.

My office looked like a hurricane had been through it, but I pushed things aside and sketched out potential scenarios for the murder using sticky notes and markers. All ideas, even crazy ones, went up on the wall, organized into plausible process maps for how each version of events could've occurred.

I asked myself questions like: If the whole thing happened at Fred's tank, what was Fred doing while Jane was being strangled? Would he have tried to intervene? If Jane was killed at Fred's tank, one or two people of average strength could have done it. If she died somewhere else and was carried up the stairs and into the tank, the killer or killers were extremely strong. We didn't look for other potential crime scenes, but perhaps we should, now that we know she was murdered. The killers had to figure out how to open the tank.

I wondered why Ari kissed me and wished he had an alibi.

My phone rang. I saw it was Gregory and hit the ANSWER BUTTON.

"Hellooo!"

"You OK to talk early tonight? The wife wants me to take her to Indika for dinner. They've goat masala tonight."

"I love Indika, used to go there all the time. She's got great taste. Sure, let's do it. Talking early works for me, too. I'm going to take another look in Jane's house later."

I sat and opened the document I had saved on my laptop with our questions.

"Be careful," Gregory pleaded.

"No sweat. I know where the key is and I'll drive around to make sure I'm not tailed," I said before switching gears. "Before we go through the questions, can I asked a hypothetical?"

"Sure," he said, eager to play along.

"Imagine that Jane and her killer stood next to Fred's tank, on the top of the stairs. The tank was open. The killer grabbed her throat and pressed her backward so her head submerged."

He interrupted. "Was the edge low enough that this was possible?"

"Yes. It comes waist high. The killer forced Jane underwater and squeezed and pressed her neck at the same time. What did Jane do?" I asked.

"She tried to beat her assailant with her arms and kicked to try to free herself."

"Yes, I agree, but we found no signs that she did this. She must've been subdued or weakened."

"Possibly, but wouldn't drugs have showed up in her bloodstream? Maybe her hands were full?"

"With what?"

"Fred?"

"Jane had a few hickies in addition to the marks on her neck," I said. "I wonder if Fred would've intervened. Perhaps Jane tried to protect Fred from the killer."

"Great question. Too bad you don't know any cute octopus experts."

"Funny."

"Seriously, ask your client. If you're sure he didn't do anything wrong – you think he's innocent, right? – you might as well put his expertise to work."

"OK, fair point. Let's go through our questions so you can get to your goat."

∼⊙

I drove up the alley at the back of Jane's house and parked by her backyard gate. Seemingly on cue, the ten-pound pom-poo-terrier mix went apeshit as I got out of my car.

I sighed in frustration. Galveston's most popular home security system was a dog barely contained behind a rickety fence. If I could sell the setup in my spy shop, I'd make a mint. The yappy dog that lived in the house next to Jane's must've been inside when Ari and I were there, because I didn't remember it.

I looked around to see if anyone noticed, but my car was hidden from view. I closed the door and dashed toward Jane's house and into her backyard. I moved closer to the dog to shush it, extending my hand close to the wire fence that separated us. It barked. I moved a bit closer and spoke in baby talk: "Hey, little fella, you look like a nice doggie." It barked, wagged its tail, and came to me at the fence. I moved toward Jane's house and it barked again. I moved closer and he quieted, wagging his tail. This dog had a range of yappiness and I was stuck inside it. I walked along the fence line, mutt in tow, to the front yard and ran over to Jane's front porch. It barked for a few seconds and stopped once I was out of sight. I found the hide-a-key where Ari had left it and entered the house.

I turned on my red headlamp, which was less likely to be noticed by passersby. To be safe I closed the blinds and curtains. New mail was fanned out on the floor under the slot in the front door. I opened a package from Amazon to find a book about ground water contamination. Why did Jane buy this? I stuck it in my bag. The rest of the mail was of no interest.

I went into Jane's bedroom and scanned back and forth with my headlamp. Something looked different, but it was hard to figure out using the red light. I took a chance and turned on a lamp on the bedside table. The formal dress I noticed on the first visit was gone and the closet seemed less full overall. Someone had been here.

I took more pictures, turned off the lamp, and moved to Jane's office. As I sat in her office chair and looked through her desk drawers, I found pictures of Jane and others at BARL in scuba gear out in the field. Several included Ari.

The dog next door started yapping again. I worried that

someone might discover my car and report it as suspicious, so I looked out the back window to see what was going on. I could see the dog barking, but not my car because it was parked behind Jane's back hedge.

After a couple of minutes, the dog was quiet again. I went back to Jane's office but kept thinking about the dog. What if he started barking again? I cursed myself because I should've parked farther away. I hurried to finish, took a few more pictures, eased out the front door, and slinked toward the back of the house. The dog barked, then quieted when I got close and whispered to it. We trotted along the fence line to the backyard.

I looked at my car and planned how I'd get in and leave before the dog attracted more attention.

Something did not seem right.

Looking around, I realized that this was where I'd seen the dog barking while I was in the house. He had faced the direction of my car. No one around. A horizontal shiny streak near the bottom of my driver's side door caught my eye. That wasn't there before; I hadn't washed my car in weeks. Did someone or something touch my car? Go in my car? Under my car? My heart raced. I knelt and looked around to see if I was being watched while one hand petted the dog through the fence. I switched my headlamp back on and crouched low to see under my car. Nothing looked out of order, but car bugs and bombs don't have blinking red lights like in the movies.

I assessed my options and decided to play it safe by using my remote starter to get the car going and unlocked. I grabbed my keys and got ready to take cover farther down the alley but stopped and looked over at the dog.

If something happened, and it was here barking at me, it might get hurt. *Shit.*

I turned off my headlamp, ran back up the fence to the front of Jane's house, the dog barked again, I got the key, unlocked the front door, went inside to the kitchen, and opened the fridge. Nothing good there. I left the fridge door open to use the light and checked the cupboards.

Peanut butter.

I took the jar, left, and relocked the house. The dog barked until I got to the fence to quiet it. We ran along the fence line and stopped at the end. I kneeled, opened the jar and let the dog smell the peanut butter, holding it up to the dog's nose. I then threw the open jar as far away from the alley as I could. The dog ran after the jar, and I ran down the alley and pushed the remote starter.

I heard the engine sputter a moment then start.

Then … BOOOM.

An ear-shattering explosion and simultaneous wave of what felt like concrete swept over me and threw me on the ground as my car blew up.

I rolled a few times, then righted myself.

I looked back to see the dog was startled but OK. He (or she) resumed licking the peanut butter jar. The back part of the fence was blown to bits. I looked around to make sure no one else needed help. Luckily the hedge, now a tangle of bare twigs, took a lot of the blast and no houses seemed damaged.

I made a quick body check and found a few wet spots on my face, which turned out to be bloody scrapes from the hedge twigs. Also, a swelling on my cheekbone and a sore elbow.

I pulled out my cell, called 911 to report the explosion, and asked the dispatcher to send the fire department and to inform BJ. Several neighbors came out and hurried over to where I was still sitting on the ground.

"That your car ...? Are you OK?"

"Just fine," I mumbled, spitting out some gravel that had been blown into my mouth and wiping off the blood on my cheek. "I'm a friend of Jane's from BARL, looking after her plants. My car must've overheated, caught fire, and exploded."

The owner of the dog came out and frantically looked for her pom-poo-terrier. I pointed to the side of the house.

She ran over to the dog in animated distress. "Bear-Bear, are you OK? How many times have I told you to stay out of the trash?"

My car was barely recognizable and it looked like nothing was salvageable. My body ached, and I'd have bruises on top of my bruises tomorrow. I sat on Jane's front porch and waited for BJ to arrive while it started to sink in.

Someone had tried to kill me.

No one knew I was going to be here and I made sure no one followed me. In fact, I had been extra careful since the incident at the Shrimp Festival.

Maybe a GPS tracker?

Five minutes later, BJ marched onto the porch steps in a huff. "What the hell happened here?"

"Jane's killer tried to kill me," I said, as the idea settled in.

He stepped closer to me, crossed his arms, and wrinkled his forehead. He was pissed. "What? Why were you here? I thought we agreed you weren't going rogue!"

"I was checking on a clue. This was Jane's house," I said. "I knew where the key was hidden."

"You could have been killed!" he yelled.

"I know!" I yelled back.

"Hell, the way that thing went up, you should have been killed. How is it that you weren't in your car when it blew? Did you hear or see someone?"

"No. Well …" I pointed to the house next door. "I heard the dog bark at something close to my car and saw a fresh hand swipe print."

"Dog?"

I pulled my car keys from my bag. "Used my remote starter."

"Well, you're one lucky lady," he said, a little more softly, and sat on the half wall. "Now, tell me what's going on and why you're on someone's hit list?"

An hour later, I swallowed four Advils with a glass of wine, sat on my porch, and called Ari. "There are two good things that have come from someone trying to kill me tonight," I said, nonchalant.

"What?!" he exclaimed.

"My car is toast, which leads me to the first positive thing:

I now have a perfect excuse to buy a Tesla. Electric cars don't blow up, right?"

"What? Blow up? What the hell happened?" I could hear Ari breathing heavily on the other side of the phone. "Do you need me to come over?"

"No, I'm fine. A little sore, but fine. Do you want to know the second positive thing?"

"Sure."

"BJ has agreed to reopen the investigation into Jane's death …"

After helping Ari process the news, I poured a Scotch, slinked down each stair slowly, went to my office, plugged my phone into my computer, and downloaded the pictures I'd taken. I compared the pictures I took in Jane's bedroom on the first and second visits.

I knew it!

The gala dress was gone, along with several other items from the closet. I went back upstairs, called Sparky, and told him what happened.

"Man, that's some heavy shit," he responded. "You should've called me to go with you."

"I know. I wish I had, but it all worked out OK. We can talk about it more tomorrow," I said, not wanting to rehash the same conversations I'd had with BJ and Ari.

"I need your help," I said.

"Sure. With what?"

"Better security cameras at my house. Covering three-hundred-sixty degrees, like you have. I looked at the camera footage from before I went to Jane's house and couldn't see anything. You'd have to stand right in front of my house to show on the camera. No one is that stupid."

"For real. I'll pick up what we need at the shop and get it installed tomorrow. Backyard, too?"

"Yes. Eyes on all sides. And I want to stream to the Cloud."

I looked outside while sitting on my porch. No lights on.

"You got it," he confirmed.

"One more thing. When you go to the shop tomorrow, pull the video from the gala. Text me a still picture of Laura Block. I want to see what she wore."

"Sure. We'll talk more tomorrow?"

"Yes. BJ wants me to come by the station Friday morning to share everything we know. I'll need you and Dora to help me prepare."

We both were quiet. Me, because I was staring out the porch screen.

"Do you want me to come over there?" Sparky asked.

"No. I'll be fine. It's what we do," I replied.

"I know."

"I paid off that car last month."

"Damn fine car."

"Thanks for installing the remote starter, by the way. Turned out to be a useful hack."

"Top of the line, that one was. I bet we sell out of them at the shop once this hits the news."

"Don't make me laugh; it hurts like hell."

Chapter 13
Day 10, Thursday

The Starbucks on Harborside Drive is a popular spot for both locals and tourists, especially those going on or coming off one of the cruise ships docked across the street. During the week, it is also a frequent stop for university students heading to class. I preferred the Mod over this place and I didn't attempt to order my usual cortado because it required too much finesse to get right.

There were a lot of people in line but I quickly identified and found Ansel thanks to the briefing document Dora prepared for me, which included a physical description and his picture.

> *Dr. Ansel Homer, 36 years old, born of wealthy and successful parents; second-generation American, from Scandinavian and German roots; six feet three, blond, mustache.*

"Hello, you must be Dr. Homer. I'm Xena Cali," I said.

"Hömer," he corrected.

"Sorry, Homer."

"Never mind," Ansel complained dismissively as he rolled his eyes.

We ordered and took our coffees to one of the outside tables at the Jimmy John's sandwich shop next door, which didn't open until lunch. He wore a red Ralph Lauren shirt with the large embroidered jockey on the chest, a chunky diamond watch, and he carried a Tumi pad holder. His haircut was fresh and perfectly gelled, and he obviously combed his mustache. His nails looked manicured with a clear coat of polish. Not what I would've expected from an up-and-coming researcher.

Ansel's words only confirmed my first impression that he was a raging narcissist. "Ms. Cali, I've a busy day with important client meetings. Please jump right into your questions." He opened his pad folio and handed me his card. ANSEL HOMER, LEAD RESEARCH ASSOCIATE.

"I appreciate you meeting with me," I said. I lingered a moment to see his reaction.

"What questions do you have?" His response seemed cold and too apathetic – detached – to be protective in nature.

I opened to a fresh page in my notebook. "Tell me about your role at BARL. How long have you been there?" I already knew the answer was three years.

"I've been at BARL nearly five years and am their lead research scientist for foreign body water intrusion issues."

"What does that mean?" I asked.

Ansel gave me a bored look, as if he was wearing pince-nez reading glasses, which he wasn't. "In lay terms, stuff that ends up in the water that shouldn't be there. I'd be happy to send you my detailed CV if that's of interest. I know you're looking into Dr. Moore's death. I didn't work with her often and didn't know her well." He shifted his seating position to look over the harbor area. "I'm afraid I can't be more helpful, but please ask any substantive questions you have."

I can play it this way, you ass. I dropped my smile, sat straighter, and looked directly into Ansel's eyes. "Dr. Moore asked you to check out a potential pollution site. She was frustrated with your poor responsiveness on this issue. Why was that?"

"You're referring to P67, I presume?"

I nodded and smiled again, even though I had no idea what P67 was.

"Those situations are need-to-know and she didn't. That incident wasn't under her purview or in the scope of her work."

"What was P67?"

"That's confidential. But the matter has no connection to your case."

"How do you know?"

"It involves no controversy," he said. "Dr. Moore alerted me to a potential source of pollution. I assessed the situation, contacted the owner of the source, who hadn't realized the leak occurred. The owner agreed to remedy the situation."

"If it's resolved and there was no concern, can you tell me the company involved?"

"No. Do you have other questions? I need to get to my next meeting." He closed his folio.

Whoa, big fella!

"Was there tension between you and Dr. Moore?"

"None on my part, she was of no consequence to me," he replied. "This wasn't her project, so I felt no need to keep her informed." Ansel adjusted his shoulders back and scrunched his eyes. "She always wanted to be informed, but not every project at BARL revolved around her."

I leaned in and mirrored his intensity. "Were you jealous of Dr. Moore's stature in the community and at BARL?"

"No."

"Where were you the evening that Dr. Moore died?"

"Am I a suspect? Because of this tiny project? Jane was no one. I didn't care about Jane or her work."

"Where were you last Monday evening?"

"At my apartment with my girlfriend. All night."

"And what about last night?"

"Same. What happened last night?"

"It's confidential," I said.

He stood and looked down at me. "Are we done here?"

I shook my head and motioned for him to sit again. He stayed standing.

"Let me help you figure this out. Jane reported I was being difficult …" He then sat and rested his hand on the table. "I wasn't jealous of Jane. She was the one who was behaving inappropriately. She was fascinated by me, and wanted me to be interested in her. But I wasn't."

"Really?"

"She came on to me and I rejected her," he said. "Women who feel rejected sometimes say things that aren't true. I'm sure you can understand this."

I stood. Ansel stood. I stepped close, into his personal space, and whispered, "Let's cut the crap, Dr. Homer. Jane wasn't interested in you romantically. The tension between you and Dr. Moore was related to your envy of her notoriety and success." I paused, but not long enough for Ansel to say anything. "Let's review. Someone murdered Dr. Moore. I'm going to figure out who did it. I've credible information there was tension between you and Jane. I can't help you unless you're straight with me."

I then handed one of my cards to Ansel. "Call anytime if you'd like to try this conversation again."

I walked out to the parking lot to my car and watched him for a few moments. Ansel stood still next to the table for a moment. He made a call, walked back to his car, and left.

I texted Sparky and asked him to work with the BARL IT department to explore whether Ansel might have been the one to delete Jane's files.

~◉

As I drove my rental car south on Twenty-Ninth Street and up to my house, I noticed a pile of boxes, ladders, and large coils of wire in my front yard.

Sparky.

"You sure I need all this?" I asked while looking at and into the boxes.

Sparky had climbed the oak tree in front of my house and was attaching something to one of the branches. "You said you wanted eyeballs on all sides of your house, right?"

"Yeah … these cameras are big."

"You know how the security tapes they show on TV news always seem so grainy?"

"Yes."

"That's because they use crappy cameras."

"OK …"

"I got this, Xena," Sparky declared and smiled at me.

I threw up my hands in surrender. "Maybe the cameras will catch whoever is letting their dog poop in my rock garden."

Sparky climbed down the tree, pulled out his phone, and showed me a picture from the gala. It was Laura Block in the dress from Jane's house.

"Nice. She wore Jane's dress. She knew how to get into her house." I smiled. "Laura Block and Jane. I need to go to the shop. You OK if I leave you here to finish?"

"No prob. I'll text you the link and password for the new system once it's up. We'll use the same app as the cameras at the shop."

"Cool. You're the best."

"I know."

"Please don't step on my agave."

~⊚

Dora waved me over to the right side of the spy shop as soon as I walked in.

"Look!" she trilled with glee.

She had filled the shelves against the north wall with stuffed animals. Shelves and shelves of animals the size of frozen turkeys. Bears, birds, dogs, cats, horses, gigantic red lips, and more. I stood and stared for a moment, not sure what to say.

"What do we have here?" I asked.

"Watch this!"

Dora stepped in front of the shelves, moved back and forth, and did something that looked a bit like a stork's mating ritual. The animals' eyes followed her left and right, up and down.

"They're nanny cams!" She opened her arms up wide. "And you can watch much more than babies with these fuzzies. Pets! Roommates! Pet sitters! Grannies! Even coworkers."

She gave a sly look, perhaps forewarning?

"These are all cam systems?"

She nodded. "Uh-huh."

"That's so cool. It's a bit freaky the way they follow all our movements. Tracking up and down is uncommon."

"I know, and I love it. If it becomes too much, we can turn the eyeballs off and they'll stay in one position."

"We talked about getting some of these. I had no idea they came in so many variations."

I walked up to the shelves and inspected a few of the animals. Several batted their eyes at me as I picked them up.

"Isn't it wonderful?" Dora asked. "I especially love the rainbow-colored unicorn for our gay friends, the largemouth bass for fishermen, and the flamingos for the birders on the island."

"Impressive. This potato is odd."

Dora laughed. "That's Einstein!"

"We're going to have a great holiday season."

Dora agreed.

I walked passed the gallery of cyber eyes – that's what I decided they were – to my office. Dora followed.

"Did you find the info I asked for?" I asked. "I need to make a few calls."

"The complete work up on Ansel Homer is on your desk and Laura Block's cell number is next to your desk phone."

"Thanks, that's perfect."

I sat at my desk, checked email, and then called Laura's number. She picked up after a few rings.

"Laura Block?"

"Yes. Who is this?" she asked tentatively.

"It's Xena Cali. We met at the gala? I'm investigating the death of Dr. Jane Moore."

"Yes," Laura said slowly, still unsure as to where this was going.

"I was wondering if we could meet and talk for a few minutes," I said in a nonchalant tone so she wouldn't overreact. "It would be helpful for our case."

"Why me?"

"I saw you at Jane's funeral and I know you were close with Jane."

"You do?"

"Yes."

"Will this be off the record?"

"I'm not a reporter, but sure."

"OK, I'm working on the landscaping outside the Rosenberg Library today. You can come by at five."

"Great. I'll see you soon." We hung up and I took notes about the questions I wanted to ask Laura. I printed photos of Laura at the gala and the dress she'd been wearing hanging in Jane's closet and put them in a folder with the notes. My phone pinged from an incoming text. I hoped it was from Ari, but it came from an unfamiliar number.

This is Ansel Homer. We need to talk. Tonight at Menard Park at 10 p.m.

I stared at the screen for a moment. Maybe the egotistical bastard realized it was in his best interest to cooperate with our investigation. I texted back.

OK.

I walked to the front of the store and showed the text to Dora and told her about my earlier conversation with Ansel.

"You should call BJ," she suggested.

"Not yet. I don't want him to spook Ansel."

"Please take protection."

"Of course."

Dora went to the main counter and waved for me to follow. "I charged this up today."

Dora pinned a poodle head–brooch camera onto the lapel of my denim jacket.

"Your bag full?" Dora asked, referring to the cross-body tote bag I always carried.

My bag contained a cornucopia of spy gadgets and personal protective devices. Sparky, Dora, and I had perfected the mix of items to be both comprehensive in supporting a wide variety of challenging situations – muggings, buggings, surveillance, escapes, and break-ins – while adding only a pound of extra weight to the bag and little bulk. Everyone on my team carried a ditty bag with a common core inventory of devices and some personally curated ones. Mine was black and with several secret pockets and liners where I kept a trove of basic elements that any MacGyver could use to do nearly everything. String, foil, zip-ties, double-sided tape, face paint, and a baggie of seedless raisins. Stuff like that.

I use the face paint to quickly transform into a scary clown, readers; I know you were wondering. Even hardened criminals are batshit afraid of clowns and rightly so.

"I think it is, but it wouldn't hurt to check. Maybe fresh batteries for my headlamp." I handed her my bag. I examined my jacket lapel. "Nice pin, by the way."

After Dora checked and refilled my bag, I left the store to meet with Laura Block. The wall of stuffed animals tracked my position with their beady little eyes.

The Rosenberg Library was at the northwest corner of Tremont and Sealy, and about four blocks from the spy shop. Dora went there often to research local archives. Beautiful inside and out, it was the oldest public library in Texas in continuous operation. And like many buildings and sites in Galveston, some historians and locals believed it was haunted.

I pulled into the parking lot next to Laura's landscaping van and got out. The sliding door was open, revealing a portable garden shack with planting bench, shelves of supplies, and a few power and hand tools. Laura was sitting on the floor of the van with her legs dangling outside the door.

"Hello again," I waved.

Laura stood and we shook hands. She sat back on the van floor.

"Did you find me OK?" she asked. "What am I thinking, you're the spy. Of course you found me."

Laura blushed awkwardly.

"My spy shop and PI practice are right up the street. We come to the library often. It's beautiful."

"We didn't get to talk much at the gala. Sam was focused on winning his silent auction items." Laura paused. "I meant to ask where you found the dress you wore at the gala. It was like nothing I've ever seen."

"Yes," I admitted and bowed my head. "My assistant found it for me on Craigslist. My decision to attend the gala was last minute, after being assigned Jane's case."

"Have a seat." Laura pointed to the van floor next to her. "It's a bit dirty but comfortable."

I sat and took my notebook out of my bag. "Thanks for agreeing to meet me today."

"Might as well get this over with," she said. "Off the record, right?"

I acknowledged.

"Are you recording this conversation?" she asked.

"Good question. No." I liked Laura's directness and respected her with mine. "I've no interest in embarrassing you or sharing private information."

"Thanks."

"I wanted to talk to you about *your* gala dress," I said. I pulled the two photos out of my bag and handed them to her.

Laura looked at the photos and sighed. "Jane was an amazing woman and I miss her so much."

"What was the nature of your relationship?"

Laura crossed her arms but I could see her hands tremble a bit. Her legs swung back and forth like a child sitting on the edge of a dock. "It's complicated. I'm not gay, you know. I'm married. Hell, I'm not sure what I am anymore. Jane upended my life in the most wonderful and unsettling ways."

"The best things in life often do. How'd you and Jane meet?"

"Sam invited her to our annual charity dinner for the Conservation Fund as a special guest. She and I sat next to each other at dinner. We auctioned off a private nature dive, with Jane as the guide." Laura paused and her legs fell still. "She amazed me. Her intelligence. Her wit. Her realness. When you live with a politician, you spend a lot of time with people who say they're your friends but rarely are. I'm not talking about Sam, he's a good man. It was the world that swirled around Sam and other council members that I found uninteresting."

I twisted and pulled one leg in the van so I could look Laura more direct in the eyes. "Jane was different?"

"She was luminous and funny and beautiful. By the time the auction started at the end of the night I was so enamored with her that I outbid everyone so I could spend more time with her. Sam wasn't thrilled I'd spent the money!" Laura smiled and held her face with her hands and sighed.

"How long ago was this?"

"About a year ago. I asked Sam if he wanted to go on the dive with us, but thankfully he declined. Jane and I had an amazing time." Laura paused for a moment, looked at me. "I loved her."

"Was that why your gala dress was at her house?"

"Yes ... well, no. We'd been flirting and skirting around our feelings for months. Acting like best girlfriends, but feeling something deeper. I was never more happy and more scared in my life."

"Scared?"

"Of what might happen next," she said.

"You mean if Sam found out?"

"God, no. Sam and I are married for show. For his political career. It's an arrangement. I promised him I'd stick it out through his mayoral bid. That's *very* off the record. He hasn't announced yet."

"Sure. Were you aware of the rumor in town that Sam was having an affair with Jane?"

"Yes, we both laughed about it. It's funny how people jumped to conclude that it was Sam instead of me."

"You're being open about all this. I'm surprised."

Laura looked down. Her eyes teared up. "She was special and I'm broken. Honestly, you're the only one who knows. I haven't said a word to anyone else."

"I'm so sorry." We sat quietly for a couple of minutes.

She wiped her tears in determination. "Thank you. I'm

also sharing this with you because I want to help. I'm so pissed that Jane is gone. Do you think someone killed her? I assume so, or there'd be nothing to investigate."

"We do. The evidence suggests that she was murdered. It's not public knowledge, but the police have reopened the case."

Laura dropped her head.

"Can you think of anyone who might've wanted to hurt Jane?" I asked.

"No." She paused. "You can cross Sam off your list. He's on your list, right?"

"Yes."

"He, like everyone else, assumed we were just friends."

"Would he be upset if he knew you loved her?"

"I doubt it. Perhaps he'd be jealous that I found someone." She grunted. "My husband is a simple man, Xena. I know he didn't kill Jane. And to answer what I assume was your next question, we were both in Houston the night she was killed. At a charity event for ALS, surrounded by hundreds of people. We stayed overnight at the Hilton Americas so we didn't have to drive back so late."

"Did Jane tell you about any conflicts she was having?"

Laura got up to stand between our vehicles. "We didn't talk about work, except for Fred."

"She talked about Fred?" I smiled and thought about him myself.

"She was fascinated by Fred. How he hugged her, how his tentacles were ticklish at the tips. How he was getting stronger each week."

"Did you ever meet Fred?"

"No, I never went to her workplace."

"Is there anything that you can remember from your time with Jane that might help me find her killer?"

"Not specifically. She believed city politicians were all corrupt and could be bought."

"What do you mean?"

"Corporations and developers could pay to get their way, even if it was bad for the bay. It's true, but hardly motive for murder." She leaned against my rental car. "She loved Galveston Bay and was frustrated that others didn't show the same commitment."

"With anyone in particular?"

"Someone named Ansel. Called him a jerk. But it didn't seem like a big deal."

I switched gears. "How'd you get in her house? Did you have a key?"

"No. But I knew where she kept her spare. We drove up to Clear Lake to shop for gala gowns. That was hers, by the way. I decided I needed to wear it. To feel near her. We wear the same size."

"You said that you and Sam were in Houston the night she was killed. Did you know what Jane's plans were that night?"

Laura sat next to me and pulled out her phone. "Would you like to see her final words to me?"

"Yes, thanks."

She pulled up her texts from Jane and handed the phone to me so I could read the screen.

Jane: *How are things in Houston?*

Laura: *Fine. Boring. The auction starts in 15 min. Usual stuff. How're you?*

Jane: *Getting caught up. Meetings. Will say hi to Fred.*

Laura: *Cool. Can't wait to see you tomorrow.*

Jane: *Same here. Tacos?*

Laura: *Uh-huh. I'll bring the ingredients.*

The final text was time-stamped at 5:24 p.m.

"She liked my homemade tortillas," Laura remembered and smiled. "I bought her a press so I could cook real tacos for her. These Californians don't know what a taco is supposed to taste like."

"Had she mentioned upcoming meetings?"

"Nothing specific. She had a lot of meetings."

I motioned for her to unlock the phone screen again. "May I scroll up?"

"OK," Laura said, but I could tell she was unsure.

I read several other text conversations between Jane and Laura that confirmed Laura's characterization of their relationship as evolving. I gave the phone back to Laura.

"Thanks."

"I'll go back through my emails and texts from her."

"That'd be great. Sometimes small, seemingly unrelated pieces of information break the case open."

I handed Laura my card and stood up.

Laura embraced me. "I hope you find who did this."

"I will," I assured her.

I got in my car and noticed that Laura was sobbing. As I pulled out, I decided that love wasn't likely the motive for

Jane's murder. I made a note to look closer at Jane's schedule the day she died because this was the second time someone told me she stayed late for a meeting.

Menard Park was one block from my house, along the seawall and two blocks away from the Pleasure Pier. It was a great meeting place because it was public but not crowded. I arrived a few minutes before ten and sat on a bench between the dog and skateboard parks. It was relatively quiet compared to a weekend night, but there were plenty of lights and sounds from the Pleasure Pier to keep things interesting. I watched what was going on throughout the park. To the east, several teens were practicing their moves in the skateboard park. To the west, a dog and its owner waited in the off-leash area for someone else to come play. A young couple walked by the tennis courts as an old man rode by on his bike.

Ansel wasn't here yet.

After twenty minutes, I started getting irritated, and after thirty, I was worried. I sent Ansel a text.

Are we still meeting?

I practiced walking handstands down the half wall along the sidewalk. My phone rang. It was BJ.

"Where are you?" he asked in a huff.

"Close to my house. Why?" I looked around so I didn't scare off Ansel if he heard me talking to someone. "Do you need something?"

"Where, specifically, are you?"

"Menard Park. What's up, BJ?"

"Were you supposed to meet with Dr. Ansel Homer?"

My stomach tightened. "How do you know?"

"He won't be making your appointment. He's dead," he barked with anger in his voice. "Now get over here and tell me what's going on. I'm at his apartment. I'll text you the address."

Ansel's apartment was swarming with cops and media, including Steve Heart, who saw me and tried to pull me aside to see what was going on. I put my hand up, indicating I wanted him to wait. I didn't want BJ to think I was blabbing to the press.

BJ saw and waved me in past the cops guarding the taped perimeter. The apartment's living room looked undisturbed except for the forensic team's equipment.

"No pictures," BJ informed.

"Sure," I agreed.

BJ grabbed my arm and led me into the next room. Ansel was sitting up on his bed, slumped over, with a rubber tourniquet around his forearm. His nose and mouth area were encrusted with dried blood. He was wearing black boxer briefs and nothing else. Ansel's hair was disheveled and he looked unkempt. Not like the man I met this morning.

"Heroine OD with some possible body trauma," BJ explained.

"I would've guessed he was more of a coke guy." I wasn't being flippant about his death; cocaine is the drug of choice for narcissists. It's true; you can look it up.

"How'd you know the deceased and why were you going to meet him?"

"Ansel worked at BARL. I interviewed him this morning for the Jane Moore case. He texted me about 4 p.m. and asked me to meet him at Menard Park at ten. He never showed. You know the rest," I said. "He was a suspect in Jane's murder, but I didn't see this coming."

"You were going to meet a suspect at night, on your own, after you received a suspicious text, and you didn't call me?"

"Menard Park isn't exactly in the middle of nowhere. And I knew I'd be talking to you and your team tomorrow morning."

"What's this guy's connection to the biologist other than he worked at the lab?"

"Jane asked him to research some pollution in the ship channel and was frustrated with his lack of attention and responsiveness."

"That's it? This guy wasn't fast enough and he ended up dead?"

"There's obviously more to it than this. And something must've happened between the time I talked with him this morning and 4 p.m., and again between four and ten, so it might be worth tracing his steps today."

"Obviously."

"Are you thinking accidental overdose or murder?"

"Definitely murder," BJ snapped back. "Made to look like an accident, but unconvincingly."

"Was anything missing?"

"Aren't sure yet. We have his phone, that's how I found

out he was meeting you. Your text came in shortly after we got here."

"What tipped you off?"

"Neighbor complained about loud music and the manager found him."

"The killer wanted you to find him quickly."

"That's what we think, too," he agreed. "It's pretty brazen."

"Yes. Do you know time of death?"

"Around 6 p.m., give or take. Autopsy will confirm."

"Did you find a computer?"

"Not yet."

"If you do, have forensics look for Jane's missing files. He might've deleted them from BARL's shared drive."

I started to look around, but BJ stopped me. "You should go now." He guided me out of the room. "And no talking to your reporter friend. Got it?"

"Yes. Is there a girlfriend?"

"The super says he lives alone. We found no evidence of a girlfriend."

So who was his alibi for Jane's murder? "He told me he had a girlfriend. Who're you notifying?"

"Looking for next of kin now. His name won't be released until we reach them. We'll contact the lab director, too."

"Do you still want me to stop by in the morning?"

"Even more so now."

I left the room and moved past the growing crowd of onlookers. Steve followed me.

"Xena, wait up," he said.

"I can't comment," I replied. "I'll let you know what I know when I can share it. BJ put a gag order on me."

I turned to leave but he tapped my arm to stop me. "One question. Does this have anything to do with the death of Dr. Jane Moore?" He looked direct into my eyes and waited.

"You mean the *only* case I am currently working on?" I paused. "No comment." Which was code for *Hell yes.*

As I walked to my rental car, I phoned Ari on my cell. He answered after two rings.

"Hey, whatcha doing?" I asked. "Got a minute?"

"Are you OK?"

Ari sounded worried and nervous, so I cut to it. "I'm fine, but Ansel is dead."

"What! No, this can't be."

"Sorry, it's true."

"How?"

"Heroin overdose. Not a word of this to anyone, but Detective Rawlins is thinking it's murder disguised as accidental suicide."

"No!"

I thought about how to help Ari process this news. This week was full of shocking events he had never had to fathom.

"Is this connected … to Jane … your car?" he asked.

"I'm working to figure that out. The pieces are coming together and I think they're all linked."

"Xena, please, I want to see you …"

"Sure, but not now. There are some things I need to do. Gotta run … Try not to worry about me."

I hung up and drove home in a daze, wondering how everything was supposed to fit together. And if it did.

Chapter 14
Day 11, Friday

I went down to my office to prep for the meeting with BJ and look at the video feed from the new cameras Sparky installed. My computer screen displayed six boxes, each with a different camera feed. I didn't have time to review the history from last night, but found it addicting to watch live.

As I drank my coffee and organized my notes, I learned a few new things about my neighbors. First, it was the lady three houses away who was letting her dog defecate on my rock garden. I made a note to think through possible solutions after I solved this case. And I can tell you, readers, I followed through. It's amazing what a well-placed motion sensor connected to an annoying dog whistle can do! I also learned the guy behind me is hung like a horse and likes to pee on his wife's prized rose bushes. I was sure there was much more to this saga than needing to piss.

I saw Sally go by with her early morning Segway tour group. They didn't stop at my house. Perhaps she was still annoyed with me for kidnapping her Segway during the Shrimp Festival and embarrassing her in front of her tour group. Of course that's not what happened at all, was it? The group loved watching my little interruption and maybe that's what she was angry about. My disobedience was the highlight of their tour! We like to think that people are interested in history when they sign up for a historical tour, but they couldn't give a shit about the hurricane of 1900. What they want is to see Miss Shrimp Festival stripped of her skirt and flash her butt cheeks.

I texted Sparky.

The cameras look great.

Thanks. Top of the line. See anything?

Poop, dick, Sally. Nothing concerning.

Ah, ok … Want me to look for anything unusual last night?

Sure, that'd be great. Heading out to see BJ now.

Need anything else from me or Dora?

Think I'm set. Will stop by the shop after my meeting with BJ.

Roger that.

BJ escorted me to the meeting room, which was also an interrogation room with two-way glass, a linoleum table, metal chairs, and nothing on the wall except a clock that was one hour behind. Did they forget to "fall back" or was it intentional so suspects in their third hour of questions think they've been here only two?

We went in and sat down, joining two others who were already there. No one smiled, but they didn't seem pissed-off either.

"This is Nancy and Tim," BJ said. "Nancy is the newest

member of my team and was an investigator in New Orleans."

Nancy bobbed her head in acknowledgement.

"And Tim has been with the GIPD longer than I have. Back to the Stone Age." BJ snickered.

Tim pointed a finger gun at me.

I reviewed my case notes, told them about Ari's expert opinion on the autopsy, my PM and PS charts, Jane's journals, the funeral and my discussion with Jane's brother, Jane's will and life insurance beneficiaries, meeting the BARL team at the gala, the Segway chase through the Shrimp Festival, potential cases involving Jane that Steve told me about, Laura Block's confession about having a relationship with Jane, my exploding car, my interview with Ansel, Ansel's text and his death, and meeting Fred.

"That was a lot of information," BJ said.

"Until he was murdered, Ansel was on the top of my potential suspects list," I said.

"Was he at the gala?" BJ asked.

"Not that I saw or was told. At the time, I didn't know what he looked like. But he wasn't with the other BARL researchers, because I sat at their table."

"I saw your picture in that dress," Nancy offered with a laugh. "What was the story behind that? You got it from a family in South America?"

"Actually, it belonged to a fifteen-year-old who has terminal cancer and I told her I'd wear it in her honor," I said, offering my sixth explanation.

"That's cool." Tim thankfully changed the subject.

"Captain Rawlins, do we have anything preliminary from forensics on the murder scene from last night?"

"Not yet, other than that heroin overdose was the likely cause of death. They took several bags of evidence and lifted a lot of fingerprints," BJ said. "This thing has ramped up."

BJ glared at me. My theory was that he was torn. He preferred that I was doing most of their work but didn't like the lack of control and the surprises. BJ was near retirement and it made sense that he didn't want to get his hands dirty.

But what about Nancy and Tim? I assumed they were not happy that I was getting up in their business, but who knows, they said very little and didn't ask questions.

"Let me know how you'd like to proceed," I said. I needed to follow their lead but had no intention of sitting on the sidelines now.

"What do you have planned?" BJ asked.

I considered whether to reveal my entire agenda and didn't.

"I'm going to attend the city council meeting next week, and I've an appointment to meet with Judge Buddy Sassoon late this afternoon. Tomorrow I'm going to go talk to the *Elissa* ship crew to find out about the pollution they told Jane they saw. See if it's still there or resolved like Ansel led me to believe."

"That all seems harmless," BJ concluded. "I know Buddy has nothing to do with this. So knock yourself out. But don't do anything else without letting us know *before* you do it."

"I understand."

"Let us focus on investigating Ansel's murder. There has to be a connection to Dr. Moore's death."

"Agreed. And what about the person who blew up my car?"

"We'll look into that, too," BJ said.

~⊙

I walked into the spy shop and found the stuffed animals were now on the other side of the store. They all still followed me with their eyes as I went to the back counter.

"We're testing different places for the animal farm," Dora explained.

"That's what we're calling it," Sparky clarified.

"It's important that shoppers notice them, but we don't want to creep anyone out," Dora continued.

"Yes, it's important we don't creep out our already outside-the-norm clientele," I joked.

"We took a video of people seeing them for the first time, showing how their eyes are multi-directional, and put it up on the shop's Facebook page. It has gone viral. Three million views so far. That's just this morning," Sparky bragged.

"Wow," I said. "It *is* hard to take your eyes off them."

"They feel the same about you!" Dora exclaimed.

"Let's not anthropomorphize these furry things. I'll have nightmares," I said. "Will you both join me in the meeting room? I'd like to update you on the meeting with BJ and our plan the next few days."

I put on the conference table the book Jane bought from Amazon, the journals that mentioned Ansel and the *Elissa*, and my notes from my discussions with Steve at the Olympia Grill and Ansel at Starbucks.

"We don't know if the request Jane made to Ansel regarding the pollution is connected to either of their deaths," I said. "I'd like to confirm how these events are related or rule it out so we can solve these crimes before our time runs out. And before anyone else gets hurt."

I reviewed my notes from my meeting with Ansel with Dora and Sparky.

"Something doesn't seem right about what Ansel told you," Dora said.

"The girlfriend the landlord says doesn't exist?" Sparky guessed.

"No. What he said about the owner of P67 agreeing to take care of the pollution like that was no big thing," Dora said.

"So?" I asked.

"I'm skeptical that any landowner would be so quick to resolve concerns – it never even became an official BARL project." Dora sat back. "I've been living here forever and cleaning up even small amounts of pollution – unless spilled from a boat that can be moved – is usually a big deal. Most developers fight hard to avoid the extra costs, and these things often end up as huge lawsuits involving the EPA and other federal agencies."

"Good point," I agreed. "It's important that we talk to the *Elissa* crew and determine how large or small a problem this pollution might've been. And perhaps whether it likely came from a ship or some development along the channel."

"I'll put together a summary document listing the most likely contaminants and their qualities so you can take it with you to the *Elissa*."

"That'd be great Dora, thanks," I said. "I don't know enough about pollution."

"I want to know more about the girlfriend comment and whether Ansel had an alibi for Jane's murder," Sparky said.

"That's important, too. Will you see what you can figure out?" I asked. "Maybe social media accounts or other online accounts? I'll ask Ari if there's anyone who might've known more about Ansel's personal life. I promised him I'd call him tonight. He was pretty unnerved when I told him what happened to Ansel."

"It's a lot for a squid man to take in," Sparky proclaimed.

"Exactly. I need to remind myself that for most people, murder, violence, and corruption are unreal things that make for great TV."

"You saying we're jaded?" Dora asked.

"Goes without saying," I replied.

We updated the charts on the wall, reviewed the rest of my notes, and each of us left with a list of to-dos that we hoped would help us wrap up this case before anyone else died.

~⊙

I arrived at Judge Buddy's office in the courthouse at 4:30 p.m., a time chosen because it was after his cases and paperwork were all wrapped up. His assistant escorted me to an outer office and knocked on his office door.

"CEEOOme on in!" he bellowed in his slow but singsongy southern accent, which was more pronounced now than at the gala.

The assistant opened the door, I walked in, and she left, closing the door. Buddy had his feet propped up on his desk and he was holding up a glass of some kind of liquor. He was dressed in 1980s Hilfiger from head to toe. Do you remember when designer Tommy Hilfiger was in the red, white, and blue block color phase? Buddy had white TH tennis shoes, matching socks, white TH jeans with a pressed crease – I've never understood why people iron jeans – a red TH golf shirt, a blue TH sweater tied around his neck, and a white TH ball cap.

"XEEna, my friend!" he egged on. Buddy stood and walked over toward me. "Can I pour you a Scotch? It's a nice sherry cask-aged one."

Did he know that was my favorite type of Scotch? Had to be a coincidence.

"No, thank you, Judge Sassoon, I—"

"Buddy! What's this 'Judge Sassoon' nonsense? We're friends, you and me. We're partners, and I love everything you do at your little store. By the way, I told that man of yours, Stevie, that I couldn't have done my latest security install without his significant expertise." He motioned for me to sit by the window in one of three plush chairs separated by glass coffee tables.

I happened to know the latest installation was *not* for security purposes, as all the cameras were installed on the inside of an area he called his "romper room." "Sparky," I corrected.

"Whatever ... How about that SCOTCH?"

"Thanks, I'll pass for now."

"For NOW? Oh, are you flirting with me?" He grinned as if he had just sucked a lemon.

I pulled out my notepad, hoping he'd see I was here to discuss business. "No. I've been hired to look into the death of Dr. Jane Moore."

Buddy sat in the chair next to me, crossed his legs, and put his Scotch on the end table between us.

"Such a TRAgic loss, I don't know HOW I can help at all but certainly WILL TRY. But before we move on to SERious talkin', I simply must ask if you still have that PRETTY little dress you wore to the GALA." Buddy's face lit up. He uncrossed his legs, and turned toward me. "You looked like a young VIXen angel in that dress. Innocent and SEXually CHARged. I can't get my mind off that dress! Will you wear it for me again?"

I sat tall and struggled to hold back busting out laughing. Or strangling him. I wanted to do both. "Ah, no. I don't have that dress and there was no vixen-ing going on, Buddy."

I lowered my eyebrows to appear serious, knowing it would be tough to get him to focus on the case.

Buddy sighed and made a *hmph* sound. "Suit yourself. For NOW." He downed the rest of his Scotch.

I pressed on. "I found in Dr. Moore's notes that she was going to be working on a case that you were overseeing involving flounder. Is that right?"

He thought for a long moment. "Yes, it'll be HEARD in a few weeks."

"What's being decided?"

Buddy got up and refreshed his drink, holding his glass

up with a questioning look to see if I changed my mind and wanted one. I shook my head no.

"The SANchez brothers want to create a big farm for flounder. They've a small one a bit further south, but now they want to create a LARGE flounder farm in Galveston Bay. The challenge has always been HOW to get them to SPAWN in a farm environment. Flounder like to fuck in the open waters. Pretty particular for flat, ugly fish, they should take what they can get." Buddy had this sinister smile on his face like he was trying to imagine how flounder mated.

"The SANchez brothers said they've a plan to make the big farm work. Maybe fish aphrodisiac, no just kidding. Their hope is to get flounder back in the grocery stores like it used to be. That damned TRASH fish tilapia has taken over because it's so easy to farm and fish. They're less particular about their bedroom habits, apparently."

"Why was Jane involved?"

"Why are scientists EVER involved? There's always someone worried about the enVIRonment. The county agency that regulates commercial fish licensing ORDERed a marine life risk assessment."

"Do you know what Jane's position was on this case?"

"I have NO EARTHLY IDEA, but based on what I've HEArd, the Sanchez Brothers have a winning idea. It'll provide two hundred and fifty new jobs and the oil industry is strUGGling right now. That's two hundred and fifty more happy voters, XEEna!"

I took notes and looked up, hoping he'd say more.

Buddy paused and sighed. "Talking to ME about this

woman's death is a WASTE of time. This flounder case is immaterial. Let's talk about something else, all this about fish sex has got me humming."

"Would it surprise you if I told you she was against the building of the farm?"

"God NO!" he shouted. "I would've BET on it. She oppOSed everything. I assumed that was her JOB. No biggie."

Buddy twirled his glass in his hand. He smiled wide and held his glass out to me several times to entice me to drink with him. "I sure do enJOY visiting with you, but I don't know anything about what happened to Jane. These issues are just business and no one seems to get too RUffled."

"A lot of money is at stake," I said.

"You BETCHA. But the one who has the most usually WINS." Buddy busted out laughing and didn't stop for nearly a minute. "Way it goes around here, XEEna. Jobs and tax revenue are KING, and I'm a guardian of our values. If given the choice between fish and MEN, I side for men nearly EVery time. If GOD didn't want us to figure out how to farm FISH and harvest oil, he would've given the PELicans the brains and we'd be living in TREES eating fire ants like idiots. I'm proud of my record."

I couldn't help but laugh with Buddy. Damned if he didn't seem totally believable! Buddy was a creepy, perverted, and honest guy. I was disappointed but not surprised.

"Buddy, did you ever see anyone get real upset with Dr. Moore?"

"Nope." Buddy slid forward and smiled so wide I could see all his silver fillings. "Now, little LAdy, how 'bout we talk about you COMing over and giving me a proposal on ways to further SECURE my beach house?"

He was done with talking about Jane and seemed to care less about it. Only innocent people cared this little.

"Sparky's the equipment guy, and I'd be happy to send him over," I said.

"AAH, I was hoping I could SHOW you my new top floor SUN room and get your PROfessional opinion as the woman in CHARge."

"The room where Sparky helped you wire twelve cameras on the *inside*? 'Romper room,' I think you call it? I saw the pictures, Buddy. Listen, I've been in this business a while. Be careful what you film."

He grinned, put his index finger to his lips and whispered, "I keep my private collection safe, rest assured."

I stood and turned toward the door. "I should go. I appreciate your time."

"Any time you want to LIVE out your fantasy – whatever it is – will you PROmise to let me know?" Buddy coaxed as he walked back over to his bar cart.

One of the reasons Buddy kept getting reelected was that he was an exceedingly likable slimeball. He flirted with anything that wore a skirt and treated every man like a lifelong fishing buddy.

There was no way Buddy would've risked screwing up his idyllic, greasy life by murdering Jane. Killing is an emotional act most of the time – unless we're talking about some sociopaths – and Buddy has plenty of emotion. But none of it, not even a little, was directed at Jane or the cases she got involved in. Partially because she never won any of her cases.

BJ was right about Buddy. I left his office feeling as though I needed to take another shower. I'm sure if Buddy knew, he would've misconstrued my comment to mean he'd gotten me hot and bothered instead of coated with verbal drivel.

~☉

There's a good reason, readers, that I never tell my clients – even, and especially, ones that I'm attracted to – everything. It's about leverage, situation control, and the importance of managing the flow of information.

When Ari called me from his cellphone, he would've had no way of knowing that I recently installed new video cameras. Nor could he have guessed I had six crisp video feeds recording anything and anyone within three blocks of my house in all directions. He certainly had no idea I could see he was sitting in his car one block away when he called.

"Are you doing OK?" I asked.

"Yes, I'm worried about you," he replied. "Do you want me to come over to your house?"

"You don't need to worry about me. What're you up to?"

"I'm straightening up my home office. Busy work to get my mind off things. Playing some music."

I continued to watch Ari and encouraged him to embellish his story. "What kind of music?"

"Foals. Stuff like that."

"I love Foals, too. It's so moody."

"We've several things in common, Xena. I want you to know that I'm not at all sorry I kissed you."

I zoomed in the camera to get a closer look at Ari's face. It was dark, but the light from his cellphone enabled me to see his expressions. "It was nice, I'll admit. But we need to focus on the case right now. I don't want to make any mistakes. It could be dangerous."

"I understand, though I'd like to be more involved in the case. You call me with shocking news every day, then I go to work and try to trudge on. I don't want to do that anymore. I'd like to help." Ari was wiping his face with his free hand, frustrated. He pulled his hair back and held it away from his face.

"How about this," I offered and immediately second-guessed myself. "Tomorrow, I'm going to meet with the crew of the *Elissa* about some pollution they told Jane about. Would you like to come with me?"

"Yes! I would. I know the crew."

"Meet me at Pier 21 at 9 a.m.?"

"Sounds good. Are you sure you wouldn't feel better if I came by tonight? Aren't you worried about the person who rigged your car?"

"No, my house has security cameras and can see anyone who comes close from any direction."

The look on Ari's face was precious! He nearly dropped his phone looking around trying to determine if he was going to get caught by my cameras. He crouched low in his seat so his face was no longer visible.

"My car and bike are locked in the garage," I explained. "So I don't pay attention to the cameras unless something makes me suspicious."

Did I feel bad about lying to Ari? No, I did not. I was letting him off the hook.

"OK, well, I should let you go," Ari said.

"See you at 9 a.m. tomorrow."

"I'll be there. And thanks."

"For what?"

"Letting me tag along with you. I won't get in your way. Promise."

"I'm not worried about it."

A lie; I was concerned about exposing Ari to killers. Killers act and think differently than non-killers.

Ari sat in his car for an hour after we hung up. I'm not sure if he stayed there to protect me, or if it took him that long to figure out how to ease out of the street without being noticed by my security cameras.

Either way was OK with me. I enjoyed watching and thinking about him.

Chapter 15

Day 12, Saturday

I parked in the lot next to Nonno Tony's, walked up to the main walkway of Pier 21, looked around for Ari, and spotted him sitting on a nearby bench with a tall Starbucks coffee from across the street. He was dressed in a navy jogging suit, the second one I'd seen him wear.

"Good morning!" I met him halfway and I pointed at his suit. "Do you run?"

"No. It's just comfortable." He blushed.

"I know what you mean. I'm the same way with yoga pants." I smiled at him, and we started walking toward the *Elissa*. Although it had started to get cool in the mornings, I wore shorts, a sport tank top, and fleece pullover because I knew it would warm up soon.

"You look like you run," he said.

"I freerun," I said.

"What's that?"

"It's cool. I'll tell you about it sometime."

Before boarding the ship, we stopped to read a small plaque mounted next to the gangplank on the dock.

Elissa is a beautifully maintained 205-foot, three-masted sailing ship that was built in 1877. She carried a variety of cargos to ports around the world, and her working life as a freighter ended in Piraeus Harbor, Greece, where she was rescued from the scrapyard by ship preservationists who refused to let her die. Elissa is both a floating National Historic Landmark and a fully functional vessel that continues to sail yearly during sea trials in the Gulf of Mexico.

A deckhand greeted us at the top of the gangway. "Hello! Can I help you?" the young man asked.

"I'm looking for Chris," I replied. That's the name Jane mentioned in her journal.

"I'm Chris," said a slightly older but still young man about ten feet away. "Are you Xenia?"

"Xena, yes. Is now still a good time to meet?" He looked as though he was in the middle of painting the deck.

"Sure." He walked up and recognized Ari. "Hey, Ari, I didn't know you were coming. Great to see you again."

"BARL is my client," I explained.

"It's been a while. Sorry it's under these circumstances," Ari said.

"We were all so shocked to hear about what happened to Jane," Chris said. "She was an important supporter of the *Elissa* and an amazing human being."

Chris led us amidships.

"I'm sorry for your loss and appreciate your time." We

walked to the edge facing the water. "A few weeks ago, you asked Jane to look at something floating in the water. Can you tell us about that?"

"Yes, that's right. We noticed a shiny film on top of the water" – Chris pointed at the water line – "that smelled different than what we were used to."

"Pardon my ignorance, but this place is full of ships, rigs, and equipment." I indicated the cruise ship docks and the oil rig equipment right across the channel. "Isn't there a lot of stuff in the water?"

Chris shook his head and looked down at the water. "You might be surprised to learn that most of what's in the water is a different variation of basic diesel fuel. The regulations are pretty tight right now, and this ship channel in particular doesn't carry a lot of the freighters you see anchored off the beach coast. They go up the bay."

Chris motioned for me and Ari to follow him back down the gangplank and onto the dock. He pointed to where the water met the bow. "It was here."

"What did it look like?" I asked.

"It was much thinner than oil or fuel. It looked almost like a thin shellac and it smelled sweet."

"And this was new to you?"

"Yes. Our deckhands working in the water got dizzy. They complained that they felt like they had sniffed a bunch of toxic magic markers."

"And it's gone now?"

"It comes and goes with the tides. The tide is going in right now. I don't see anything."

"What does that tell you?" Ari asked.

"Good question. That tells me it was coming from the west," he concluded as he pointed down the ship channel.

"Has anyone else from BARL come to look at or talk to you about the substance?" I asked.

"No," Chris said. "I saw some guy looking around the docks over there by the hotel, but didn't talk to him."

"Tall blond guy with a mustache?" I asked.

"Yes, that's the one," Chris said.

"Ansel," Ari said.

"Xena?" Chris asked, hesitating with a worried looked on his face.

"Yes?"

"This whole mess didn't have anything to do with Jane's death, did it? One of the BARL people I know – Roberta – mentioned at Jane's funeral that someone was investigating."

I gave Ari a look not to say anything. Last thing I needed was him taking Chris down the rabbit hole of why Fred was innocent.

"She was talking about me. We're not sure what might've happened, but you reporting this pollution wasn't what got her killed," I said, not completely convinced that this was true. "Please don't blame yourself. It was the right thing to do."

"I could've called the EPA but they make you do a lot of paperwork even if it ends up being nothing of concern."

Ari nodded knowingly.

"Chris, what you did was fine and right," I assured him.

We walked along the dock and admired the *Elissa*'s design.

"Thank you for sharing this information with us. Here's my card if you think of anything else," I said.

Chris took and looked at my card. "The spy shop, huh? My girlfriend goes there a lot."

"Thank you for that, too."

Ari also handed Chris his card. "Will you call me when the smell returns? I'd like to take a look at it. I'll bring one of our chemical experts."

"Sure, no problem," Chris said.

"Let's get together and talk about Jane's replacement for the onboard marine biologist, too."

"That'd be nice, Ari. Thanks."

We left Chris and walked off the *Elissa*'s pier and back out to the parking lot. As Ari and I walked to my rental car, I noticed someone sitting in a parked car across the street looking this way and wondered if it was my skinny friend. It was a different car than the one along the seawall. The driver in the car left as I got near mine.

Probably nothing, I thought. "Do you want to get coffee and talk about what we learned and the next steps?"

"Yes, I've a few ideas," Ari said.

"Where'd you park?" I asked.

"Across the street. It's fine if you don't want me to go with you," Ari said.

"OK, let's go to the Mod. Better coffee there."

~⊙

The Mod was busy, but we got a table outside under the jasmine arbor. A lovely breeze swirled about as people browsed the art studios in the area. It was easy to tell the tourists apart from the locals, because the locals looked sloppier, or more comfortable depending on whose filter you saw things through. The tourists were more likely to wear impractical plastic shoes and carry cavernous, back-breaking bags appliquéd with starfish and sand dollars.

Wisps of Ari's hair swirled around in the wind. Have you noticed that stores don't sell hair accessories for men? Lots of men let their hair grow and many don't know how to contain or tie it up. They use their hands and hats, and some use plain rubber bands. Marketing people are quick to paint male-oriented products pink to sell to women, so why don't they come out with a line of macho barrettes or beefy headbands just for guys?

Ari gave up trying to keep his hair out of his eyes and sent a few texts after we sat with our coffees. I enjoyed watching him. He was neither cocky nor weak. He was present and OK with himself. I thought about offering him the leopard-patterned hair scrunchie I kept in my bag for situations like these, but decided against it.

"I sent a text to my friend who manages the BARL motor pool," he said. "Anytime we take a vehicle to a research site we have to sign it out. Dates, times, destinations."

"I'm not following."

"It's worth a shot to see whether Ansel signed out any vehicles recently, and if so, where he went."

"Brilliant!" I said and meant it. "Can you also find out which company was associated with P67?"

"Director Larson will have to give that to me. He went

to Houston after the funeral and won't be back in town until Monday. I'll ask. Client names are closely guarded."

"Interesting," I said.

We watched a group of tourists walk by and remarked on how they seemed totally focused on shopping and oblivious that they were walking by beautiful and well-preserved historic buildings. The paradox, of course, is that tourism dollars – those T-shirt and trinket purchases – helped fund our preservation efforts. It'd be nice if they noticed them!

"I can see why you like this line of work. Fascinating puzzles to solve," Ari said.

"Yeah, it's invigorating, scary, and intellectually challenging. Most the time, anyway. Some cases are pretty boring."

"Not this one!"

"Nope. Not on any level ... Last month a widow hired us to stake out a cemetery once a week for the entire night. My client put flowers at her husband's grave every week. She noticed that instead of dead flowers the next time she visited, she found nothing. The flowers were stolen. She went to the police, but they told her they couldn't help, so she hired us."

"No offense, but that seems like a big expense for missing flowers," he said.

"I agree! But she believed her dead husband could tell that the flowers were there and that they would comfort him."

"Did you find the thief?"

"Yep. Turned out to be an enterprising raccoon using the flowers for nesting material in its burrowed-out tree house. My client saw this as a sign that the raccoon was the reincarnated soul of her husband, Wally. She continued to bring Wally the raccoon flowers, called out his name, and hoped he'd eventually let her pet him."

"She should get a rabies shot."

"Exactly. Every case has its own peculiarities. Yours especially." I smiled and raised my eyebrows at Ari.

We drank our coffee and went over the information that Chris had shared. I pulled out the chemical chart Dora had created for me and we narrowed down the type of pollution based on weight (floats) and smell (sweet).

Ari's phone pinged. "Jackpot!"

"What?"

"My friend Roger. He sent me the details for the last motor pool vehicle Ansel checked out. He went to Pelican Island with a chemical test kit." Ari paused for dramatic effect. "I have the coordinates of where he was heading."

"Excellent. Where on Pelican Island was he going?"

"On the shore of the ship channel. Looks west of the *Elissa* on the other side. Just like Chris guessed."

"Great. Forward the info to me. I'll take Sparky out there to check it out."

"You and Sparky?"

"Yes. Why?"

"I want to go with you."

"Well … I don't know," I waffled.

"Come on, I don't know a lot about chemicals but likely more than you do," he pleaded. "We rescue marine life from polluted waters all the time. What if we run into animals in distress?"

"You're stretching it. It could be dangerous."

"I know."

"No, you don't. No offense, but this isn't what you do. Three nights ago, someone blew up my car. I could've been in that car. Most people would've been in the car."

"You'll be there. Sparky will be there. It's daylight."

I tapped my nails on the café table. Thinking.

"This is important to me," he declared.

"I know, but every part of me is screaming that this is a bad idea."

Ari placed his hand over mine to stop the tapping. "I know the coordinates and you don't. I'm going."

"Shit!"

"Thank you," Ari said.

I called Sparky and we decided to meet in an hour at the spy shop. Sparky offered to drive so I didn't risk messing up my rental car on the mostly gravel roads on Pelican Island. And although Ari had coerced me into letting him come, what he didn't know is that I was leaning toward giving in to him anyway. He's the scientist, after all.

I then remembered my agreement with BJ and decided that we didn't need to tell him the three of us were driving over to Pelican Island. If we saw something important, we'd call him.

~⊙

The Volkswagen Type 181 is a screwy, two-wheel drive, four-door, convertible, off-road car manufactured from 1968 to 1983. In the United States, it was called the "Thing" and I cannot imagine a more apt name. They came in Pumpkin Orange, Sunshine Yellow, or Blizzard White and featured a stripped-down interior and easily removable body parts. Sparky's partially restored 1973 Thing was yellow with a black top.

Ari and I pulled into the spy shop parking lot. I realized that Ari had never been to the shop, so I was worried about what his first impression would be of our product offerings. Would he see all these gadgets as promoting behaviors that degrade our community? Or as fun and useful things? I believed the latter and was proud of our eclectic and unusual offerings.

Sparky pulled into the parking lot as we were about to go into the shop.

"Hello! Are you ready for some adventure?" Sparky asked. "It's a beautiful day, so let's go top down."

"Sounds good to me!" Ari said.

I flashed Sparky a look that communicated my unease with taking Ari with us. We went around to the front of the spy shop and entered. I looked around, moved closer to Sparky, and whispered, "Jesus Christ, she has animals on both sides now."

As we walked in, hundreds of stuffed animals looked at and followed us. Ari noticed immediately and walked back and forth to test them. He laughed and looked at a few other things. Night vision goggles, safety bags, safes that looked like books.

"You didn't tell me you had so much cool stuff in here!"

I breathed a sigh of relief.

"We serve an eclectic customer base." Dora joined us. I introduced her to Ari.

"I'd love to look around sometime." Ari scanned the shelves.

"So what's the plan?" Sparky asked.

"Let's grab some gear and head out before it gets too hot," I said.

Sparky and I collected a few things to take with us. I was careful not to show Ari our meeting room. I didn't want him to see all our charts, especially his name on the PS list, because I realized I hadn't yet crossed it off and didn't want to explain it to him. So we went out the front door again, down the alley to where Sparky had parked his Thing.

I climbed in the back "seat" because I was the smallest person and it really wasn't a full back seat. Ari sat up front with Sparky.

"I've always wondered what these Things were like," Ari said. "This'll be fun!"

"My first boyfriend had a Thing," I interjected. "His name was Guy, pronounced *Gee*, and he was French. He bought Partager wine, which I thought was fancy and fine. I later found out it was French two-buck-chuck and practically undrinkable for anyone with good taste."

"How old were you?" Ari asked.

"Fourteen."

"Xena!" Sparky exclaimed.

"Don't *even* try to tell me you two didn't drink by the time you were fourteen," I warned. "I won't buy it."

They both nodded their heads in agreement and laughed.

Sparky pulled out from the alley and confirmed Ari was going to be the navigator.

~⊙

The entrance to Pelican Island was less than a mile from the spy shop. As we went over the drawbridge, a flock of pelicans flew overhead. Did they know the island was named for them? Perhaps they had rookeries here? I made a mental note to ask Dora why it was called Pelican Island.

We took a right down a narrow road that led to an industrial area along the ship channel. A large pickup truck came up behind us, going fast. I could see that it had jacked-up wheels.

"That guy is awful close. Why doesn't he pass?" I asked.

"Guys in trucks think they own the road," Ari said. "No offense," he then said to Sparky.

"None taken, although I'm shocked you think this is a truck. It's a utility vehicle and a chick magnet." Sparky looked back at me with a broad grin.

The truck's windows were tinted so we couldn't see who was inside. It was a few feet away and speeding up. He moved to the side and started to pass but instead came closer to us on the side.

"What the hell?!" I exclaimed.

Sparky laid on the horn, which sputtered softly.

"Hang on!" he yelled as he tried to speed up and away from the truck.

Sparky's attempts at losing the guy didn't work. The truck stayed right beside us and came closer. It turned into us and forced Sparky off the road.

"Shit! What's he doing?" Ari exclaimed.

"Here we go!" Sparky crushed several bushes and slid in the loose dirt. A cloud of dust kicked up, and I could see the truck turn and come back toward us.

"He's coming back!" I shouted.

Sparky turned the wheel and managed to get it back on the road. The pickup truck played chicken with us and forced Sparky off the road again.

The Thing hit a rock and went over on its side. I fell out on the ground – the back seat lacked a seat belt – and Sparky nearly landed on top of Ari. They released their seat belts and climbed out. The truck kept going, turned left, and didn't come back.

"Everybody OK?" Sparky asked.

"Yes," I said. "A bit dusty."

"I'm good, but mad. Who *was* that?" Ari asked.

"*Why* might be a better question," Sparky said. "Probably not random."

The Thing didn't look so good. The crash caused the windshield to crack in several places and left serious damage on one of the doors that now wouldn't close. Sparky surveyed the damage and shrugged.

"Do we need to call for a ride?" Ari asked.

Sparky messed with the windshield. "We'll be back on the road in a minute," he declared.

He took off the windshield as Ari and I pitched in. We removed the passenger side door and turned the Thing right side up. Sparky threw the loose parts in the back and started up the car, which purred back to life.

"Hello Banana Mama." Sparky smiled. Then he turned to Ari. "Where to, navigator?"

"Well ... OK! The spot's another mile down this road."

Sparky drove south, slowing as we came closer to the water and then came to a stop along the shore of the ship channel, across from where the cruise ships docked.

"This is where Ansel stopped," Ari confirmed and looked at me for what to do next.

"Let's look around," I said. "But keep your eyes open for that truck."

Sparky parked on the shoulder. We walked close to the shore, where we saw a dead egret about one hundred feet away. The air smelled unnatural, like gasoline but sweeter.

Ari crouched at the water's edge. He cupped water in his hands and brought it close to his nose to smell it. He then tasted the water with his tongue.

"Ari, stop," I urged. "Are you crazy?"

He released the water from his hands. "This isn't good," he said. "This water smells and tastes like benzene."

"The name is familiar. Was that on our shortlist of possible chemicals?" I asked.

Ari looked across the water's surface. "Yes. I could be wrong, but if it's benzene, this is fresh. It's light and evaporates quickly."

"How bad is benzene?" Sparky asked.

I pulled Dora's chart from my bag and looked up benzene. "Says here that widespread use of benzene was outlawed because it causes cancer. It hasn't been used in any commercial operations for over fifty years."

"Where do you think it's coming from?" Sparky asked.

"Hard to tell with the currents, but not far," Ari replied. "Likely somewhere on east end of the island, or the west end of the Bolivar Peninsula."

"Do you think someone is using it illegally?"

Ari stepped back from the water and we followed him. "Seems doubtful. Maybe it's coming from an older site that has been newly disturbed."

"Might Ansel have come to the same conclusion?" I asked.

"He was an expert in this stuff. He could've quickly pinpointed the source. I'm surprised he didn't share his findings with others. Maybe he did. Seems like something we'd be concerned about."

Sparky and I bobbed our heads in agreement. We headed back to the Thing.

"Let's assume for a moment that this is all related to Jane's death. What might've happened?" Sparky theorized. "Ansel uncovers the pollution. Owner doesn't want to pay to fix it. Owner bribes Ansel. Jane continues to bug Ansel about the pollution and he sees her as an obstacle."

Ari stared, stunned by the notion, yet not sure what to believe anymore.

"Let's get the gull in the air and get some close-up pictures of this," I suggested.

"Great idea. Hope it didn't get damaged when the Thing turned over.

"What's the gull?" Ari asked.

"One of our drones," I said. "Looks kind of like a seagull."

"Can I help?"

"Sparky and I will handle this. You want to take a closer look at the water? No more tasting."

"You got it," Ari said.

The gull had suffered some damage, but Sparky and I managed to get it put together and in the air. Sparky used it to take video footage of the water that we hoped might help identify the source of the benzene, or at least the general direction from which it was flowing. I called Dora and asked her to research the most likely sources of benzene on the island, especially older sites.

The gull made a weird clicking noise and began flying crooked.

"This thing is real quirky, Xena, I'm not sure about this," Sparky warned.

"We've got good footage of the water, so let's bring it in before we lose it in the channel," I suggested. "We don't want to go swimming in there to retrieve it."

Sparky piloted the gull over land just in time. It sparked, fell, and landed on the roof of a warehouse-type building.

"Shit! It landed inside the fence. Do you know anyone at Rolls-Royce?" Sparky asked, looking at me.

"Rolls-Royce?" Ari asked.

"Marine, not cars," Sparky explained. "The gull landed on their property."

I walked up to the fence and assessed where the gull had landed. It was lying one hundred feet inside a chain-link fence, on top of a garage surrounded by a six-foot-tall concrete wall.

"I'll get it," I said. I pulled on my bag's hidden waist

straps to secure it and ran toward the fence.

"What's she doing?" Ari yelled.

"Careful!" I heard Sparky call.

The fence had a metal arch around the opening to help support the weight of the swinging gate. The gate had a padlock so I climbed the vertical post and used my momentum to swing over to the other side. I rolled a few times to break my fall then sprinted to, and vaulted onto, the concrete wall. I balanced, then walked along the wall and jumped up to hang on the roof of the garage. After pulling myself up onto the roof, I retrieved the drone. With the gull in one hand, I dropped to the wall and again to the ground.

"A little help here?" I ran to the fence.

Sparky and Ari met me at the fence and caught the gull after I threw it over. I shimmied back up the pole and over the fence.

"How'd you do that?" Ari asked, his jaw slack.

"That's freerunning," I answered.

"You looked like Spider-Woman!" Ari said.

"That's nothing," Sparky said. "I've seen her run in a handstand and jump across alleys, stories above the ground."

"Sparky, stop," I implored.

"Impressive!" Ari exclaimed.

"The gull's memory chip looks undamaged!" Sparky proclaimed.

We went back to the Thing and left Pelican Island. I watched for the truck on the way out, but didn't see it again. We dropped off Ari at his car and returned to the spy shop to process through all the data we had collected. Ari promised not to tell anyone about the benzene until we talked again, but said he'd have to report it soon. I wanted to map out everything to make sure we didn't step into the killer's trap – they knew we went to Pelican Island.

~⊙

It was a beautiful night on the island and a perfect time to be sitting on the porch with a glass of wine. Instead, I talked to Gregory from my home office while I stared at my security camera feeds. Ari was back in his car, parked on my street, watching my house.

"How long has he been sitting there?" Gregory asked.

"About an hour. The same place as last night," I said.

"He doesn't know you're watching him?"

"I don't think so."

"Hmmph."

"Yep," I agreed.

"So you think this benzene spill is related to Jane's murder?" Gregory asked.

"I need to connect several dots, but yes, I do. It feels right."

"Motive, money?"

"Yeah, and maybe fame, too," I proposed. "Here's my challenge. I need to place someone in the cephalopod tank area at BARL that Monday night and I haven't been able to do that yet."

"And find out the company name associated with P67," Gregory added.

"Especially that. Dora's researching possible producers or

users of benzene on the island. We're going to meet early tomorrow morning to go over it all. Maybe that info will help narrow the options," I said. "And I've been reading the book that Jane bought. Did you know that chemicals move *through* soils and the water table?"

"That's why bad shit happens with superfund sites. The companies say they've contained the contaminants, but fail to mention that small amounts almost always escape. Next you know, the stuff enters the water table superhighway and pops up in elementary school water fountains."

"Water table superhighway. Scary."

Chapter 16
Day 13, Sunday

Every Sunday I drive to the Sunshine Bakery when it opens at 7 a.m., order a fresh-out-of-the-oven cinnamon roll and bottomless cup of black coffee, sit outside (except in August), and read the Sunday paper front to back. Not this Sunday. Things were heating up with the case, and I didn't want to lose momentum by taking the morning off.

I got cinnamon rolls and coffee to go and arrived at the spy shop a few minutes before Dora. I divvied up our breakfast items, peeked at the Sunday paper, and dug into my cinnamon roll before it cooled off. I swooned at the warm, oozing cream-slash-butter-slash-sugar frosting that enveloped it. My eyelashes fluttered as I inhaled scents of exotic cinnamon and sour yeast. My fork glided silently through the pillowy white layers and dark gooey center chamber. As I savored my first bite, I experienced a vision of what heaven must be like.

"Mmmm," I murmured as Dora walked in. "This is the best thing in the world right now."

"It's good tasting but not good for us!" Dora started eating hers.

"Don't start preaching the food pyramid."

"I'm just providing a reality check," she insisted.

"I know that this cinnamon roll is less nutritious than a can of aerosol paint. I know that its nine hundred calories are more than skinny people consume in a week."

"You're skinny," she said.

"Thanks, but I'm not nine-hundred-calories-a-week skinny," I replied. "I'm fully aware that carpenters make permanent glues out of ingredients similar to those I'm consuming right now."

"You're funny," Dora said.

"This is serious," I retorted and started using my hands. "The cinnamon roll from the Sunshine Bakery is a perfectly designed delivery system for peace and happiness. When properly consumed – without fear or guilt – it releases all the good hormones and comes as close to emulating love as I've found in the legal world of options."

"Scientists have estimated that up to seventy percent of all illnesses are related to stress," Dora said, finally coming around to my way of thinking.

"That's a lot!" I agreed. "Have you tried eating tofu 'chicken' marsala? I have, and it was a stressful experience. I'm sure I produced a few cancer cells that day. Kale chips? Stress. Broccoli juice in the morning? Double estresso! When we're under stress, we produce cortisol and this causes belly fat. So maybe uninteresting salads with no-oil dressings are causing more diseases, obesity, and premature deaths than the affordable and luxurious cinnamon roll."

"Wow, someone already had a cup of coffee or two."

"Two," I placed my hands on the table and sighed with contentment.

"Anything good in the paper?" Dora asked.

"Yes, very good in fact. Steve's feature article on Sparky's demonstration at Cerulean Sky landed on the front page."

We took a few minutes to finish our cinnamon rolls while skimming Steve's article called *Cerulean Sky: Blue Skies or Gloomy for the Island?* It included a profile of Vicki Moon, her vision for Cerulean Sky, and a fascinating look back at the businesses that had occupied the site where Cerulean Sky was being built. At 8 a.m., I looked at the clock and pushed the paper aside.

"Shall we delve into the world of benzene pollution?" I asked.

"Yes, let's," Dora agreed. "I've created a chart with type of uses going down and time going across. You said you wanted to consider older sites."

"Yes. Since it's no longer legal for most applications."

"And there are better alternatives even if it were."

"Good to know …" I scanned Dora's chart.

Benzene, the chart read, was "a hydrocarbon, a by-product of oil production and refining, used as a solvent for degreasing metal."

"We have a lot of refineries," Dora explained. "But most of them are farther up the bay."

"I'd assume all the shipping companies along the ship channel probably used benzene at some point."

"That'd be a fair guess," Dora said. "Now, check this out. Benzene was used – although less commonly – as an aftershave lotion because of its pleasant smell."

"No! Imagine being told that benzene was a carcinogen after using it on your face for years!"

"I know. Tragic. I wasn't able to find any reference to companies in Galveston that produced the eau de benzene."

"I'm glad to hear that," I said.

"Benzene was also used to decaffeinate coffee – it's how Sanka was invented."

"Yuck …"

"Yes, and benzene was used to extract hop oil for beer production."

"Wait." I cut in. "Beer production?"

"Yes. Not for fifty years or so, but it was an effective extractor."

"What about the brewery?"

"The big brewery?" Dora asked. "You mean where Cerulean Sky is now?"

I grabbed Steve's story and found the part that discussed the site's history:

The old brewery site has been empty and in decay since 1982. Various companies produced beer there from the 1890s until the 1980s. Most notably, the Campeche Brewery operated for fifty years and its best-selling beer was the Pirate Island IPA. It was a successful business until the patriarch of the company died and his two sons bickered the company into the ground.

"Well, I know one thing from personal experience," Dora said. "You need a lot of hops to make IPA."

If that name – Campeche – is familiar to you, readers, it's because it goes back to Galveston's pirate roots. The French pirate Jean Lafitte was the first non-native to settle in Galveston in 1816. He led a pirate kingdom of nearly one thousand called Campeche until the US Navy chased him away. Imagine the volume of beer that a pirate *kingdom* would consume!

"Check this out," I said, reading more from Steve's story:

> *This site attracted beer makers because it was one of the few places on the island that had a water well. In fact, it was an unusually high yield well and you needed a lot of water to make beer.*

"The well ... it's the clue we've been missing."

"Are you suggesting that Vicki Moon might be involved in this pollution?" Dora asked. "It makes no sense, Xena. The site is inland by nearly a third of a mile and landlocked."

"Water table superhighway," I mumbled, recalling my earlier conversation with Gregory. "What if the development of the site is somehow pushing the pollutants out and into the underground water sources?"

Dora and I spent the day cross-referencing information from the book Jane bought on groundwater contamination and our research on the uses of benzene. We process-mapped potential scenarios for how Vicki and the Cerulean Sky project could've been connected to the pollution, Ansel, and

Jane. By early evening, we agreed that we were close to a possible breakthrough but that we were in way over our heads with the science. We knew it was time to get together with Ari, BJ, and the EPA to review the information. Sparky was still working on the drone footage and said he'd have it ready to review by early morning.

After Dora left the spy shop, I reread Steve's story from beginning to end. It was a balanced piece with coverage of the demonstration juxtaposed with positive remarks about the economic development that Vicki and her husband provided to the island over the years. A sidebar highlighted the mystery of Vicki's husband's disappearance and presumed death. A body was never found and the police had no strong theories about what happened to him. After three months with no clues, Vicki had her husband declared dead so that she could manage their estate. She promptly sold their chain of Vape Escape vapor cigarette stores for $1.5 billion. I googled news stories about the incident because I find unsolved crimes irresistible!

I circled the sentence in Steve's article that said Cerulean Sky was going to have the island's first high-end tattoo shop. *Right on, Vicki!* Not that I'd have gone there, readers. My tattoo artist, Vix, was a master with subtle shading, crisp detail, and vivid colors. I'd never cheat on him.

~⊙

I locked up the spy shop and got in my car to head home. I couldn't get Vicki and Cerulean Sky off my mind, so I drove there, parked a block away, and walked to the site. It was dark, but I sat under a tree across from the main entrance to better stay out of view. There were several guards that came, went, and walked around the outside of the property. The building looked nearly complete except it needed to be painted and a few floors didn't yet have windows.

There was a light on in the fourth floor. I stared at it for several minutes. A large black sedan drove up to the main gate. Guards allowed it through and it sat idling outside the front entrance. Someone was being picked up. I moved to get a better view in time to see the light on the fourth floor go off. A couple of minutes later, Vicki emerged and got in the back of the car. The driver backed out and left.

I bet Vicki's work or living space is on the fourth floor.

I decided to go in. After walking a wide perimeter to assess the best point of entry, I kept to the west side of the scaffolding because it wasn't well lit. I climbed and vaulted the perimeter fence and jumped onto and through the scaffolding like a jungle gym.

I could hear Gregory's voice in my head saying, *just because you can climb scaffolding doesn't mean that you should.*

That was true, but I needed to find something that connected Vicki and Cerulean Sky to this investigation. The case was in that dangerous in-between place where inaction could be deadly but the facts weren't clear enough to get BJ and his team involved.

This particular scaffolding was well constructed and it was easy to swing between the diagonal bars between each platform level. I entered the building from the fifth floor, through one of the openings the workers were using to pass supplies. Even if it were open, which it wasn't, I wouldn't have entered on the fourth floor where I saw Vicki because it was more likely to have alarms and cameras installed.

I made my way through partially constructed hotel rooms or offices across the floor to the side of the building where Vicki's office was located and exited onto the balcony right above hers. I used my telescoping mirror to see into Vicki's office. No one was there, so I hung on to the railing and slipped onto her balcony. The patio door into the office was unlocked.

Vicki's office was gorgeous with a large seating group in the center, a long desk, and two more chairs on the end opposite the office door that led to the elevators. A large abstract painting filled one wall opposite the balcony and pictures from her travels were displayed on both sides of the glass doors leading out to the balcony. I noticed one picture where she was in scuba gear and wondered if she had ever met Jane.

I walked over to her desk and sat in her chair. The desk's surface was clear and tidy. The first drawer had Cerulean Sky stationery and pens. Another drawer contained brochures and marketing materials and a third contained folders with what looked like potential investors.

In the bottom-right drawer – it's always in the bottom-right drawer – I found a folder labeled AH. I opened the folder and found a remediation report.

Jackpot!

It wasn't an official report on BARL letterhead; it was plain-looking and unsigned. A small sticky note on the first page read, CALL TO DISCUSS, ANSEL.

Off the books work, I assumed.

On the first few pages Ansel defined the scope of the benzene pollution and confirmed that "the construction site is causing the soil below the main building to compress and push contaminants into the well water." And because the well is capped and not in use, the polluted water is flowing through the soils and into the ship channel.

I read further and found the smoking gun.

Ansel detailed several recommendations for how Vicki could handle the benzene leak, including letting the new cruise ship terminal project take the fall for it. Based on the construction plans filed with the city, Ansel estimated:

> *They'll be disturbing the area saturated with the benzene in the next four weeks, so you'll need to monitor and clean the current benzene floating in the ship channel. Once the construction for the new dock begins, the leak will be discovered and, with a favorable analysis from me on behalf of BARL, the city would find the cruise ship terminal developers responsible. Even if they assigned partial responsibility to the Cerulean Sky site, you'll pay a fraction of what it'll cost to clean it up.*

I took pictures of each page of the report and put it back in Vicki's desk. I synched up the pictures to my Cloud Drive to make sure we could access them later. As I sat in Vicki's chair, I ran through possible scenarios in my head.

Did Vicki pay Ansel to provide her a way out of the remediation expense and then eliminate the only person who could implicate her?

Was Ansel so eager for a big payoff that he was willing to risk his life and Jane's?

Did Vicki get rid of Jane because she kept inquiring about the pollution?

I'd found what I came for and was looking forward to sharing the evidence with Ari, Sparky, Dora, and BJ. I climbed back up to the fifth floor, onto the scaffolding and down to ground level outside the complex. A guard saw me as I walked around the corner.

Shit. Keep it cool.

He waved to me like a "Hello" wave, not a "What the hell are you doing here" wave, and I waved back. He was motioning me to come closer and I did.

"Good evening, Ms. Moon. Can I help you find something?" he asked.

No … He thinks I'm Vicki.

It was dark, this was her place, I looked like her, and I was dressed in all black, making the subtle differences in our appearance less noticeable.

I shook my head *NO* instead of speaking. Our voices were not similar.

The guard, who I noticed was armed, opened the door for me so I could go inside, which he likely assumed was what I wanted to do. Once inside, I saw other guards, but kept my head down and walked with a purpose.

"Good evening, Ms. Moon," each of them said.

I walked to the elevator, hit 4, and in less than a minute

I was back in Vicki's office. I stood for a moment and didn't know whether to laugh or cry.

I can't get out!

I headed toward the balcony to leave again, but the elevator opened. The real Vicki stood there with two guards.

Change of plans.

"Grab her," she snapped at the guards. She shook her head at me.

"This *is* a surprise." Vicki walked around me, looking me up and down. "When the guards said they'd just escorted *me* in, I knew it was you. I should ask the police to arrest you for trespassing."

"You can't. Your guards let me in," I said.

"Because they thought you were me."

"I didn't know that."

Vicki stopped in front of me. She was acting different; not the bubbly person I'd talked to at the gala. Serious and put out. This was the real Vicki.

"I think you did," she said. "How'd you know to go to the fourth floor?"

I smiled at her. "Lucky guess."

Vicki did not smile back. "Right. What're you doing here? Are you curious about Cerulean Sky? I would've been happy to arrange a tour by appointment."

"I am working on a murder case and it led me here."

I left it at that to see how she'd respond.

"Murder? That's fascinating and unsettling. I hope you weren't looking for dead bodies!" She laughed, which prompted her guards to laugh. She motioned for the guards to make me sit.

Vicki sat in the chair facing mine.

"No. But I was looking for a killer," I announced, hoping to provoke her.

"I'm sorry I can't help you there." She looked at the guards. "Leave Xena and me to chat, but please remain outside the door to escort our friend back to her car once we're done."

The guards walked out. Vicki said nothing and just stared at me.

"I was looking for signs of remediation on your construction site," I said, while keeping constant eye contact with her.

You might be wondering, readers, what the signs of remediation might look like. Depending on the situation and conditions, I might expect to see differences in soil and fill that indicate a recent dig or removal of contaminated soil. Trenches and grout curtains are often used during remediation. And I'd look for evidence of containment walls, cement caps or wells below ground level and equipment that seemed out of place for standard building construction (like large tanks used to extract and separate contaminants or vapor treatment units).

"I'm not sure what remediation is, but I know that we're building Cerulean Sky to the best standards. Sparing no expense to do this right. It's going to be amazing for my customers and this island." She frowned at me, crinkling her brow. "So again, tell me why you are here?"

Meeting her intensity, I said, "I was confirming leads that suggest Dr. Jane Moore was killed to cover up a new source of pollution the killer wanted to conceal. The highly toxic chemicals are coming from a new construction site near the cruise terminal."

"And you think it was coming from here? Cerulean Sky isn't on the water!" she said conclusively and waved her hand, dismissing the idea.

"Did you do any remediation of the toxic substances in the soil below this structure before starting to build? Were you aware that this site used to be a brewery?"

"Yes, of course, anyone living on this island knows that many breweries operated from here over the years. I've been here all my life and I'd never do anything to harm this place."

"Part of the beer-making process involves using a chemical called benzene to separate hop oil from hops."

"So?"

"Wide-spread use of benzene has been illegal for over fifty years because it causes leukemia."

"I know nothing of this. If you have questions about our construction processes, you'll have to talk to my contractor."

"Did you know Ansel Homer?" I asked and glared at her.

The question surprised Vicki. She got up and moved behind her desk, where she grabbed and started smoking a vapor cigarette. With a deep breath in, she scowled and raised her voice. "What a little conniving bitch you are, how *dare* you break into my building and interrogate me in this way!"

The guards heard her and came back into the office.

"I wanted to know if you were greedy enough to kill for this place," I said, trying not to seem ruffled.

"Little Miss Spy Shop is way out of her league. Pity, I thought I might come to like you." Vicki motioned with her hands for the guards to converge on me. "She has threatened me and I feel as though I'm in danger. I'd like you to restrain her until I decide whether to call the police."

They held me down, removed my bag, and handcuffed my wrists together behind my back. Vicki took my bag and emptied it onto her desk.

"Let's see what she has here and if there were any devices I wouldn't want watching or listening to me. I'm sure you understand." She bowed to me condescendingly.

Vicki put the pepper spray and stun gun aside. "I'll keep these," she said.

She then picked up my phone and hit the power button. "You've a new message from Gregory. He wants to know if you can chat. You're a popular girl." She glanced at me, but I said nothing. "Seems you're indisposed and not available to chat." She started typing, speaking the message out loud as she did. "'Sorry, Gregory, I'm very busy. New project. Exciting stuff. Let's talk later in the week.' Send. Goodbye, Gregory."

Vicki threw my phone with all her strength on the marble floor. It smashed into many pieces.

"Let's see if you're wearing a wire. Search her well," Vicki instructed her thugs.

The guards held me still while they fondled around my belly, back, and breasts. One of them stuck his hands inside my bra and whispered, "Just doing my job."

"Don't get her excited, Carl," Vicki said to the guard, then turned to me. "Are you saving yourself for your exotic-looking little client?"

Vicki's verbal jab pissed me off but not enough to distract

me from thinking through two questions: How can I get her to talk? How will I get out of here?

"Maybe under different circumstances," I hissed.

"She's clean." Carl squeezed my breasts for the third time.

"No recorder, no wire. Hmmph. Aren't you being brave all on your own. It's time that you and I cut the crap, don't you agree?" Vicki pulled a chair in front of me and sat close enough that our knees nearly touched. "I thought mentioning Ari would pique your interest. He's cute. But I like a bit more meat on my men, how about you?" She paused, then bent toward me to whisper, "I knew they'd hired you to investigate the biologist's death the moment I saw you sitting with the lab rats at the gala."

She sat back and sighed. "Did you think our meeting in the ladies' room was an accident?" She laughed and drummed her hands on her thighs. "What a fucking ridiculous dress! Where do you shop?"

"Did Ansel Homer kill Jane Moore for you?" I asked.

"If you believe Ansel killed the lady, go pester him."

"He's dead."

"He must've been the weaker man." She smiled. "Insignificant gnat."

"I met with him hours before he was killed. What would you say if I told you that he gave me a copy of the report he did for you where he recommended how you could get out of paying to clean up the benzene leak? As I recall, that report also mentioned that Jane's questions about the pollution were problematic and needed to stop."

Vicki paused and was quiet for a moment as we stared each other down. "Ansel came to see me. He offered to help me with my permits if I gave him a large research grant. But that's not how I work, and I could tell he wouldn't be useful to me. Whatever you think I bought from him, you're wrong. Whatever you think he meant to me, wrong again. He wasn't my collaborator in any way."

She looked at me, smiled, and motioned across the room. "Carl, bring me the packing tape from over there."

"Too bad you didn't bribe better scientists," I said. "The benzene will be traced back to this brewery. Your precious Cerulean Sky will be shut down, perhaps torn down." I bent forward as far as I could to whisper in her ear. "No matter what happens here today, tomorrow morning the GIPD will have a copy of Ansel's report." I paused, smiled, then continued. "And how's this for a kicker? They'll have all the information I've collected to support reopening the cold case for your husband's disappearance."

I was bluffing about that last item but I had a hunch that Vicki had to have been involved.

"How does it feel to be poor street trash dressed up with stuff bought with other people's money?" I asked.

"I want you to shut up." Vicki put tape over my mouth.

Besides keeping an eye on what Vicki and her guards were doing, I had been looking around the room for resources, and so I was pleased to add packing tape to my mental list.

Vicki got up, walked to the abstract painting, and swung it out from the wall to reveal a safe. She put in the combination and opened it.

LISA HANEBERG

"Carl, I need you to keep an eye on the main entrance. Take the radio and let me know if you see or hear anything."

"No problem." Carl left, leaving the other guard in the room.

"Here's what you're missing, Little Miss Spy Shop." Vicki brought a box from the safe to the seating area and put it on a coffee table. "I was the brains of our business. I built the chain of Vape Escape stores from one to two hundred. I made the money. All my dipshit husband had to do was spend his allowance and stay out of trouble. When a trusted contact told me he was trying to buy a young girl from the trade up in Houston, I got a little upset."

She paused, opened the box, and pulled out a vial of clear liquid and a needle.

"He wasn't smart enough to buy a newly harvested hooker and avoid getting caught. I gave him some money and kicked him out. Never saw him again. I heard he hopped on a ship heading to South Africa. Maybe the pirates got him."

I remembered that Ansel had died of a heroin overdose. My time to act was running out. Luckily neither Vicki nor her guards had noticed that I'd taken the pick from my watch band (it has a file, too; we sell them at the shop) and placed it in the lock of one of the handcuffs.

I turned the pick, pulled hard, and was out. I kicked the coffee table up and into Vicki and ripped the tape off my mouth. The vial and syringe flew across the room, but not before she'd filled the syringe with whatever drug was in the vial. I grabbed my bag and put back in the pepper spray and stun gun.

The guard launched toward me with his gun drawn. I rolled sideways to escape his shots and pepper-sprayed him from one side of his eyes to the other. He stumbled, fell to his knees, and dropped his gun. I went for the gun and saw Vicki coming at me with the syringe in her hand. I used my bag as a shield and jammed the stun gun onto her neck. I pulled the trigger and Vicki fell into me. The syringe went through my bag and hit my forearm. I pulled it out before she could push the plunger and rolled away from Vicki, who was writhing on the floor.

I got out the heavy-duty zip-ties from the lining of my bag, hog-tied the guard and Vicki, and taped both of their mouths with the packing tape. Standing over them, I made sure they wouldn't be able to get up and planned my escape. I ran toward the elevator – but jumped to the side when the floor bell rang.

The elevator door opened and Carl ran in the office with his gun drawn. I hit him with the stun gun from the side, took his gun, too, and hog-tied him as well.

The elevator door opened again and I nearly slammed into BJ, investigators Tim and Nancy, and several uniformed officers I didn't recognize.

"Stand down!" BJ yelled.

I handed him a handful of guns and relaxed. He and his crew rushed into the office, where they secured custody of Vicki and the two guards.

"What's going on here? Oh, and thanks for calling me *before* you got into trouble," he growled as he looked around.

"Nice timing," I admitted, clearly confused why he was here, but thankful.

"Sparky called me. He said a friend of yours named Gregory got a weird text so he looked up your location on some app and it showed this as your last known location."

"The case led me here," I said. "Vicki killed Ansel and Jane, or had Ansel kill Jane for her. You can find a report that Ansel completed for her in her desk."

"Anything else you haven't told me but should?"

"Lots more. Just getting started."

"Where would you suggest I look for this report?" BJ asked.

"Bottom desk drawers are always the first place I look."

BJ asked me to stay and give a statement of what happened while his team searched Vicki's office. In addition to the report, BJ and his team found more guns, heroin, and Ansel's laptop.

~⊙

I drove back to the spy shop after BJ let me go to make a few calls because I didn't have a landline at home. BJ seemed mad but also grateful. This was a big break in the case.

My first call was to Sparky. I let him know what happened and that I was OK. I asked him to text Gregory for me, too, and let him know I'd call him in an hour or so. I called Steve and suggested he drive to Cerulean Sky for a scoop on the arrest of Vicki Moon. Then I dialed Ari's number.

"Hey, you. What time is it?" Ari said.

"I'm calling from the spy shop."

"So late?" he asked in a groggy voice. "What happened? Something bad again? You OK?"

"They arrested Vicki Moon for Ansel's death and they think she might be implicated in Jane's murder. Or Ansel killed Jane for her."

"What? Who is Vicki Moon?"

"P67. She's building Cerulean Sky."

"The source of the pollution? Ansel killed Jane? That doesn't make sense to me."

"Captain Rawlins and his investigators are going through Vicki's office now. Maybe they'll find something conclusive."

"Why are you at the spy shop?"

"Vicki destroyed my cellphone."

"Wait. You were *there*?"

"Yes. She tried to stick me with heroin and her guard tried to shoot me. But neither were successful, and I'm fine."

"Do you need me to come over there?"

"No, there's nothing to do tonight. It's over. I need to make a few more calls but wanted you to know that we caught them."

"I feel lost. It's good, don't get me wrong, but unexpected. Can we meet tomorrow morning?" Ari asked.

"Yes, let's meet at your office mid-morning."

"OK. I feel so confused about everything … Hey, Xena?"

"Yes?"

"Congratulations. I don't know how you did this."

After I hung up, I made a pot of coffee and called Gregory to proclaim him the king of guts.

"How'd you know?" I asked.

"This question process of yours is gospel. You'd never put me off for a few days. So when I got the text I knew that either you were writing this to me as a call for help or someone else was doing it."

"The latter. Vicki took it upon herself to answer and smashed my phone. It sucks because there isn't an Apple store on the island. I now have no phone and am driving a crappy rental car."

Gregory huffed. "Vicki killed Jane?"

"She did or maybe she had Ansel do it. She definitely killed Ansel."

"Was she on the PS chart?"

"Not exactly," I admitted. "I'm looking at the list now. We had listed P67, but we didn't know who that was until today. Cerulean Sky wasn't on our radar for this case."

"Do you think the motive was money?"

"Yes, billions. Cleaning benzene that's underneath a huge building will be a massive undertaking."

"So that's it? Case closed?"

"Ask me again tomorrow. I want to see what BJ and his team find and make sure we know who killed Jane."

Chapter 17

Day 14, Monday

I was dazed and tired, as though I'd never left the spy shop. I wore a ball cap to hide my messy hair. Dora brought coffee and scones from the Mod and helped me reorganize the war room. She was clingy because she was worried about whether I was OK about what went down.

"How do you handle it? How do you mentally process that you were being attacked?" she asked.

"It's an in-the-moment thing. I didn't feel the gravity of it until I got home after 2 a.m., and by then I was relieved."

"Because the case was solved?"

"No. Well, that too. Relief that I knew what to do." I grabbed my bag and put it on the table. "We tell people what to carry and how to use these things, but it's a moment of truth when you're faced with having to do it."

"You should share your story at the next Personal Protection class we have here."

I glanced at my bag and tapped it in agreement. "We need to do more practicing. Actually *using* the items." I opened my bag. "This one needs some serious refilling after last night. I used everything I had, even the pick from my watch and the raisins!"

We laughed. I looked at the charts and let out a heavy sigh.

"Had we known what P67 was earlier, we would've had Cerulean Sky in our sights," said Dora.

"Yes, but I don't know if it would've made sense without the backstory from Steve's profile story in the paper," I remarked. I removed the newspaper clippings we had posted on the wall.

Dora started to take down the PS and PM charts.

"Hold on for a minute. I want to leave these up for another day or so," I said.

"The case is closed, right?" she asked.

"Hopefully, but I want to take some time to process through the loose ends to be sure."

We packed everything except the PS and PM charts before the shop opened. I called Jane's brother, as promised, to let him know about the break in the case. He was disappointed they weren't filing charges for Jane's murder yet, and I told him to have faith that it'll happen. Dora came back to let me know that Steve was on the phone for me. I picked up the receiver and punched the line on hold.

"Did you get the scoop last night?" I asked.

"Yes, thanks for the heads-up. It's quite a story. I've a short piece in this morning's paper, but I'm working on a longer feature for tomorrow or Thursday."

"Cool. I look forward to learning what you, BJ, and the DA find out. We've uncovered a lot in the last two weeks, but I'm glad there will be more eyes, ears, and noses looking at everything."

"Noses?"

"You know what I mean. Nosiness."

"Yep, I do. I'd like to interview you and Ari. Can you help me arrange that with Ari as soon as possible?"

"I'm meeting him at his office around ten. Why don't you plan on coming to BARL at noon? He might have to clear it with the director, so I'll call if anything changes."

"That's perfect. Do you think there is a chance I can meet Fred?" Steve asked.

"Oooh, great idea ... I don't see why not! I'll ask Ari. I'd like to see Fred again, too."

I returned to the chore of tidying the meeting room. Dora took over and suggested I rest. I went to the Mod, sat at a corner table, and stared at my cortado until it was time to head to BARL to meet with Ari.

~⊙

The receptionist waved me back. Ari welcomed me into his office, shut the door, and hugged me for a long minute.

We sat at his table and I told him what happened at Cerulean Sky and how our discovery on Pelican Island, Dora's research on benzene, and Steve's profile story about Vicki and the brewery site helped me pinpoint Cerulean Sky as the source of the pollution.

"One of the issues I had with the pollution being a motive for murder was that, even with Jane out of the picture, it was likely that someone else would discover and report the pollution," I said.

"I wondered about that, too," Ari said.

"Ansel's report identified a motive for murder we hadn't considered. The new cruise terminal project offered Vicki a fall guy – a way to pass off the blame to someone else. Vicki needed a month of hush time and—"

"Jane was in their way." Ari air swiped an imaginary person. "Damn it. It's hard for me to wrap my mind around the idea that it was one of her BARL colleagues who sold his soul and sacrificed hers. For what? For money?"

"It's always love, money, or fame," I explained. "In this case, Ansel seems to have been motivated by money and fame."

"I guess you never really know people." Ari slumped back and ran his fingers through his hair.

I tapped on the table to get his attention. "Sure you do. That's how we started on this journey, remember? You told me that you knew Jane and Fred, and you were right." I placed my hand on his for a few seconds and gazed into his eyes. "You didn't work with Ansel."

"True."

"We may never know what exactly happened the night Jane was killed, but at least we know who was responsible. That's something."

"It's a lot."

We sat and reminisced about everything that had happened in the last two weeks until the receptionist called Ari to say Steve was here. We both walked to the lobby to greet him and got settled in a meeting room right off the lobby – the same room where I'd interviewed Roberta.

Ari and Steve spent several minutes getting to know each other. Ari was fidgety, eager to contribute. He was probably star-struck by the idea of being interviewed, especially when Steve made it clear that he and Fred would be the stars of the story. My new disposable phone rang and I excused myself because only a few key people had this number.

"This is Xena."

"BJ here. I didn't wake you, did I?"

"No way, I'm at BARL right now. Steve from the GPI is interviewing Ari."

"Glad he's there and not here. I wanted to let you know that District Attorney Brenda Lomis reviewed everything we have so far and has filed charges against Vicki for Ansel's murder and several related charges for pollution spills and the attempted cover-up. She doesn't have enough to charge her with Jane's murder yet, though."

"OK, I understand. I assume she'll keep looking?"

"Absolutely. The DA likes Vicki for Jane's murder, but we don't have anything that places her or her thugs at BARL on the night of the murder. We think we might find something once we investigate Ansel's history a bit deeper. I wanted to give you an update."

"Thanks, I appreciate it. I'll let you tell Steve about all the charges."

"Yes, please. A release is going out to the local media in about an hour."

I went back to the meeting room and could see that Ari and Steve were already deep in conversation.

"Ari," Steve was saying, "what you're saying about octopus behavior is amazing. I can't wait to meet Fred. How's he doing, by the way?"

"He's doing OK, but it's apparent that he feels loss and grief, or some octopus version of these emotions. He's much clingier with me when I visit him. And with the other staffers, too. We try to give him lots of attention. And fish."

"What's his favorite?"

"Blue crab!" I piped in.

"Xena, let me ask you, what was your first reaction when Ari asked you to take the case?" Steve asked.

"I had no idea if he was right, but I never doubted that he believed Fred was innocent and that was enough for me to jump on board. I consider myself lucky because this was a fascinating case. As an investigator, I live for these opportunities."

"Me, too," Steve agreed.

"No one else could've solved this case," Ari declared. "Xena and her team saw things and connections that others would've missed."

I had to hold back tears because I felt proud and happy. But I wasn't complacent, however, because there were a few dangling items that were not yet resolved or clear to me.

~⊙

Once inside the tank area, Ari took Steve up the stairs to meet Fred, who immediately swam to greet them. Fred even showed an interest in Steve, who was simultaneously freaked out and blown away feeling the octopus's touch. I was sure this was exactly what Roberta saw when she was watching me meet Fred for the first time.

As Ari and Steve interacted with Fred, I observed from

ground level and let my mind wander back into the case. I pondered what Fred may remember from the night Jane was killed and if he *thought* about it – or if any of that was even possible. I reflected on what we'd learned about Vicki and Ansel and how these developments in the case should affect our working theories about what happened the night Jane was murdered. I wondered how could we test our best hypothesis and bring closure for Ari, Bernie, and the BARL team.

I had an idea. I knew it might not work and could backfire. It would be a big production. I looked around the tank area, second-guessed myself, shook my head, and whispered to myself as I watched the guys interact.

Don't blow things out of proportion.

Let the police and DA fill in the rest of the details. You did your part.

I was hired to solve JANE's murder, that's my job.

This might be the only way I'd know for sure what happened.

Steve and Ari came down the stairs after feeding Fred. Steve showed me his soon-to-be octopus hickies.

"Look!" Steve said.

"Fred likes you," I swooned and smiled.

"Yes, he does," Ari agreed.

"What a cool creature!" Steve said. "Thank you for this experience."

"You're welcome. Thanks for sharing Fred's story," Ari said.

"I have an important request," I announced to both of them.

"Sure. What?" Steve asked.

"Steve, I'd like you to ask the director to hold a press conference, right here, in front of Fred's tank. Will you do that?"

"Sure, it's a great idea." Steve smirked. "Especially since I already have the exclusive."

To Ari I asked, "Do you think the director will agree?"

"Absolutely, he loves the media. Especially when he gets to play the hero."

"Why do you want the press conference?" Steve nudged me and smiled. "Are you looking for some publicity for your business? My story will help there, too."

"No, I don't want to be mentioned. The focus should be on the director telling the press there has been an arrest in Ansel's murder and that Fred has been exonerated of any fault in Jane's death."

"Why is this important to you?" Ari asked.

"It'll help bring closure to things," I concluded.

I regretted not being more forthcoming about my motivations but I needed Steve and Ari to act naturally at the press conference or my plan wouldn't work.

Ari called the director and requested the press conference. The director loved the idea and agreed to hold it in front of Fred's tank, the next day at 4 p.m., a perfect time for maximum TV coverage. Ari and Steve discussed logistics for the seated area across from the tanks.

I stared at Fred and whispered to him very softly. I stood three feet away from his tank and could see he was watching me. I did the octopus dance and he responded. This was going to work. I called Sparky and told him I was on my way to the shop. I asked him to get the van ready for tomorrow and to pull up the pictures from the gala. I wanted to look at them one more time.

Chapter 18
Day 15, Tuesday

BJ went along with my plan for the press conference after Sparky and I assured him that it wouldn't be a waste of his team's time. Sparky set up in his van outside while Ari and I went over final arrangements inside. The podium was placed in front of Fred's tank and Ari had arranged his feeding schedule so he'd be out and alert. It would make for better media coverage if they could see Fred in the background. I practiced standing behind the podium.

"What're you worried about?" Ari asked.

"I want to make sure the positioning is correct. Can Fred see me?"

"Sure, he's watching you closely. He's probably wondering why you're ignoring him!"

"Good. Not the ignoring part, I mean" – I turned to Fred – "I'd love to come say hello later, Fred."

By 4 p.m., the room had filled with members of the media from as far away as San Antonio. This was the kind of story that drew them – murder, strange animals, and an excuse to take a paid trip to the beach. The chairs were set in front of the podium, and cameras and long boom mikes suspended like an Alexander Calder mobile along both sides, pointing to the podium and Fred's tank.

As the press conference began, we took our places. The BARL staff stood in a line to the left of the podium, I stood against the wall toward the front on the left. BJ, Tim, Nancy, and two of his officers were with Sparky outside in the van. Sparky streamed video and sound from three cameras that we had placed earlier.

The director entered the room and stepped to the podium.

"Hello, I'm Dr. Mark Larson – L-A-R-S-O-N – director here at the Biological and Aquatic Research Labs, or BARL, and I'm pleased to share the following statement."

He looked up from this paper, and smiled for the cameras.

I looked to the left toward the director and Fred's tank, then to the right at the media. Everything seemed calm, which worried me, but only for a moment, since my hunch began to play out.

Fred started to move.

"This Monday evening," Larson droned, "police arrested Galveston native and developer Vicki Moon and have since charged her with the murder of BARL researcher Dr. Ansel Homer. We here at BARL are grieving Dr. Homer's loss and are glad that a perpetrator has been charged with his murder."

The director looked up, noticed that people were looking past him, and turned around. Fred was flashing and had puffed himself up to look large, like a vampire with tentacles stretched wide to show the webbing between each arm. Ari looked confused.

Fred turned dark red, swelled with water, and shot it against the top of his tank. A few reporters reacted – "*Whoa! Wow! What's happening?*"

Ari kept looking back and forth between the director and Fred, concerned.

"Look, Fred is excited, too!" The director gestured in triumph.

Several journalists laughed and clapped.

"And he *should* be happy because this week's arrest also produced information that has cleared Fred of responsibility in the death of Dr. Jane Moore, another beloved BARL researcher we recently lost."

Fred shot more water to the top of the tank and turned black. The director turned and pointed to Fred, as if he were a lion tamer and Fred was his performer. I could see that Ari was upset.

I moved toward the podium and shouted, "This is *not* what an octopus does when it's happy! Am I right, Dr. Pani?" I turned toward Ari and glared into his eyes to encourage him.

Ari stepped close to the podium and nudged the director away from the mic. "Excuse me, Director Larson." He then addressed the assembled reporters. "I'm Dr. Ari Pani, cephalopod team leader here at BARL, and Ms. Cali is right. This isn't what octopuses do when they're happy."

The director moved into the mic. "Excuse Dr. Pani, he—"

"Fred isn't happy, so please don't laugh," Ari implored.

"What you see him doing right now, flashing dark colors and spraying water, these are signs of aggression. This is what octopuses do when they face an adversary."

The director tried again to reclaim the mic. "Dr. Pani, Fred has been cleared. We don't need to be telling people he's aggressive."

Ari asked the entire BARL team to leave the room while the director tried to get the press conference back on track. "As I was saying, the police have charged Ms. Moon with the murder of Ansel Homer, and have cleared Fred in the death of Dr. Jane Moore. I don't have any more information regarding Dr. Moore's death at this time."

Ari watched Fred, whose behavior hadn't changed since the BARL team left the stage.

"It's you!" Ari yelled while pointing to the director.

I walked to the podium. "Fred thinks you're his adversary, Dr. Larson. So, did you kill Dr. Jane Moore?"

Mark Larson looked shocked, his mouth open, face turned red. "What? No, step away, Ms. Cali, or I'll have you removed by security."

"The press would like to know why you and Vicki Moon conspired to kill Jane and Ansel," I said.

The room was stirring and the reporters moved closer.

"You shut off the security cameras, didn't you? You strangled and threw Jane's dead body in Fred's tank. You told Vicki that Ansel was meeting with me. How much money did she promise you?" I asked.

The director pushed me aside – hard – and called for security. "Guards, please remove this lunatic." He then turned to the press. "Excuse this ridiculous outburst."

But the assembled reporters were paying more attention to Fred, as he released a dark cloud of black ink in his tank. The press area ruptured in hysteria. Reporters fired questions at the director.

Did you kill Jane?
Did you work with Vicki Moon?
Was Vicki paying you off?
Did you cover up the pollution?

The director tried to answer each question, but got more upset and flustered by the minute. The press conference had turned on him and he was no longer in control.

I looked at Ari and he glared back with dagger eyes, showing pain and anger because he knew that I'd set him up. I wanted to explain that I needed him to do exactly what he did. I knew he'd step in if the director misrepresented Fred's intentions.

And then it happened.

"Stop!" the director yelled at the top of his lungs. It got quiet.

"You've no idea how things work," the director protested. "Who do you think funds ninety percent of our environmental research? Dolphin lovers? No. Corporations. Who do you think paid for all those oyster beds we put in the bay? The oyster producers. Who do you think is going to fund our research on pollution control? The biggest damn polluters in the state, that's who."

The director turned to look at Fred, but the tank was still dark from the ink. He spun back around and threw his arms onto the podium in disgust.

"Our corporate partners pay our bills and paychecks." He pointed at the BARL team, who had come back in and were now along the back of the room. "All you researchers have jobs because of the developers and oil refineries. Jane was beloved by the people who have no money but hated by those who do. Her righteousness was endangering BARL's existence. I couldn't let that happen. Your work is too important and I'm the only one who is really fighting for you. I did all of this for you."

The director saw that he had everyone's undivided attention and was buoyed.

"All that bitch had to do was be patient – a few weeks of peace and quiet. But no. She was ready to go to the freakin' EPA. Bureaucrats up my asshole ... you've no idea what I do for you and this city. This business is give and take. We can help the environment because we help big business, too. But you all don't understand business."

Steve stepped closer to the podium. "Dr. Larson, did you kill Dr. Jane Moore?"

"Go screw yourself," the director replied.

He was about to leave the room when BJ walked in with his officers. "Mark Larson, you are under arrest for the murder of Dr. Jane Moore. You have the right to remain silent ..."

BJ hustled the director outside of the room to get away from the press. I looked back at Fred's tank. The water was becoming clearer and Fred was stuck to the side of his tank, apparently calm, changing to a soft tan color with a few flashes of a bright red. Several of his tentacles were moving back and forth in a way that looked like he was waving to the cameras!

Such a ham. Such a star!

I went outside to check on Sparky in the van. He replayed key pieces of video for me. The part where Fred released the ink was surreal! Steve walked in.

"How'd you know?" Steve asked me.

"Off the record?" I replied.

"Sure."

"I was never comfortable with Ansel being a killer. He didn't seem that invested in anything. And what he would've gotten in return for committing murder wasn't enough of a motivator. He craved fame above all else and killing Jane wouldn't have made him famous in the way he sought."

"I can see that," Steve said.

"I couldn't figure out how Vicki or one of her thugs could've gotten into and out of BARL undetected. It had to be someone else from BARL."

"Glad it wasn't Ari!" Sparky said.

"Me, too!" I exclaimed. "And there was the guy who followed me a few times. Sparky found his image on video feed from the new cameras we installed at my house. Sparky and I went over the tape again last night. He's Vicki's nephew. We also have him on tape talking to the director at the gala."

"Lots of people talk to people they don't know at parties," Steve challenged.

"It looked like something a bit more than this," I said. "We also found pictures from the gala that showed the director had round red marks near his wrists and presumably farther down his arms."

"Octopus hickies," Sparky said. "Which he got when Fred tried to intervene as he was strangling Jane."

"Wow," Steve murmured.

"That evidence is gone now because the bruises have healed," I explained. "He was careful to wear full-length sleeves but we caught him reaching on video."

Steve and I left the van to go back inside.

"And there was the money," I said to Steve. "Love, money, or fame. It was hard to ignore Vicki's wealth and her motivation to compensate those who would help her shift responsibility for the cleanup onto the cruise terminal project. The director had a lot to gain from an alliance with her."

"That's true. I won't quote you, but I plan on digging deeper into the money trail for subsequent stories."

"Please do. Who knows what else you might find."

Steve headed across the parking lot to where his photographer was waiting. He stopped, and turned back in my direction. "It's always a real adventure working with you. Let's do it again sometime soon."

"I'm sure we will. This is an interesting town."

I went back inside and found Ari sitting in his office. I sat in the chair in front of his desk and rested my elbows on my knees and held my face.

"Are we OK?" I asked.

Ari glared for a moment and then softened his posture.

"Yes. I hate what happened and how it happened, but I understand why you did it."

"We didn't have enough to give BJ the director. We needed Larson to implicate himself, and I knew Fred could help. I'm sorry I didn't tell you ahead of time."

"How'd you know I was going to step in?"

"Because you've always told the truth about Fred and you explained why he could never have killed Jane, that's how this whole thing started."

"True. But it was a big risk. The whole thing could've failed. What if Fred hadn't reacted?"

"You taught me well and told me that he'd remember people. And when I mapped out what likely happened that night, I knew Fred must've tried to intervene to save Jane. And if that hypothesis was true, then we could conclude that he'd remember the killer. Even more, he might've left a few marks – hickies – on him or her."

Ari was tracking well and his whole body nodded in agreement.

"And guess what?" I continued.

"What?"

"We went through all the footage from the gala again, frame by frame and found one shot that showed that Larson had hickies on his arms."

"No way! Really?"

"He tried to keep his skin hidden with a long turtleneck but we caught a glimpse when he raised his auction paddle high in the air."

"He's never interacted with the octopuses. He doesn't

know anything about them."

"He learned a few things tonight," I observed. "Courtesy of Fred."

"How'd you know Mark would lose it?"

"I didn't know for sure, but he seemed self-absorbed and driven by being right and in control. That type of leader often gets tripped up when their standing as the smartest person in the room is challenged. When pressed hard enough, they snap. The next thing you know, they proudly share and justify their reprehensible behavior, and reveal their flaws and limitations in a glorious blaze of defeat. Happens all the time in corporations."

Ari raised his eyebrows and shook his head.

"Sometimes you have to go big or go home," I pronounced and placed my hand on his desk. "In the unlikely event that Fred didn't react or Mark didn't flip out, it would've been a normal press conference. No biggie."

"Do you do anything normal?" he asked with a half-smile.

"Not often," I admitted and sighed. "Not ever."

"There's no other way to say this. You were magnificent."

"You were, too."

Chapter 19
Day 16, Wednesday

It was Wednesday morning and, other than the fact that I ached all over, I was in great spirits. Another case solved. Two killers arrested. Justice prevailed.

I arrived at 9 a.m., late for me, and had fun distributing the stuffed animal cams throughout every aisle, at varying levels, behind the counter, and in our meeting room. When Sparky and Dora arrived at a more leisurely 9:30, two or three sets of eyeballs followed us no matter where we went.

I placed a box of scones I'd picked up at the Mod in the middle of our meeting room table. Sparky made coffee and took a seat. I looked at him.

"Wow," I began.

"Indeed," Sparky agreed. He had noticed the half-hidden stuffed unicorn cam right away and given me a look that said, *Wait.*

Dora came in the back door and bounded into the meeting room.

"Hello, all! I was—aiiiiieeee!" Dora shrieked as she was surprised by the unicorn's following eyes. "Sparky!"

"Hey, don't look at me," he protested as he pointed to me.

"A bit too Stephen King for you?" I asked, smiling.

"Yes," Dora said.

She sat at the table but kept looking around for hidden mice or cockroaches.

"Glad we're together. I don't have much to share other than my deepest thanks for being amazing partners," I said.

"I've something to share," Dora responded. "Sparky, you're going to love this. It's hot off the press." He perked up. "The city council held an emergency meeting this morning where they suspended all active permits at Cerulean Sky and authorized funds for an independent study of alternatives for cleaning up the benzene – once and for all. They made a big deal about it."

"Yes!" Sparky yelled, and drummed the table.

"I'm not surprised," I said. "They don't want tourists thinking they'll get cancer if they swim at the beach."

It was likely the idea of the city's PR department to have the emergency meeting to figure out how to milk the draw of the octopus story and diminish the story about the pollution. People think the mayor and politicians run the city, but in a struggling beach town, the tourism board rules the roost.

"Xena ..." Dora added mischievously, "Sparky and I spent the afternoon yesterday making something for you."

I looked at them with excitement. I love surprises!

"Did you clean out the old stock of Polaroid cameras?" I asked.

"No," Sparky jumped in. "It's related to the case. And those are coming back, by the way. We should put them on eBay."

"Or place several out in the store where tourists can take pictures with the mural or Lafitte mannequin for a dollar," Dora suggested.

"Done and done," I proclaimed, pointing to the two of them. "Make it so."

"That's not the surprise." Dora pointed to the TV and clicked on the remote. "Sparky and I put together a 'best of' reel for the case."

"You didn't," I implored.

"Yep. We put together—" Sparky started to describe the video, but Dora stopped him.

"Just watch." Dora turned on the monitor and started the video.

The first five minutes was a montage of the stories I'd concocted about my gala dress. I laughed so hard I almost peed my pants. My favorite was the one I told the executive director of the Galveston Bay Foundation, that the dress was made with one hundred percent organic and sustainably harvested dyes to promote cutting our reliance on chemically produced colorants. I was impressed that he immediately came back with a statistic about how artificial colors were linked to brain-related ailments like Alzheimer's, schizophrenia, and the tendency to run for political office.

The next part of the video included clips I hadn't seen. "There's Judge Buddy at the gala," I narrated as though it was no big deal.

"Keep watching," Sparky warned.

I then saw Buddy follow the mayor's wife and air-cup her ass as she walked.

"Buddy, Buddy, Buddy, will you never change?" I said. "I wonder if he wanted to take the mayor's place!"

"Watch what you wish for," Dora teased. "I heard Buddy is thinking about running for mayor next year."

"No!" I watched for the next clip.

"He'll win," Sparky joked in a high-pitched quip. "People relate to him in some weird way. Not that they've anything in common with him ... Perhaps it's his charisma."

The scene changed to an overhead view. "What's this? The Strand?" I asked. They both smiled but said nothing. The camera zoomed in and I could see it was the Shrimp Festival.

"Oh, shit," I blurted.

"You're going to love this," Dora said. "Sparky tapped into the city cams and several of the shops had footage."

"I didn't catch the whole chase, but we got the best part," Sparky boasted.

I covered my eyes but peeked at the screen. The skinny guy, who I didn't know at the time was a guy named Ken Moon, ran right into Miss Shrimp Festival. Her skirt got caught in the truck wheel well. But the clip was in slow motion. Sparky transformed what took two seconds into two minutes of frame-by-frame drama.

"A couple of inches closer and she would've been a goner," he said.

I then noticed something I did not remember from that

day. "Is that guy smiling and sticking his tongue out at Miss Shrimp Festival?"

"Yes," Sparky said. "You will be glad to know that he later was identified as Lenny Boudreaux, Miss Shrimp Festival's father."

"My goodness. Judge Buddy has competition for the slimiest old man award," I said.

"Shall we marvel at your Segway crash? Watch this!" Sparky pointed to the monitor.

I was on the Segway in the background coming forward. I hit the pothole and went airborne. Sparky slowed my crash footage to show each painful frame.

"I can't believe you didn't break anything," Dora said.

"I almost crashed on the Segway a second time while trying to find the guy," I said.

"One more scene," Dora responded in anticipation.

It was of my house from the new security cameras that Sparky installed. So clear and crisp it looked like high definition! This clip was from the front, looking down the street toward the seawall. "I don't see anything," I said.

Sparky stood, walked to the monitor, and pointed. "Do you see this car?"

"Yes." It was a small car sitting a block away from my house with someone inside it. The time stamp a few minutes past midnight. "Who is it?" I asked, already knowing the answer.

"You might recognize the car if I zoom in." Almost on cue, the video switched to a tight shot. "It's Ari," Sparky said softly.

"The night after your car blew. After the explosion was cleaned up he came and sat for a couple of hours, just to make sure you were OK." Dora put her hand on my arm.

"Can I tell you both something?" They nodded. "I know about this. I've watched him from the monitors. He did it several evenings. He even called me – reportedly from home – and asked if I needed him to come over. I told him no."

"He's a good guy," Dora added.

I sat straight and looked at them. "We'll never show this to him. Do you understand me?" They agreed. "We're spies, we do these kinds of things, and we like to watch people when they don't know they're being watched. But he's not like us. I doubt he'll ever tell me he parked outside my house and that's OK."

"WE'RE SPIES!" Sparky proclaimed and raised his arm. His drama broke the softness of the moment and we laughed.

"SPIES!" Dora announced proudly and pumped her fist as she walked out of the meeting room.

Dora and Sparky went to the front of the store to help a customer. I sat, picked at my scone, and grabbed my new cellphone. I dialed Ari and smiled when he answered right away.

"Am I calling at a bad time?" I asked.

"Not at all," Ari said.

"Can I see Fred?"

"Of course," Ari said softly. "The police have the tank area taped off, but they agreed to release the scene before the weekend."

"OK, good."

"Why don't you come by on Friday morning? We missed each other at the station yesterday. BJ mentioned you were there documenting your statement for the official report. I'd love to see you."

"I'll see you Friday."

I sat there after I hung up, still, long enough that Sparky came back to check on me.

"You cool?"

"I'm cool, Sparky. Couldn't be cooler."

Chapter 20

Day 17, Thursday

Do you have tattoos, readers? If not, why not? Are you worried about what happens when you get old and your skin sags? Or maybe you fear you'll change your mind or not like the way it turns out?

Forget those worries and take my advice: be brave, not boring! And find the right artist. That's important. And when your clown tattoo starts to droop, turn it into a cool piece of weird abstract art.

This was my first case-inspired tattoo. I started thinking about it soon after meeting Fred and Ari and had been refining the design in my head since then. It was amazing, if I do say so myself!

I walked into Aasylum Tattoo and embraced Vix. "Thanks for doing this on such short notice. I know you're booked for months."

"For you? Anytime," Vix said. "Besides, my girlfriend wanted me to take her shopping in Clear Lake. You gave me a great out."

We walked back to his workstation and I sat in his chair.

"I got the picture you emailed and I've created a design," he said. Vix handed me the drawing. I stared at it for a long minute. "Come on … do you like it? You're making me nervous."

I looked at Vix and smiled. "It's perfect. You've captured Fred's personality as if you knew him yourself!"

"Well, you went on and on in your email, so I kinda do know him."

Fred's body in the design was red and ochre and purple, with large black eyes. His mantle was inflated with water and strips of green seaweed intertwined with his body. His tentacles stretched out in many directions, each heading for a unique adventure. One was wrapped around a blue crab and another was clutching an eyeball.

"I love the eyeball!" I exclaimed.

"You asked for it. I can turn it into a Diet Coke can if you prefer."

"No. I want the eyeball. It's a symbol for what happens when we plunge ourselves into unknown worlds without understanding them."

"That's deep," Vix said.

"Let's do this!" I took off my jacket. I was wearing an old black tube top so Vix could access my right shoulder.

"This will look nice with the dragon on the other side."

I'd been saving my right shoulder for the perfect artistic inspiration.

"Here we go," announced Vix as he started his pneumatic tattoo machine. It took ten hours for Vix to create the tattoo, not including two rest breaks. It looked amazing.

Chapter 21
Day 18, Friday

I was looking forward to seeing Fred and Ari, and smiled wide as I walked into the lobby and greeted the receptionist. I wore a dark turtleneck to hide my freshly tattooed shoulder because I wasn't ready to show it to Ari. Or anyone. Ari met me in the lobby and we went back to the tank area. Roberta was there waiting for us.

"Hello, Roberta," I said. "How are you?"

"Coming to terms with everything." She managed a smile.

I stood in front of Fred's tank and looked for, but didn't see him. "How's Fred doing?"

Ari climbed the stairs and waved me up.

"Hey, Roberta," I called and started to do the octopus dance. She laughed and joined in.

"Goofballs," Ari said from the top of the tank. He smiled but didn't dance.

"Hey, it's working!" I exclaimed as Fred came out of his lair and propped himself on a rock. "Hello, Fred." I then stopped dancing and joined Ari up top.

"He's doing pretty well," Ari said. "He was a bit perturbed about all the police here the last several days. They're strangers to him and he didn't like them hanging around. But let's see if he wants to visit us!"

Ari opened the lid. We both watched for a moment. Nothing.

"He's starting to move," Roberta said. She could see better from her vantage point at the bottom of the stairs.

We crouched and looked down at Fred. His tentacles moved out wider from his body, furling and unfurling. He floated in the center of his tank and spread his arms, showing us his full size, like a giant vanilla and caramel mottled starfish. His mantle expanded with water and he propelled himself to the top of the tank, where he looked at us mischievously with his dominant eye. He turned pinkish. His pupil was a flat bar and he stared at us while two of his now orange-on-top-pink-on-the-bottom tentacles came out of the tank and started exploring the outside of the glass.

Ari pulled the tentacles off the glass and back into the tank. "Whoa, there, fella, where do you think you're going?" He handed me one of Fred's tentacles. I held it with my left hand to stay away from my tender tattooed area. "Remember Xena?" he asked.

"You know me, Fred, I'm the one who set you up and made you upset," I confessed. "I'm sorry I did that to you, Fred, but you were extraordinary. You caught Jane's killer."

I pulled up the sleeve of my turtleneck and put my left arm in the water so he could taste me further. Another tentacle grasped me and started moving along my arm. I tugged back and forth a bit to test his strength.

"He seems strong and playful," I said.

"Yes. Precocious as hell." Ari smiled and pulled off one of the tentacles that was inching its way out of the tank again.

I stared into his eye and believed he was staring at me. His pupil transformed from a bar to a starburst.

"That's cool," I whispered.

"Imagine being able to change everything about your appearance based on how you feel." Ari placed his right arm in the water to give Fred more stimuli. "Color, patterns, skin texture, all custom for the moment."

I asked Roberta to come up and take a few pictures of Fred, Ari, and me tangled together. She took several close-ups and a few wide shots. Ari then asked Roberta to take his place next to me with Fred. She pulled two tentacles off Ari and took them for herself.

"Let's see if we can get him to show us his mouth," Ari said, now standing behind and between the two of us. "Stand a little higher to bring his body out of the water."

Roberta and I stood taller and stopped. We had Fred in our hands and his center was facing us. Ari grabbed a tiny fish from a pail and moved between us to place it on one of the tentacles about four inches from the center.

"Here's an appetizer, Fred. One of your favorites."

The fish adhered to Fred's suction cups and we watched while he slowly brought it to his mouth. Ari took my phone from Roberta and got ready to take a picture. Just before the fish reached his center, Fred pulled back the fleshy part covering his mouth and we saw his beak-like mouth open.

"Cool," I whispered, hoping not to startle him.

"Got the shot!" Ari shared proudly. "You'll need to send me these pictures." He put the phone tenderly in my back pocket. "Ease him back in the water and let's allow Roberta to finish feeding him."

Ari helped pull off the two tentacles wrapped around my left arm and placed them in the water. He removed the arms wrapped around Roberta. Fred floated, bobbed, and stayed near the top of the water.

Roberta grabbed the pail and fed Fred as Ari and I went down the stairs to watch from below. He checked his watch. "I'm late for a meeting." He then looked up the staircase. "Roberta, I need to leave. Please finish for now."

As she closed the lid, Ari walked close to me. He stared at me with smoldering eyes and a soft smile, but spoke in a loud, businesslike tone. "Give me a call when you want to go over the final details of the case, Ms. Cali." He then moved closer and whispered softly, "Don't wait too long."

Chapter 22
Day 21, Monday

I sorted through the mail that had been pushed through the slot in my front door, threw the junk in the nearby bin, and headed up the stairs. My phone rang. It was Ari.

"Hey!" I said.

"Do you have a minute? Are you near your computer?" he asked.

I went back down the stairs to my office and sat at my desk. "Yes and yes. Something wrong?"

"I sent you an email with a link. Click it."

I started to worry because Ari was being vague. My computer took what seemed like forever to wake. I found the email and clicked the link. It was a video taken inside the BARL tank area.

"What am I watching?" I asked.

"Look toward the top of the screen."

After a few seconds, I saw something move outside the tank. "Is that an octopus?"

"It's Fred. He escaped over the weekend."

"Oh my god! Is he OK? Did you find him?"

"We eventually found him." Ari then paused. "Whether he's OK or not is a matter of interpretation. He broke into Ethel's tank and got inside."

"No! Really? Wow!" The video showed Fred get on the grate that connected the tanks before the feed cut out. "How'd he do it?"

"We aren't sure because the cameras didn't capture that part. We believe they mated."

I fell back in my chair and sighed because I knew what this meant. "How do you know?"

"We don't for sure, but will soon enough. If he mated, we'll begin observing signs that he's dying."

Ari's words were heavy. I gulped and exhaled slowly.

"Fred took destiny into his own hands. I respect that," I said.

"Me too," Ari agreed. "What he did was extraordinary. We've separated them for their own safety. Fred is back in his tank, and we reinforced the closure mechanism."

"You might have octopus babies!" I sputtered, thinking about the ramifications.

"Yes, a whole new adventure perhaps. We won't know until Ethel lays her eggs and we see if there are little octopuses inside. All females lay eggs and then die, even if the eggs are not fertilized."

"Will you keep me informed about what you learn? I'm officially an octopus fan!"

"Of course." He paused again. "Can I ask you a question?"

"Sure."

"The Affaire d'Art shop has agreed to auction off an original painting of Fred at the next ArtWalk this Saturday. I sent their resident artist several pictures to use as a reference. The proceeds benefit BARL."

"Cool. I love ArtWalk."

"They've asked me to represent BARL. I seem to be the spokesperson du jour since Steve ran that article in the paper. Would you like to go with me to the auction? We could grab dinner afterward."

Moment of truth, readers. Did I ask or did I *not* ask?

I asked.

"Do you mean like a date?"

"Yes. A date," he replied confidently.

I breathed a silent sigh of relief. "That sounds nice."

"Wonderful. I'll let you know how things go with Fred, but I'm glad I caught you."

"Me, too. Talk to you soon."

I then watched the video several more times. Fred was an amazing octopus!

Chapter 23
Day 22, Tuesday

Gregory drove down to spend the next day with me on the island. He brought some cool new gadgets to show Dora and Sparky and would leave with a carload of stuffed animal cams. We went to the Ocean Grill and had lunch while watching the tide come in. People in rented bicycle cars fought the crosswind coming off the gulf.

I had the fish and chips and Gregory enjoyed the oyster po' boy. We had a couple of beers and relaxed.

"The city council pardoned Fred," I said.

"I'm sure he's relieved." Gregory smirked and drilled half his beer.

"We know it's not for Fred. It's for those people." I pointed to a young couple walking by with their beach bags.

"I see Steve is doing well and keeping busy," Gregory added. "You still not interested in him?"

"Romantically? No way. We work better as friends. Besides, I have a date. With Ari."

"I knew it!" Gregory gloated.

"I shouldn't have told you."

"You deserve a little happiness, my dear. I kid, but I'm happy for you."

"Thanks. It's next Saturday evening. They're auctioning off a painting of Fred to benefit BARL. Dinner afterwards."

"Be sure to send your final invoice before you sleep with him so you're not tempted to discount your fees."

I laughed a bit. "I'm way ahead of you. That's already done."

"What's next for you?" Gregory asked.

"Running a spy shop. Selling creepy animals that watch your every move to impulsive tourists!"

We laughed, swapped stories about our more interesting and eclectic spy shop inventory items, and split a piece of key lime pie.

Chapter 24
Day 24, Thursday

I walked downstairs to review the video feeds from overnight after I noticed a fresh pile of dog poop in my rock garden. As my computer came to life, I noticed that I received an email from Ari at 2 a.m. The subject: Fred.

Dear Xena,

Fred died tonight. I didn't call because it's late and I'm too upset to talk. Upset not because this was a surprise, we've known he was dying for over a week, but because I didn't think he'd go so soon.

Maybe Fred and Ethel fought the night they mated and that weakened him.

Could've been worse, female octopuses often kill and eat the male after mating.

It was his choice and his time, but I'll miss him terribly.

Cycle of life, eh?

Ethel has laid her eggs. We think we'll have around 200,000 little octopuses in about a month. A whole new set of challenges and opportunities. The Cousteau group will be helping us release most back into the wild. Maybe some will be social like Fred was.

Ethel will die of starvation shortly after her eggs hatch. It's their way.

I'm so glad you got to know Fred and he got to know you. Jane would've been so proud of the way he helped you catch her killer.

Jane would've liked you, too.

Fred was an amazing octopus. He came to us dying, toxic with pollutants, and showed us how to live and love more fully.

Looking forward to Saturday.

Love, Ari

I walked upstairs, poured a tall Scotch, gulped it, cried a bit, put on "Everybody Hurts" by R.E.M., cranked the volume, and did a slow version of the octopus dance in Fred's honor.

Chapter 25
Day 26, Saturday

I was excited about my date. Excited to see Fred's painting; excited to hold Ari. I put on a sleeveless black turtleneck, blue jeans, and black cowboy boots. It would be chilly, especially later, so I wore a red leather jacket on top. My hairdresser had freshened my black-blue highlights and trimmed my thick bangs earlier in the day. I looked good.

I went downstairs to find my favorite dangly earrings and saw the mail had been put through the slot in my door. Mostly bills, but one envelope with a handwritten address and no return address captured my curiosity. I opened it. My stomach tightened and my face went flush.

We see you made the papers again.
Whose life have you ruined this time?
Watch your back.

I knew where this had come from. I took a picture of the letter and texted it to Gregory.

Received in today's mail, Houston postmark.
Will call you later tonight.
Might be late.

A loud knock at the door startled me and I nearly jumped out of my skin. I looked through the peephole, relaxed, and opened the door.

Ari smiled. He looked great in a tan turtleneck and black leather jacket.

"Are you ready?" he asked.

I hit SEND on my phone and put it and the letter in my purse and smiled.

"Yes, I can't wait to see the painting of Fred!" I confirmed. "But first …"

I stepped closer to Ari, curled my hands around the back of his neck and kissed him for a long time. He drew me in closer. After a moment, I pulled my head away and teased, "I probably shouldn't have done that."

"Done what?" Ari winked at me.

"Let's go," I said. "We need to see who'll buy Fred."

We arrived at Affaire d'Art a few minutes later and the reception room was already full. The owner took us back and an assistant took our coats. Ari beamed when he saw my shoulder.

"Is that new? It's amazing!"

"Yes. Had it done last week. See the eyeball?" I lowered my shoulder and pointed.

He looked closely at the tattoo. He traced every tentacle with his finger. "I want one."

"You have to do your own design, but I can hook you up with my guy, Vix."

"Vix?"

"His name is Victor Miller, but he didn't think that was a good street name for a badass tattoo artist," I explained, as we walked through the crowd toward the painting in the middle of the room.

"Indeed."

The painting of Fred was luminous. He was swimming on the seafloor in teal waters with orange and white starfish nearby. It was large, too, about four feet square. Ari shared a few words about Fred, including that he'd escaped, mated with Ethel, and recently died. He assured everyone that Fred had fulfilled his destiny.

The auction began. Several bidders drove the price to the better than expected winning bid of $32,000 placed by Laura Block. As people started leaving, I walked up to Laura and embraced her.

"Nicely done," I said.

"I wanted something that'd help me remember Jane's buoyant spirit," she told me.

We took a few selfies with the artist, Laura, and her octopus painting. Laura seemed both sad and thrilled, excited and melancholy, but mostly she was at peace.

Ari walked up close from behind and ran a soft finger over my tattoo of Fred. It tickled.

"Are you ready to go to dinner?" he asked.

"Yes! I'm starved."

We walked east along Post Office to the Gumbo Bar. I

paused and grabbed Ari's arm. "I want to say something now so you don't misconstrue it later."

"OK, should I be worried?" he asked.

"Not at all. I'm looking forward to dinner, but I'll need to leave after dinner."

Ari cocked his head and seemed concerned. "I don't understand."

"There's something I need to take care of. A call that can't wait," I said, already feeling guilty. "But I'd like to pick up wherever we leave off tonight." I held his hand. "How about dinner, my place, tomorrow?"

His face relaxed and he smiled. "Another mystery to solve?"

"Something like that."

As we walked, I looked at Ari and realized I was doing what I always did: putting work above life. It was time to let joy in. And besides, Ari was hot from the inside out!

"This can wait," I whispered.

"Pardon me?"

"Sorry, I was talking to myself. Hang on." I stopped, pulled out my cellphone and dialed Gregory. "Xena here. I'm calling so you know everything is OK. You don't need to worry or have Sparky track me. To prove it is me and not some darker version of me, I'm going to remind you that the holidays are coming up and your wife Lynn wants you to take her on a trip to Paris. She deserves a vacation, Gregory."

Ari looked confused, so I held up my finger and winked at him.

"Gregory, we'll talk about the letter tomorrow. I've got a hot date tonight."

I hung up, turned to face Ari, and kissed him. We didn't make it to the Gumbo Bar. We went to Ari's house, where he heated up something. Me.

Request for Reviews

Reviews are the most powerful tools in my arsenal when it comes to getting attention for my books. As an indie author, I don't have the financial or marketing muscle of a New York publisher. Honest reviews of my books help bring them to the attention of other readers. If you've enjoyed this book I'd be very grateful if you could spend five minutes leaving a review on the book's retail page.

Thank you very much.

Reader Newsletter and Free Book

Building a relationship with my readers is very important to me and one of the best things about being a writer. I occasionally send newsletters with details on new releases, humorous essays, and other news. If you sign up for my mailing list, you will also receive a free copy of the Spy Shop Mystery Series prequel novella, *Ghost Rat*.

You can sign up at: www.lisahaneberg.com

Acknowledgements

Thanks to my husband Bill, for directly and indirectly encouraging me to bring my foolish ideas to fruition. Thanks for putting up with, then accepting, and then enjoying, our adventures with our beloved money pit on Galveston Island.

Thanks to my human resources colleagues and friends, especially my Houston-based teammates; you're amazing! I wrote this book while working with you, but remember it's *fiction*. I'm not the main character, and I've not done the things I've written about here. It's all made up. Every single bit of it. *Hehehe.*

Lori Knowles, you get special thanks and a shout out for your tremendous support, friendship, and great taste in wine. You have a healthy, albeit somewhat twisted, sense of humor no matter what people think about you.

Thanks to Alan Rinzler for being a remarkable mentor and creative developmental editor. I learned much from you, including when to let the crazy rip. You greatly influenced the shape of this book.

Thanks to Jim Spivey and Mark Swift, you're two of the

most talented editors with which I have worked. You helped *Toxic Octopus* become the book I dreamed of. (I ended that sentence with a preposition, and I'm not changing it.)

Thanks to Stuart Bache for designing a rocking-awesome cover befitting the spirit of the book. I love it.

Thanks to Seamus Kraham, for your encouragement and for being one of my earliest test pilot readers. Your friendship has made my time in Galveston more interesting.

Finally, thanks to the city of Galveston, Texas, for being enigmatic, gritty, fun, scary, smart, ridiculous, and so many other adjectives all rolled into one. I could not think of a better real setting for this fictional mystery series. I'm proud to call Galveston my second home town.

About the Author

Lisa Haneberg is the author of over a dozen nonfiction books covering human resources, leadership, and personal success. *Toxic Octopus* is her first novel in the Spy Shop Mystery Series. She lives with her husband and two dogs in Lexington, Kentucky and Galveston, Texas. Her online home is at www.lisahaneberg.com. You can connect with Lisa on Twitter at @lisahaneberg, on Facebook at www.facebook.com/lhaneberg, and you can send her an email at lisa@lisahaneberg.com.

CPSIA information can be obtained
at www.ICGtesting.com
Printed in the USA
FSHW010903060919
61650FS